Ian Watson was born in Tyneside in 1943. He studied English at Balliol College, Oxford. His first speculative fiction stories were stimulated by his three-year stay as a lecturer in Japan. In 1969 *Roof Garden Under Saturn*, a short story, was published in *New Worlds* magazine, and since then his stories have appeared in various magazines and anthologies. They have also been published in book form in two collections, *The Very Slow Time Machine* and *Sunstroke*.

Ian Watson's first novel, *The Embedding*, was published in 1973 and received enormous critical acclaim. His second novel, *The Jonah Kit*, became a British Science Fiction Award winner as well as confirming his position in the front rank of contemporary writers. He has been features editor of the journal *Foundation* since 1975 and a full-time writer since 1976. His most recent novels, *Chekhov's Journey* (1983), *Converts* (1984) and *The Book of the River* (1984) are all published in paperback by Panther Books.

By the same author

IAN WATSON

The Book of the Stars

PANTHER
Granada Publishing

Panther Books
Granada Publishing Ltd
8 Grafton Street, London W1X 3LA

Published by Panther Books 1986

First published in Great Britain by
Victor Gollancz Ltd 1984

Copyright © Ian Watson 1984

ISBN 0-586-06388-9

Printed and bound in Great Britain by
Collins, Glasgow

Set in Plantin

Contents

PART ONE
Doctor Edrick's Revenge

There are always loose ends. Nothing is ever tied up neatly and completely. At times life seems to be one long loose end after another; and if you've read *The Book of the River* by Yaleen of Pecawar (and who hasn't, I wonder, along the east bank of our river?), then you'll know how many loose ends there were for me personally at the end of that book – not to mention all the loose ends left over by the war with the west.

I still had to visit my parents in Pecawar – and see my little sister for the first time. And on the way there I had to visit Verrino to find out whether Hasso had survived, and repay him a kiss.

Most of all, I had to keep out of the clutches of the black current, which had plans to send me (somehow) to Eeden, that planet of a distant star from which we all originally came, and where the Godmind ruled. Whatever the Godmind really was!

Ironically, it was something which I thought *was* all tied up and done with which proved to be quite a ticklish loose end.

You may recall when I was last in Aladalia how I enjoyed a sweet liaison with a boy named Tam. That was in my innocent youth – which wasn't so very long since! – and back then Tam had seemed quite the young man, though in retrospect I knew he had just been a grown-up boy.

So here was I back in Aladalia once more, busily writing my book whilst lodging in a couple of upper rooms rented to the guild for my use by a weaver called Milian, when who should turn up but Tam?

By then I was well into my writing stint, and was dealing with the Port Barbran fungus drug which would inspire Doctor Edrick to start the war – whilst in the now-world the war itself was really getting under way. (It was Edrick who started it; not I!)

But first, a few words about the progress of the war . . .

Initially I'd taken to calling at the quaymistress's office every two or three days to enquire about the latest developments. This, despite the fact that bulletins were posted regularly in town. I fancied that there might be some extra bit of news, which I uniquely was privileged to know – not that I ever learnt any such thing by bothering the woman, and really the bulletins were quite adequate and up to date.

Since the black current had returned to most of the river, women could sail our boats safely again, unmenaced by the Sons of Adam. Thus north–south communications had been restored, on which I rather prided myself.

Had I thought this through properly, I might have realized that yet again, full of good and bold intentions, I had buggered things up!

When I gaily rode the Worm downriver, only the first detachments of junglejack soldiers had actually reached Guineamoy (to guard the town while the factory guild there turned out weapons for them). Oh, and a small advance party of 'jacks had sailed on towards Pecawar. The remainder of the army had been delayed in Jangali, awaiting more boats from other southern towns to ferry them. Though it finally set sail, that part of our army had only just cleared Croakers' Bayou.

At least I'd thought to tell the crew of the *Yaleen* to signal ahead to warn our own men off the water, otherwise the situation would have been even more of a mess. It could have been a total disaster. Naively, I'd imagined the sound of applause as I rode the Worm north. In reality there was a mad scramble inshore somewhere between the Bayou and Spanglestream to beach our troops before the

10

current arrived. Rather than cheers I guess there was a barrage of ripe curses from many of the men at the prospect of the long, long walk ahead. And in those parts there wasn't even much of a road.

What happened then, to recover the situation, was a clever tactical stroke. But it required a poignant sacrifice on the part of many young men.

Plainly, if all the beached soldiers had to walk the remaining distance, the transport fleet would have had their work cut out just ferrying victuals to and fro. So our marooned troops were divided, ashore, into those 'jacks who had already sailed the river once before with the 'consent' of the current, to marry into Jangali; and 'jacks who were born in Jangali and who hadn't yet been wooed away by any husband-hunting girl on her wander-weeks. The latter group, of men who were fresh to the river, accordingly re-embarked to sail all the way directly to Pecawar, using up their 'one-go' in the process. These men would drill in Pecawar, awaiting the transport of weapons from Guineamoy and the arrival, on foot, of their comrades. Meanwhile their comrades, who were somewhat the majority, would all have to walk.

This obviously upset the original war plan, as agreed in Jangali. Still, with the current back in place, Guineamoy was safe from attack, except overland from the north.

But before this division of forces was finalized, one brave 'jack – a settler in Jangali who had sailed once before – volunteered to step back on board a boat. His aim, to see if the Worm might perhaps be with us wholeheartedly. Maybe it would allow passage to all eastern men, irrespective of whether or not they had sailed before?

As if the Worm cared about granting a dispensation to our side!

Of course not. The Worm wanted some dead westerners for its *Ka*-store. Sons would need to die in the right circumstances for it to harvest their *Ka*s; that's to say they

11

would have to die in battle very close to the river. Which meant that many Sons would have to be killed, overall. The last thing the Worm wanted was a hasty surrender by the Sons to our superior forces.

If only I'd thought when I had the chance to plant an image deep in the Worm of immunity for all our men. So that they could sail the river as long as the war lasted! But I hadn't thought. I'd only planted the image of myself, valiantly at the helm.

Perhaps I *couldn't* have planted that other image? Perhaps it was too diffuse, too general? Perhaps the Worm would have resisted? Perhaps.

Anyway, the volunteer 'jack went mad and drowned himself.

After that, a volunteer from among the 'river-virgins' (who was perhaps even braver) had to see whether the Worm knew or cared that they weren't really virgins. They had already sailed from Jangali to that area by the Bayou. So would the Worm deal them the same death-card?

No: the river-virgins could sail on.

I'm glad I only learned these details quite a while later. Or I would have had that 'jack's horrid death on my conscience; not to mention half an army of sore feet.

When I *did* cotton on to the sore foot aspect, and to how I must have slowed up the liberation of Verrino, I fled from my writing table to the Aladalia quaymistress, full of qualms. By then I was into the last part of my book; much earlier, while I was still getting into my stride and was paying her frequent officious visits, she had reproved me thus (more gently than in exasperation): 'It isn't *your* war, Yaleen. You don't have to worry about what's going on. Everything's under control. Now please do go away, and get on writing that book!' This time she reassured me (quite falsely, as it turned out!) that I hadn't messed up anything in particular. Oh no, the run-up to the war had proceeded fine and dandy. Obviously the guild wanted my

12

book written in a not too troubled state of mind; and the quaymistress plainly had me figured as something of a brattish prima donna. But she didn't betray this. She was a cute psychologist. I must have been a real pain in the ass to the woman; she probably wanted to kick me up the backside.

Which at least goes to explain why no one made me a guildmistress for my heroism in riding the Worm down to Aladalia . . .

I now humbly apologize to all those who wore their shoes out because of my lack of imagination. And yes, to those families who lost kin unnecessarily. I can only hope they were few. May they forgive me.

And meanwhile the war was gathering momentum, even though forced marches must have been the order of the day; even though the 'jacks would have to wade home afterwards through the swamps around the Bayou; or else detour through the desert, all thanks to me. So much for all the insight I thought I'd gleaned during my travels! At the time I merely thought that whilst I was *undoubtedly* a heroine, some Aladalia folk must feel ambiguous about me – because I hadn't 'dared' go the whole hog. Because I'd stopped the Worm far short of Umdala, leaving the northern flanks unprotected. 'That's the trouble with people,' I remember reflecting at the time. 'Never satisfied!' Hadn't I made my choice of where to stop most scrupulously (with the aid of that bottle of wine)? Yet a few locals reacted as though I'd built a fine house all with my own two hands, then left the roof off so that the rain could pour in. But at least no one was offensive, not to my face.

Nevertheless, to some in Aladalia I was a heroine indeed. Which brings me back to Tam. And when *he* turned up, none of the other aspects of my Worm-ride had occurred to me . . .

Tam of the tousled hair; Tam of the knuckles.

Tam had such big hands, with unusually knobbly joints.

13

These, he seemed to be forever barking on walls and door-posts and the like. Thus he had adopted a funny stiff stride that involved walking without swinging the arms. His hands dangled sheepishly slack by his sides, to keep them out of trouble; when he remembered – which wasn't always! On my previous sojourn in Aladalia, when I got to know him well, he had told me that strange bone formations ran in his family. The bones didn't seem to know when to stop growing. According to Tam his granddad had looked like a gnarled, bobbly tree-trunk by the time he died; and Tam's knees were definitely knobbly, whilst down in the shin-bone area there seemed to be altogether too much leg, as if his shanks were turning to wood and about to bud out roots; or as if he wore boots in bed.

An apothecary had advised a non-milk diet for Tam and his kin; and apparently this was the answer. Now that Tam had eschewed milk and cheese and butter, his bone problem was under control, or at least wasn't getting worse. In any case, after our first few meetings Tam's hands had ceased to strike me as coarse or lumpish – they were so gentle and clever. When alone with me, they were never sheepish or awkward.

Tam was an apprentice potter, and sometimes it seemed as though lumps and bumps of clay had dried on him; or as if working with clay had somehow caused wet clay to seep through his skin and harden inside him, baked by the heat of his blood.

So there was I, scribbling away alone in my sitting room, when I heard footsteps on the stairs. Then a muffled thump on the door, as of someone knocking with the flat of their hand. I assumed this was Milian the weaver wanting something, since he tended to pat on my door to call me for meals or whatever, rather than batter on the wood. I didn't look round, just called, 'Come on in!'

A discreet cough. Out of the corner of my eye I was aware of somebody standing with arms dangling.

'Remember me, Yaleen?'

'Why . . . Tam!'

Of course I was pleased to see him. Yet I also felt curiously disturbed. I don't mean disturbed in my writing – for I tossed my pen down at once. I was disturbed because here was I writing a book in which I'd noted down my liaison with sweet Tam in Aladalia – without going into details. I was writing this in Aladalia; where Tam lived. Yet till now I had made no attempt emotionally to connect my last stay in Aladalia with my present stay – any more than I had made an effort to contact Tam himself. I was acting as if the Aladalia of my book, and the Aladalia of Tam, were different towns entirely.

I think I did this so that I could tell the truth.

Yet here now was the living Tam: a character stepping out of the pages of a book where he ought to have stayed.

'Why didn't you come round sooner, Tam? If you knew where I was! I mean to say . . .'

I mean to say: why did you come round at all? Why, in all these weeks, hadn't *I* looked up the person who was once my best friend in Aladalia? By accusing Tam, I absolved myself. A bit of dishonesty commenced.

'Didn't you know I was here, Tam?' I stood up, rather too late to seem spontaneous. So though we approached one another, we didn't embrace.

'Not know?' blurted Tam. 'You must be joking! Everyone knows your name and what you did and where you're staying. Even little toddlers know! I just didn't know that you'd stay on here. I thought you'd go away again . . .' He peered at my work table. 'You're busy. Writing letters?'

'I'm writing a book. About what happened. For the riverguild: they'll publish it.'

'It must take ages to write a whole book. Months and months, eh?'

'Yes, it keeps me busy.'

We were knee-deep in excuses and evasions by now.

15

I grinned. 'It's thirsty work.'

This was simply another little lie. The truth was, I didn't want Tam to look at the manuscript. Supposing he happened upon mention of our sweet liaison? That could have been embarrassing; embarrassing because it took up such a tiny number of lines . . .

'Thirst, I can fix,' said he. 'How about a pot of ale?'

Tam had filled out since the last time I saw him. He'd filled out with muscle, not with extra knobs and spurs of bone. Now he looked sleeker, his skeleton more sheathed; though I still got a distinct impression of an ill-stuffed mattress . . . Not that there had ever been anything lumpy or hard about *sleeping* with Tam, save in the most important respect. I found myself edging away from the door which stood half-open to my bedroom.

'A pot of ale would be wonderful!'

'Remember the *Golden Bugle*?'

'Oh yes! But shall we try somewhere new? A fresh venue for a fresh encounter?' (Not the old haunts. Please.)

So out we went into Aladalia town, with a haste on my part which I can hardly describe as indecent, given the motive.

We walked along wide cobbled streets. We passed the concert hall with its dome of glazed turquoise tiles which looked like a bowl of sky, but richer and deeper. We crossed the edge of the jewelsmiths' quarter; at which point naturally Tam had to enquire about my fine diamond ring.

'No, it isn't from here,' said I. 'I bought this in Tambimatu.'

'Oh?' He sounded sad, and perhaps a mite puzzled.

Actually, Aladalian artisans didn't go in much for costume jewellery; nor did the locals themselves wear many gems. The jewelsmiths of Aladalia mostly worked with semi-precious stones, and thought a bit bigger than rings. They crafted ornaments, artwork. And that's what the local connoisseurs who bought their products preferred.

Come to think of it, I hadn't noticed many Aladalian ornaments when I'd been hunting round the shops in Tambimatu; nor had I spotted any imports of jewellery from Tambimatu on offer here. There's a lot of trade between our river towns, so the distance could have nothing to do with this (though the war might have contributed). Yes, I think I'd made Tam *sad*, in his Aladalian heart. How many husbands, I wondered, were ever wooed away from Aladalia to Tambimatu? (Or vice versa?)

Tam glanced down a long avenue towards distant rolling meadows and the bushy hills beyond: a scenery of downy green thighs, with curly bunches of hair . . . It was as though he was inviting me to roam there with him – as once we had – and perhaps to penetrate even further inland to the cave-pocked mountains where the semi-precious stones were found . . .

Perhaps, perhaps. Perhaps he was just wondering whether it would rain. My mind was working overtime with images. I was the writer confronting her subject matter, which had strolled around for a second perform-ance, unscheduled, unannounced. At least we weren't heading towards the potters' part of town where Tam had his lodgings.

Oh it was quite a walk we took. Yet this was nothing special in Aladalia. The town liked to spread itself – as if all artists (of whom there were many) each needed a zone of free space around themselves. As if music required a vault to soar into; and paintings demanded breezes from afar to dry the varnish; and potters, a whole public square each to set out their wares without clutter. Everywhere I looked there was sky and long perspectives, and sights of the distant countryside with its farms and pastures.

How different the spirit of Aladalia was from that of Tambimatu with its tall houses packed tightly together, their beetling brows almost butting one another! Yet at Tambimatu jewels were truly precious. The pressure of houses, and the massive weight of the precipices, the density of jungle and the stifling tropic heat all conspired to squeeze out rubies and diamonds.

In fact, it was the sheer spread of Aladalia which had made it easy for me to leave the real live Tam out of my emotional calculations. It wasn't the case that more people dwelled in Aladalia than in other towns. No, there was simply less chance that you would bump into any particular person. If in danger of doing so, you could usually spy them from afar off and change course in good time, casually and naturally.

Though by the same token a native of Aladalia thought nothing of walking close on a league for a jar of ale and a chat. Till now, Tam hadn't done so . . .

We eventually turned off the boulevard down a lane. This lane would have been a highway anywhere else; and presently we arrived at the *Tapsters' Delight*. The long ancient yellow-brick building wore a red-shingled roof which sagged and rose and sagged again like canvas supported on poles. Orange and crimson zalea bushes grew all round the low-walled ale garden. The very air was intoxicated with sweet smells of brewing mash mingled with the scent of the flowers.

We sat ourselves on a bench by a rough-hewn table. A fat fellow wearing a chequered apron appeared in the doorway accompanied by another who looked like his twin – or perhaps his son, ripely pickled in ale – whom he directed to amble over for our order.

'That chap's an artist in ale,' confided Tam, with a nod at the proprietor.

And it *was* an excellent sup. Delicious also were the herb-speckled, coarse-cut sausages.

After the second nut-sweet foaming jar, Tam confessed why he hadn't looked me up till now.

I wish that he hadn't.

Last time round, Tam and I had been warm and casual

in our relationship. We had enjoyed each other's company, and enjoyed each other; but we hadn't exactly branded the affair into our hearts. Yet now Tam was madly in love with me. I use the word 'mad' advisedly. I suppose love always is irrational, but this was rather different. My return to Aladalia riding in the Worm's jaws had transfigured me for him. If I'd simply popped into town aboard any old boat, I imagine we could have picked up the threads once again as before. But the manner of my coming! I became his muse, his dream, his star and sun. His inspiration, aspiration. He had hauled out his memories of me from store, rejigged them and gilded them in goldleaf. Now I was his heroine, his living goddess. Also he was afraid that I might depart on the next boat or the one after. Therefore he had stayed away, the better to worship me – and to make things worse for himself meanwhile. Oh, what delirious foolishness.

The wretched thing was that he *knew* this perfectly well. He just couldn't help himself. Previously, our amorous intrigue had been like soft clay, spinning freely on the wheel of those happy weeks, moist and malleable, changing shape, able to flop down afterwards. Now this same clay had been fired by my dramatic arrival, and was a hard pot instead – within which Tam was trapped, as surely as if he had stuck his fist inside and kept it there during the baking. The pot of his passion was strong, yet it was fragile too, liable to break into tragic jagged shards.

I didn't encourage him – either on that day or on various subsequent days when we saw each other, days when I couldn't think of an excuse not to. Certainly we didn't make love again. Tam seemed to find this abstinence logical, preferable. I believe he feared he might disappoint me – I who had tamed the current itself.

But though I didn't encourage him, I fear he encouraged me – in my proud notion that I had saved him and Aladalia and everyone else in the east. He bolstered my self-esteem almightily, when I should have been volunteering to spend my next few years resoling worn-out boots and portering the wounded on my shoulders all the way home to Jangali.

Or did he really?

Maybe it was his dewy eyes fixed adoringly on mine which finally made me wake up from my delusion. Maybe his hands held bunched by his sides – so as not to touch me – at last made me grasp the actual situation.

In which case, thank you, Tam. Though that wasn't quite your intention.

Meanwhile, of course, the war was going on. Our army massed in Pecawar. Riverguild vessels ferried stocks of newly-forged weapons, and made ready to accompany the army in the role of supply boats.

And here we come to another twist of the screw concerning my heroic intervention: one which explains, when I look back, why the guild (in the person of the Aladalia quaymistress) treated me so gently despite my having trashed the original war plan. For what had I done in reality but largely restored the monopoly of the river which our guild enjoyed before the current withdrew? I'd restored the status quo all the way from the Far Precipices to Aladalia.

Once more, women only could sail the major part of the river; and maybe the guild calculated that this easily balanced off any amount of inconvenience to the army; any extra delay, any additional deaths.

Naturally the guild could never admit as much! And I would be the *last* person they would admit it to; especially when I was writing a book destined for publication. If they could have marooned me in the desert to write my book uninfluenced by current events, from their point of view this would have been even neater. Yet as it was I managed to maroon myself in a cocoon of falsely modest heroism. Maybe the one thing that did rankle with the guild was that I hadn't indeed gone the whole hog and ridden the

Worm all the way to Umdala and the ocean! Strange to realize (as I finally did) that whatever my own motives may have been, to my guild perhaps I was a secret heroine . . . of conservatism.

Oh yes indeed. I could well imagine some slick guild-mistress telling an angry council of the 'jacks: 'Look, fellows, let's be reasonable! She did stop the Worm as soon as she could. Well, okay, a hundred leagues past Verrino – just to be on the safe side. But you'll have to agree she cut the Sons' supply route at a stroke! She stopped them spreading out.'

There would have been truth in this (imaginary) advocacy. The Sons had indeed been stymied. What could they do thereafter but batten down tight in Verrino and environs?

And so the war proceeded (without any courier or spy balloons coming into play, that I noticed) – and presently the war was won. How messily, I was to learn before long. (Though perhaps the war wasn't so much messy, as simply a war.)

And so I wrote my book. And finished it; then delivered my manuscript to the quaymistress, minus my private epilogue about the Worm's dream contact with me – that, I kept about my person.

Quaymistress Larsha was a neat, composed woman in her late forties. She was neat in speech and neat in her turn-out, maybe to compensate for a weak eye which wandered if she ever got upset. She wore a pair of Verrino spectacles with gilded wire frames.

'Your manuscript will be off to Ajelobo early next week, on board the schooner *Hot Sauceboat*,' she assured me, having locked my work in her bureau for safety. 'And how about yourself, Yaleen?'

'Me? I want to go to Verrino. I'd like to help tidy up, and I have a message for somebody there: a message from a dead woman. When you read my story, you'll understand.

21

After that I want to go home to Pecawar. I haven't seen my parents for years. I'd like to leave as soon as I can.'

'The day after tomorrow, if you wish.' Larsha hesitated. 'Don't you perhaps feel that you need to pay a visit to the head of the current first? If you wish, we could sail you out.'

'There? No fear!' But I checked myself. Larsha knew nothing of what the Worm had told me the other night. 'Don't worry, it'll stay where I moored it.'

Larsha adjusted her spectacles and peered at me primly; the mannerism reminded me strongly and suddenly of Doctor Edrick. 'You're sure of that, child?'

'As sure as I am of anything.' (Which didn't, come to think of it, amount to very much.)

'Our guild will have to think long and deeply before we advise in favour of any attempt to move the current further downstream. If indeed such a move is possible or desirable.'

'I'm sure I don't know if it's possible. The Worm thinks it's a God now.'

'Well, at least we don't have to worship it . . .' Larsha's glasses caught the sunlight streaming through the window, as if winking some message at me.

This prompted me to ask, 'Is there a list of prisoners, Quaymistress?' Andri and Jothan would likely not have been with the invasion force. They would have been assigned to the wormpoison project. But Edrick could well have been one of the invaders. If so, I was wondering whether he had been killed or caught.

I do wish I hadn't thought of that man as still alive and kicking. I do wish Larsha hadn't adjusted her glasses, just so. Later on it was to seem to me as if I had recreated Edrick by thinking about him just then – and by setting out for Verrino with him in the background of my mind, hiding behind Hasso who occupied the foreground. As if I had brought him back into existence, out of the chaos of war and death.

'A list? Maybe so. You'll be in Verrino in a few days. Ask there.'

'I may. It isn't important.'

It was, though. It was deadly important.

Before leaving town, I dithered long about whether to go round to the pottery to say goodbye to Tam; but decided not to. I started a letter and tore it up half a dozen times. Now that I'd finished my book, words seemed to have deserted me. I even fancied, for half an hour, that I might send Tam my diamond ring wrapped up in a little packet by way of farewell. A grand gesture indeed, when I'd worn that ring all the way into the belly of the Worm, and back! However, Tam would never be able to slip my ring on to even his smallest knuckly finger. So I might well be taunting him by such a gift. I might be saying in effect: 'You can't slip *me* on, either!'

In the end I sent him a flower in a little box. I chose the 'farewell' Fleuradieu which blooms from midsummer almost till winter in the northern towns. The Fleuradieu starts out with light blue summer flowers but these grow deeper in hue and darker through the autumn till the final blooms of the year are violet, nearly black. It's the last flower to bid farewell to warmth and fertility.

With my remaining half-pot of ink I carefully painted the petals black before putting the bloom in its box.

Having thus solved the problem to my satisfaction, I decided to repair to the concert hall that evening. No point in brooding, eh? So directly after sharing dinner with Milian and his wife, I set out.

I'd no notion what sort of performance was billed for the hall. Some orchestral music, I supposed. But when I entered the lamplit lobby amidst a fair crush of other patrons of the arts I discovered posters announcing 'The Birds: an Operetta', by Dario of Andaji'. (Andaji being a large village not far south of Aladalia.)

What could this be? Something legendary? I certainly couldn't imagine any of the birds that I knew inspiring an artist. Tiny dowdy things they were, and rare; far less noteworthy than your average flutterbye. And as for birds singing – which I presumed 'operetta' implied – well, that definitely belonged to the land of legend. Yet to judge by the chattering throng in the lobby, Dario's *The Birds* had struck some chord.

I bought a ticket and went into the dim domed hall where I found a vacant aisle seat and parked myself. Presently a slim young man excused himself and sat next to me. He wore a long blond pigtail, bound with cord, which he arranged across his heart and held in one hand for a long while as though this was the tassel of a cap which might blow off. His skin smelled of grated lemon peel. But despite my neighbour I still felt private. The hall was dark; all the illumination of the oil lamps was concentrated on the half-circle of stage.

The musicians took their seats: two guitarists, a harpist, a fiddler, a flautist, a drummer, a xylophonist and a bugler. A canvas back-drop descended, depicting a farmyard with a rainbow arching overhead. Then from out of the wings strode the singers, extravagantly costumed as . . . a giant rooster, and a turkey-cock, and a snow-white goose.

Oh, *that* sort of bird! I giggled, and my neighbour hushed me. The music struck up, the overture sounding eerie, plangent and resentful.

'Man is of the shore,' sang the goose. 'Woman is of the river. Only birds are of the sky!'

'So, bird brothers,' the turkey answered, waddling about the stage, 'let us fly!'

Which they attempted, with no success.

The plot of the operetta concerned the plans of this trio – ridiculous, grandiose, and poignant by turns – to reach the rainbow, with ever more melancholy consequences. A farmwife soon put in an appearance, though actually this

24

was a man – a sweet tenor – wearing big false breasts; and on her head 'she' wore an enormous starched white hat looking for all the world like the sails of a boat. The wife soliloquized tunefully to herself about how she would kill and cook the birds, and what sort of sauces she would serve them up in. Her arias on the subject of cookery were lovely, but so weird.

The Birds ended on a note of gaily ironic acceptance of circumstances, with the feathered flightless trio singing their own paean of praise about those parts of their bodies which the farmwife's cuisine would transfigure from rude nature into brief-enduring art.

In short, *The Birds* was a fantastical satire, at once absurd and hauntingly melodious. But I had soon decided that the operetta wasn't about the problems of domestic birds at all. It was about men – penned in the farmyards of our various towns, while women sailed forth freely. The subtitle of the work could well have been: *Frustration*. Gaudy, lyric, manic, celebratory and comical by turns, Dario's work at heart was one of rebellion; and I wondered how many people in the audience saw beneath the surface to the tortured feelings which I thought I sensed.

After the finale the young man next to me burst into wild applause. Several voices chanted out, 'Author! Author!' – and soon Dario of Andaji stepped on to the stage.

Dario was short and tubby with little piggy eyes. He tilted his head back while surveying his audience, a mannerism which made his chin emerge more pointedly but also made him seem to squint disdainfully from under half-shut eyelids. He took several bows, resuming the same seemingly arrogant, pretentious posture after each. Maybe the truth was that he was nervous; yet I don't think that, had I seen him beforehand, I would have much wanted to see his work.

I couldn't help wondering, too, whether Dario's satire and lyric pain perhaps sprang from disgruntlement with his own body; whether his own uncomeliness made him resent women. (Had he ever made *love*?) Of course, I sympathized – and I guessed that crusaders in one cause or another must sometimes be inspired at base by personal inadequacies and frustrations. But to be honest the sight of Dario on stage did rather modify my appreciation of *The Birds*.

And maybe I was being utterly impertinent, devaluing his achievement because part of me resented its basic thrust.

Dario also wore a pigtail. His was much shorter than my enthusiastic neighbour's, tied tightly at his nape with a red bow.

As Dario withdrew offstage followed by the performers, my neighbour said to me, 'By the way, that's my brother.'

'Oh.' Apart from the pigtail they didn't seem to have much in common. 'Do you mean literally your brother?'

The young man stared at me. 'How else can he be my brother?'

'Well . . . maybe in the sense that every man's your brother, if you share his sentiments about men and women. Maybe,' I joked, 'you wear pigtails as a sign of solidarity?'

The rest of the audience was rising to leave, but the young man reached across me and held the arm of my seat so that I was imprisoned. 'Wait,' he said. Other people in our row were forced to exit by the far end.

'Okay,' he said, 'we do just that. A lot of men in Andaji wear pigtails. We have our own little artists' colony.'

'I had a brother,' I said, rather stupidly.

'Amazing. Does that make you my sister?'

'Dario resents women, doesn't he? What about you? Do you follow his lead, just because he's a good artist? Are you a good artist too?'

The young man shrugged. 'I paint.'

'Paint what?'

'Goose eggs. I paint nude figures around goose eggs,

26

after first sucking them out and cooking omelettes. Highly erotic they are. Each egg's a world of men and boys. If I don't like them afterwards, I dance on them. The fragility appeals to me. So easy to crush.' I didn't know if he was serious. 'My eggs appeal to women connoisseurs in town here. They think they're titillating, but oh so clever too, so that's all right. A friend pointed you out to me when I was last in town. You brought the current back, damn it.'

'Damn it, indeed? And how many good fellows would rather I'd steered the Worm all the way to the ocean?'

'They're women-men. Not true men.'

'Like Dario is a true man?'

'You scorn my brother, don't you?'

'No I don't. I just have mixed feelings about his work, that's all.'

'That's because you can't understand it. No woman can; because a woman doesn't share the same circumstances.'

'Look, I sympathize.'

'We in Andaji don't need your sympathy.'

'Sorry.'

'Nor your woman's sorrow.'

'That doesn't leave me much to offer.'

'A person who can *offer* things is an oppressor, lady. We don't want offers from women. Of themselves, least of all. Men can love other men beautifully. Dario and I love other men.'

'And plait each other's pigtails? Sorry, that's unworthy.' I thought of Tam. 'If what you're saying's true, then you're really in a tiny minority, Dario's Brother! Frankly, if the world was a bit different you probably wouldn't feel this way about other men at all.'

He shook his head. 'You can't understand.'

By now the hall was almost empty. I pushed his arm aside and stood up. 'In that case I suppose I wasted my ticket money. But honestly, how many people in the hall tonight saw *The Birds* this way?'

27

'Perhaps not many,' he allowed. 'Just those of us from Andaji. We who know the signals. The others saw other things. The art. The frolic.'

'Then I'd say I *did* understand. Even before you decided to rub my nose in it, friend. Because I'm already aware of the problem.'

'But we aren't a "problem".'

'I think, Dario's Brother, that maybe you're your own worst enemy. What a shame you can't paint gander eggs! What a pity male geese don't lay. I'm not your enemy, though, however much you wish to shock me and alienate me from . . . from a memorable performance, because you recognized me. So goodbye. Try to be happy.'

And I left, though there was a sour taste in my mouth as I walked back towards the weaver's house. Andaji sounded such a bitter place – though no doubt the artistic men there, who loved each other, felt that they were pure and free and astringent. Small wonder that Dario and company didn't live in Aladalia proper. Aladalia was too generous a town, too ample.

A week later I arrived in Verrino aboard a caravel.

From the river Verrino looked much the same as ever, superficially. (Already new signal towers replaced those burnt, to north and south.) Once I went ashore, though, I found the wounds of war unhealed everywhere.

The town was *seedy*. A lot of windows were broken and unrepaired. Footbridges had been hacked or burnt down, compelling long detours. Terracotta fuchsia urns were smashed into shards. Some buildings had been reduced to piles of rubble or heaps of ash.

Worse still was the spirit of the populace. No longer did Verrino folk scamper about, chattering like monkeys. Now they slunk hither and thither shiftily. Many of them appeared ill-fed, even diseased, while the vine-arbours harboured drunks – not a few of them Jangali soldiers getting smashed on crude liquor. Indeed no one seemed to be drinking wine by choice. So where had the fine vintages of Verrino gone? Into hiding? Looted by the Sons? But perhaps Verrino wines were too subtle for the men of Jangali. Soldiers wanted something fiercer to remind them of junglejack. And perhaps wines were too subtle for everyone, these days? These boozing 'jacks were amiable enough, yet at the same time they seemed lost, like tipsy ghosts drowning their sorrows at having lost contact with their own world. Verrino town was quite crowded, yet despite this the place seemed strangely uninhabited, as though people couldn't quite believe in it any longer, even while they went through the motions.

Injuries were visible: lost fingers, hideous puckered slash-marks and scar-tissue, a missing eye here, broken teeth there, blushing burns. I saw one child running half-naked with a festering blotch on her back. Maybe the fresh air would help it heal; maybe. A good deal of garbage was lying about too: rags, stinking piles of fish bones, even dried knobs of human excrement. Oh, those Sons had transformed Verrino into a fine copy of one of their own side streets! The very town itself had been wounded and was still suffering from delayed shock. I watched a small funeral cortège making its way down one street. The procession was silent, not even humming in mourning. The body lay under a dirty sheet on a litter of crudely-roped poles.

I made my way through Verrino that day with difficulty – where I had skipped before. Twice I lost my way, because the ways had changed. But when I arrived at the base of the Spire, that at least looked unaltered – as monumental and austere as ever.

I climbed, pausing a few times for breath.

On my last such halt I surveyed the view. In the direction of the glassworks off to the east I spied several new 'villages'. Villages of sorts: higgledy-piggledy shacks and canvas awnings, surrounded by spiked palisades. Each village compound was crowded with tiny dots of people doing nothing. Each compound was hidden from its neighbours by the bulge of sand hills.

Obviously those were the prison-pens. The 'jacks had separated their prisoners into four different sections for security – though from the look of it an uproar in one camp would easily be heard in the others. Out of sight, but not out of earshot.

Maybe that didn't matter. Maybe the prisoners were as stunned by their defeat as the people of Verrino had been by foreign occupation and war. And if Verrino folk looked ill-fed, the prisoners were probably weak with hunger. One could hardly starve Verrino or the army to stuff the stomachs of the Sons. So I was glad I was seeing those pens from afar.

I noticed some dark patches staining the stone steps where I stood. Dried blood? Let it be the lifeblood of the Sons!

I pressed on, through the upward tunnel, and past empty stairways and closed doors – a couple of which I pushed, only to find them locked. No hint of activity. No voices, no challenges.

I should have gone to the quaymistress's office initially and asked how it was with the Observers, instead of just turning up as though it was up to me to relieve their siege in person. I should have done. But I hadn't wanted a stranger to tell me the news. I had to see with my own eyes the outcome of events whose beginnings I had witnessed when I was Nelliam. And taste it with my own lips. Yet now that I was here, the place seemed deserted. Not ravaged, just abandoned.

The top platform was empty, save for a heliograph and signal-lantern erected by the rail. The door to the observatory building stood ajar.

I *knew* that Hasso was in there. He simply had to be. I

30

made him be there by thrusting myself into a frame of mind where no other outcome was conceivable.

I walked over. I touched the rusty bolts of the door, called softly, 'Hasso!' Then I pushed the door open decisively and stepped inside.

There was nobody in the room. Empty chairs stood behind telescopes. Every window pane was hinged wide open as though to ventilate the air of some lingering foetor.

I stood bewildered. What a weird return this was, to a place where no one was! I imagined that I'd died. I thought I was in a *Ka*-world of my own memories – a world where I could wander forever without meeting a soul because everyone else had faded away. During those few moments I felt more alone even, than when I'd found myself washed up on the west bank.

A noise from outside – a cough – broke this melancholy reverie. I whirled. I jumped to the open door.

'Yaleen!' exclaimed a voice. A familiar voice indeed!

Hasso's looks were not quite so familiar. Before he'd been slim. Now he was emaciated. His skin was sallow. His eyes looked larger, as though they'd swollen in their orbits. His once smart attire was dirty and crumpled. A ring of keys hung from his belt, which was tightened to the final notch, leaving a loose tail of leather hanging down.

I rushed towards him – then halted out of reach, like some anxious flutterbye just about to alight on a flower when it realizes that the flower is a deathbloom.

'Where – ? How – ?' (Was it his ghost whom I'd summoned to haunt me on this high and lonely place?) 'Come inside and sit down!' I made to take his arm now, but he danced back.

'Hey, I'm not about to flake out! I'm putting on fat again. Or at least,' and he grinned ruefully, 'I thought I was. The siege has ended, you know.'

'Ended. How did it end?'

'We held out. Till the 'jacks arrived. Most of us.'

31

'Most?'

'Two of us died of hunger. Or sickness. Same thing by that stage. Yosef killed himself to spin the groceries out. None of us fancied staggering downstairs with a white flag, not after some of the things we saw.'

'I saw dried blood on the stairs. Did Yosef – ?'

'Jump? No. He hanged himself. Those stains got there when the Sons made a foray. We dropped stones on them. They didn't risk it again, which is as well, since stones got hard to heave later on. Actually, Yaleen, the worst aspect was being drunk all the time and having a permanent hangover.'

'Drunk? You're joking!'

'Well, we had a decent wine cellar, so when we ran out of water . . . A glass of vintage really knocks you out when you're weak with hunger. Yosef was drunk when he hanged himself, though he left a note to say why.'

'Where are the others, Hasso?'

'Some are recovering in town. Me and Tork – remember him? – we're out at the Pens, questioning prisoners. We're compiling a real map of the west. I just popped back for an old chart. Saw you climbing up ahead of me.' He looked around. 'Actually, there ought to be a 'jack guard on duty up here – and a riverguild woman as well. Naughty, they are, naughty. Taking time off duty for private business downstairs, I shouldn't be surprised.'

Indeed it transpired that there were two guards and two watch-women assigned to the Spire. When I turned up, the night shift was down below, legitimately asleep. The day shift were merely sleeping with each other. Tousled and embarrassed, the latter pair soon emerged and got on busily with their duties of patrolling and peering.

Another symptom of disorder in Verrino? I could sympathize. They were bored; they were exiled up a shaft of rock. More important perhaps, there was evidently no

32

friction except of the fleshy sort between 'jacks and river-guild up here. When I went below with Hasso, the guard saluted me smartly (though I had to ask what the funny arm gesture meant).

Down below, Hasso let me into his quarters. He set out dry black bread and cheese, some pickles and a carafe of water. To decide which of us should tell our tale first, Hasso flipped a coin. The coin came down value side up: Hasso's turn to tell.

I said he should at least eat his meal first. He shook his head and nibbled while he talked. He ate as if he had disciplined himself to disbelieve in food, and still couldn't credit its continuing existence. But he sipped water like a connoisseur.

He was laconic concerning the siege itself. Maybe there isn't a lot that can be said about slow starvation. Maybe he said it all by the way he ate.

He talked much more about what the Observers had observed from aloft: the brutalization of Verrino. They'd spied faggots piled round a stake more than once; they'd seen women dragged shrieking to be set on fire. Yet the final stages of the war were the worst, for then the embattled Sons really vented their spleen upon Verrino town which they were about to lose.

I'd finished my own food long ago. Hasso cleared up the last few breadcrumbs meticulously upon a dampened fingertip.

'So now we have hundreds of those swine in the Pens,' he said. 'And what to do with them? Actually, a few aren't such bad chaps at heart. They regret what they did. They just didn't dare disobey their leaders. But Verrino folk aren't ever going to have them living in town. Some people say throw all the Sons in the river. Another suggestion is we march them down beyond Aladalia and ferry them across to their own side. I doubt if the Aladalians would appreciate us dumping an army opposite them . . . Hey, a fin for them?'

'Um?'

'A fin for your thoughts?'

'Oh, sorry. I'm listening, honest!' But what I was thinking was that I knew why Hasso had skated over the anguish of the siege, in favour of faithfully narrating what happened below. It was because he was fulfilling his promise to dead Nelliam. All the time he'd been talking he was honouring her memory, by being true. I knew; but he didn't know I knew.

So I started to tell him.

This had to be by a very roundabout route, via Tambimatu and Manhome South, Spanglestream and Tambimatu again; and even so I had to leave out heaps of events and skip weeks and leagues.

Hasso stared at me attentively, now and then shaking his head in amazement. 'My goodness,' he muttered once, as I was recounting my adventures, 'you're Capsi's flesh and blood all right, and no mistaking.'

Towards the end of my account he exclaimed, 'So it was *you* who brought the current back! Damn it, but it came so quickly – without warning. By the time we got Big Eye swung round . . . Well, you saved my life! That's what gave us the courage to hold out: the boats following a week or two afterwards, signalling, telling us we had an army on the way.'

This made me feel a bit better about my role. Maybe I'd slowed down the war plan – even tied a whopping great knot in it – but at least I'd given some hope to people.

I'd kept till last my revelation about how I'd *been* Nelliam just before she was killed; and how I had a kiss to repay . . .

But not now merely on the brow. That kiss prolonged itself. It wandered. Soon we also wandered, to Hasso's spartan bed.

Afterwards he lay like a cat basking beside a fire and

sighed contentedly. 'That was *good*. I thought I'd dried up completely.'

'Nonsense.' I winked. 'Starvation sharpened you, that's all.'

I spent three weeks in Verrino, helping Hasso and Tork to compile their map and gazetteer of the west bank. The riverguild gave me their blessing in this. Who better than I to catch out prisoners if they told lies about the territory from Worlzend to Manhome South? I did catch one or two out, but not many seemed to want to lie.

This new work meant that I had to travel out to the Pens by day. Nights, I spent in town; sometimes with Hasso, sometimes not. By and by Verrino began to seem less seedy and sleazy; though ugliness still simmered beneath the surface, a dark shadow upon the soul of the place.

Conditions in the Pens weren't too disgusting; no one wanted to risk an outbreak of serious disease. But life there was hardly elegant or even innocuous. I might have felt I was performing a useful penance by working there – if the 'jack guards hadn't already been doing this as routine.

The ordinary run of prisoners were just coarse, not actively venomous. The leaders were a different kettle of fish, and interrogating some of the robed ones was the nastiest but most necessary task. We had questions for them about the planning of the war and its ultimate aims.

In my final week one of the leaders sat facing our questioning committee. This committee consisted of Hasso and me, a guildmistress called Jizbel and a 'jack 'captain', Martan. We held our sessions in a tent pitched just inside the gateway to this particular pen, with bales of uprooted thornbush on sharpened stakes separating us from the largely lackadaisical mass of prisoners; these spent their time playing pebble or straw games on the sand, gambling up imaginary debts, wandering from side to side, mucking out, squabbling over rations, racing insects. Those who could, read aloud to their fellows from a pile of tatty old romances generously donated by the guild. If anyone tried to tunnel out, they wouldn't succeed; the sand would suffocate them.

The Son in question was a big brute, but now he looked baggy, as though his skin was a size too large for him. As usual the prisoner was being guarded by two 'jacks armed with clubs; they kept their swords sheathed.

'That damned Satan-Snake saved you,' the Son sneered. 'You never saved yourselves.'

'Didn't we just?' retorted Captain Martan. 'Let me tell you – '

'How do you suppose the current came back?' Hasso glanced proudly at me. He oughtn't to have done that. Jizbel uttered a soft hiss like water cast on coals to cool them. Both men shut up.

I rapped my knuckles on the trestle table. I had to take this swine by surprise if we were going to get anything of value out of him.

'So what are you, then: a Conserver or a Crusader?' I tried.

The Son's head jerked towards me – and a wattle of loose skin like a turkey cock's flopped with it.

'You!' He stared at me. 'I know you. It was you who rode in the jaws of the Snake!'

'Rubbish,' I said. 'At that distance it could as easily have been your own grandmother.'

'Witch! Damned witch – it *was* you. I saw; my eyes are keen. That's why you're here now. You're the tool of the Snake.'

'Oh, shut up about snakes. You don't know what you're talking about. I asked if you're a Conserver or a Crusader. Because if you're a Conserver – ' I hoped I was being cunning – 'then we're that much more likely to send you home to your precious Truesoil to keep it pure and secure,

36

and bore yourself to death reading junk like *The Truesoil of Manhood*.'

This was meant to impress him with how much we already knew about life in the west, so that he wouldn't lie. The effect I produced was unexpected.

'Yal . . . een,' he said. 'That is who you are! You're Doctor Edrick's waterwitch who ran away. Only she would know the names of our Brotherhood books.' He spat, though only at the sandy soil. 'The Doctor said it was you as swept by in Satan's lips that morn. Didn't know whether to credit him.'

'Drivel. Edrick couldn't spy a night-soil shack at twenty spans – even if he did loot himself a decent pair of glasses! He never was far-sighted about anything.'

Neither was I, to shout my mouth off; though why should I care if this character knew who I was? Actually, mine was a cheap jibe. To give the dog his due, Edrick had been a devious schemer. And we'd both been hoodwinked by the Worm, he and I in different ways.

What I heard the Son mutter then, was, 'Far-sighted enough to give this bloody town the slip!' Something like that. Immediately, as if realizing that I'd heard and desperate to cover his indiscretion up, the Son blustered on loudly: 'How did he know? Well, we took spyglasses off those boats, didn't we? And the Doctor had ears. He could hark the description I gave – of *Yaleen*.'

So saying, the Son launched himself out of his chair, leaping at our table.

He didn't reach it. The 'jack guards bludgeoned him senseless.

'Stop it!' I cried, nearly upsetting the trestle top myself. 'Don't hit him again!'

The way he had attacked didn't make sense. Just before he jumped, he had glanced at the 'jacks – and they were not lounging inattentively. They were alert. His glance in effect had cued them. Therefore he wanted to be knocked out. He wanted to be rendered speechless.

'Guard: did you hear what he said *before* that bit about stealing spyglasses?'

'Eh, mistress?' The 'jack guard panted.

I wasn't a 'mistress', but I let that pass. 'Think, man! The Son muttered something. I know what I heard. What did you hear?'

'Hmm . . . something about slipping . . . on all the blood?'

'No,' his colleague said, 'slipping out of town: that's what. Just what we all want to do.'

'That's enough of that!' said Captain Martan.

'What *I* heard him say,' said I, 'was that Edrick was far-sighted enough to slip away.'

'Guess I heard something of the sort,' Martan allowed. 'There haven't been any reports of runaways murdering or thieving. None that I've heard.'

'If Edrick was lying low, you wouldn't have heard anything.'

'If he's lying low, how many others are?' Hasso asked the Captain.

Martan looked more embarrassed than annoyed. 'Be reasonable. We have our work cut out here, without combing the countryside when nobody reports anything.'

I pointed at the slumped Son. 'Bring him round. We'll get some *real* answers.'

'How do you propose to go about that?' Martan asked coolly. 'Just what do you mean, Yaleen?'

The truth is, I had no clear idea what I did mean. Or rather, I did have – but I recoiled at the idea. Momentarily my head swam with images of Capsi being stretched and twisted, crushed and burnt. 'No, no, no, never!' I told myself; and I meant it too.

'We'll threaten him, with the sort of thing *they* do to prisoners,' said I.

'And supposing he clams up tight?'

I didn't know what to say.

'Threaten something, then don't do it,' Martan went on, 'and word gets round. You lose credibility. Mind you, *I* totally agree we shouldn't use – ' he hesitated – 'torture. Because, well because I wouldn't ever want torture used on me.' He gazed at me evenly as if it was all up to me to decide. How, how, *how* had I got into this fix? It had all happened so damn suddenly.

'Can't we bluff him?' I suggested.

'He's probably lying there listening to us right now,' said Jizbel, 'just pretending to be out cold.' She regarded me with interest.

Martan disagreed. 'He won't have woken up yet. *I've* had a crack on the head before. But you'll have to decide sharpish. This isn't a debating club on morals.'

Decide. *I* would have to decide.

'Hasso,' I muttered. Hasso seemed to have curled up inside himself.

'Maybe his information isn't so important,' I said.

'And what if it is?' Martan asked me unhelpfully.

Indeed, why else had the Son preferred to be beaten senseless as soon as he realized what he had let slip?

When I first came to work at the Pens, I'd asked if there was a full list of prisoners. There was; but Edrick's name hadn't been on it – and of the dead, unsurprisingly, there was no list at all. Here was the first news I'd had that Edrick might still be active; and there was only one way to follow it up. But that one way was unacceptable.

I did decide, then and there. Irrespective of what happened subsequently I'm still sure I made the right choice; otherwise I would have felt polluted.

'We'll just question him normally.'

Everyone seemed to relax. Hasso uncoiled, and stretched his limbs. 'Fine,' he said, 'fine.' Martan looked relieved. Jizbel smiled sweetly.

One of the guards dumped a bucket of water over the Son's head, then they hauled him, groaning, back into the chair.

We tried to question him normally about whether Edrick had slipped away, where to, and why. And of course it was still possible that Edrick was dead. 'Giving Verrrino the slip' could have meant just that: getting himself killed.

We tried. The Son put on a fine show of being brain-scrambled and incapacitated, confused and crippled with amnesia. We had to give up, and he was led away. If the brute *was* play-acting, he contrived to stagger and slump about so convincingly that the guards almost had to drag him.

What should happen then, but a complete volte-face on the part of the good Captain? A few minutes earlier he had quite dismissed the notion of combing the countryside. Now he suddenly leapt in the face of that resolve by announcing that he would lead a small party up-country for a day or so in search of clues.

I think Martan had decided that he simply had to get away from the Pens for a while; maybe the bludgeoning had tipped the balance. A two-day stroll around the immediate hinterland of Verrino would be unlikely to bear fruit except by wild coincidence. On the other hand, a brief working holiday might be no bad idea.

Would I accompany him and his patrol? And would Hasso?

Why yes, we would.

'If we head out Tichini way,' suggested Hasso, 'we could stop overnight by the vineyards.'

'Why not?' agreed Martan lightly. 'If any Son's hiding in a wine-cask, we'll swill him out.'

So the next morning Hasso and I rendezvoused with Martan and six 'jack soldiers, and we set off inland. All of our spirits lightened as we walked along. It was a hot summer's day but the sky remained hazy so that we weren't baked; and the dust underfoot provided a soft tread. All stones and large pebbles had been regularly raked off this road for years, till both sides were lined with low embankments, twin dry walls. A roadman was specially employed to this end by the village of Tichini. Thus empty bottles, making their way by barrow from Verrino glassworks out to the vineyards and returning full along the same route, would not get tossed around and smashed. So Hasso explained as we travelled.

But we had hardly gone half a league before we reached a long stretch of road where the embankments were broken down, kicked around, scattered all over. Amidst the golden-blooming furze bushes off to one side I spied a boot and trouser leg protruding.

I pointed.

Martan pursed his lips. 'Seem to recall a skirmish here.'

The corpse wasn't wearing a fork-toed boot, so it couldn't be an unburied 'jack.

'Maybe that's Edrick,' I said vaguely.

'Might be anybody. Shouldn't think it's him out here, if he escaped near the very end. Assuming that's so.'

'Shouldn't you take a look?'

'But I don't know his face, Yaleen – aside from your description. Only you have his features by heart.'

'Oh.' I swallowed.

'I'll come with you,' offered Hasso; and together we made our way through the furze to inspect the dead body.

The corpse lay on its back, leathery and smelly in weatherstained trousers and shirt. The face had been hacked in half, and insects had feasted. The remains weren't recognizable. They weren't even nauseating any longer. Soft torn flesh is awful, but not bone and leather. We returned to the road. I shrugged, and we carried on.

Soon shrubby cones of hills arose around us, disclosing after a further hour or more the village of Tichini hugging a hilltop. That particular hill and its immediate neighbours were all terraced around their southern slopes and neatly vine-clad. The road climbed gently, taking us up through a vineyard where swelling clusters of mauve grapes hung from the new staked growth above the twisted knobbly stocks. The soil looked quite varied between one hillside and the next. When I remarked on this to Hasso, he told me that the soil constituents – clay, limestone and porous mineral-trapping chalk – were the same, but that there were different mixtures on different hillsides. Originally, long ago, the terraced soils had all been blended by hand, to different recipes; and every winter, depending on the taste of the new wine, the slopes were top-dressed with a little more chalk or lime or clay. This, plus a variety of water sources and different vine-stocks, added up to a notable range of vintages within a comparatively small area. A few people were working on the slopes.

'Isn't it neat?' I said. 'You wouldn't think there'd been battles.'

'There weren't any out here,' said Martan.

As we rounded the flank of the hill, we came upon an old white-haired man standing by the road, leaning on a rake.

'Ho,' said Captain Martan. 'Roadside's broken down, way back. Did you know?'

The man doodled in the dust. 'You come to escort me while I rake it?'

'Why? Are there any stray Sons hiding out, so that you need escorting?'

'Who knows? When world's a pest, home's best.'

'That isn't much of an attitude,' said Hasso angrily. 'Captain Martan, here, is as far from his own home as can be. If he'd thought home was best, you'd still have the Sons on your backs.'

'Oh we had them. We had them. You needn't tell me. You can make things perfect for a hundred years – every bit of soil and pebble – then suddenly lunatics decide to hold a war. So where's the use in perfection? People might as well drink vinegar. And what's Verrino come to, these days? They blowing any fresh bottles down there?'

'They will be, after repairs to the works,' said Hasso.

'So this year we'll just cask the new wine? Or pour it into old bottles, or sluice it away, eh?'

'Are there or aren't there any Sons running wild hereabouts that you know of?' repeated Martan.

'And if there are, and one's caught here or in Little Rimo over the hills or in Bruz, do we pop him in the soil, same as we're popped in the soil when we die, so the rain can wash his foreign substance down into our vine-roots?'

Martan sighed. 'You aren't much help, old fellow.'

'Help came too late for me, soldier. Those Sons killed my boy and my boy's boy when they came here a-thieving. There was no need of that.'

'I'm sorry to hear it.'

'Don't be. I'm feeling mellow now. And I'm in my right place, which you aren't. No one here's telling me to walk to Verrino with my rake.'

We left the tetchy old man and climbed the rest of the way to the village, which was dominated by the sprawling vinthouse. A few villagers loitered in doorways, eyeing us silently. A goat stood wetting its beard and chewing on ferns growing in an ornamental basin where water bubbled from a pipe. A small boy with a stick was guarding the goat; at our approach he fled up a crooked alley. We entered a little marketplace. At that moment trade seemed to be brisk, in olives and bread, trussed chickens and oil and cheese; but as soon as the people saw us a lot of goods promptly vanished out of sight into bags and boxes. Three fat women sat outside a café, carding wool and singing; the sight of us shut them up.

I could spy no obvious damage (except in one respect), nor disfigurations, nor even signs of reduced diet, but

43

obviously the flavour of the village had soured; and in Tichini the flavour of soil and water and minerals and air was such a delicate subtle thing – blood spilt down a hillside and the smell of fear could spoil a hundred years of care and love.

The one blatant piece of damage was that the great wooden doors of the vinthouse, leading to a courtyard, hung loose – wrenched off their hinges.

We went in, spied a scurrying apron-clad boy, and asked to see the Master or Mistress Vintner, supposing that he or she was still alive. Hasso assured us that this person would be the 'mayor' of Tichini.

A man it was, and his name was Beri. He was short and fat, nearly as wide as he was tall. He welcomed us; he bustled. He quickly arranged overnight quarters: in the vinthouse for me and Hasso and Martan, in village homes for the other 'jacks. He commanded doors to open; he commanded people to step out and smile.

Beri was the sort of fellow whom you could never push over without him rolling right back up again. And, as we soon discovered, he was a repository of all human wisdom whose joy it was to preside over everyone else's foibles and follies, orchestrating popular opinion, pronouncing on anything under the sun. In other circumstances he might have struck you as an intrusive, opinionated bore. Given the current apathetic state of Tichini, though, these traits of his were a distinct plus. It seemed as if the village waited, hushed, upon his assessment of us – of our bouquet – to decide whether to spit us out or swallow us. And Beri went out of his way to give us his blessing.

He also gave us a guided tour of the vinthouse and its vaults, pointing out where the buildings had been vandalized and looted; though really neither damage nor losses would have looked too serious if a bit of mess had just been tidied up.

While guiding us, he held forth on how he had handled the Sons. 'So I said to those devils, said I, well if that's your opinion, your Honour, why fair enough; but up in the hills here we aren't dipping our toes in the river all the time, so that we aren't as unlike each other as you might suppose! Indeed, your Honour, are people ever so very different from each other as their opinions make them seem? They were brutes, Captain Martan, and murderous brutes too, but I reckon I handled them as best as could be, though I felt in peril of my life a good few times for speaking out. But I think they respected my bluntness – even if I did feel their fists once or twice. And they stole and messed things around something awful, so that we aren't even cleaned up yet. And they raped three of our women, including my own niece; and what could the women do but endure it? And what could I feel but shame and grief, and just bottle it up?'

That evening Beri arranged a celebration in the vinthouse courtyard, attended by a number of the villagers – mainly those who would host the 'jacks. A bonfire was lit. Several chickens were roasted. Bottles of vintage, which had come through the war intact, were opened. (A lot of bottles seemed to have survived intact.) A stringed bouzouki provided twangy, jangly music. And Beri held forth expertly upon the causes and circumstances of war, amidst 'jacks who had actually fought that war. Discovering that we were on the lookout for runaway Sons and had spent weeks interrogating prisoners, Beri discoursed on the psychology of the men of the west, based on his wealth of observations. Then he offered opinions on the black current and the riverguild, and wondered whether the guild ought perhaps to compensate civilian victims of war, such as the people of Tichini. And of Verrino too, of course. He invited our comments; he approved or disproved them.

After a while Martan drew Hasso and me aside. 'Would

you say,' he asked quietly, 'that our host actually . . . collaborated with the Sons while they were here?'

'What makes you say that?' asked Hasso.

'Beri's too full of how he handled the situation. And I'm sure he's lying his head off, about how rough it was.'

'What about the deaths, Martan? The damage? The broken doors? What about the rapes?'

'And why have those doors been left wrecked for so long? Could it be to show visitors how he resisted? And why does the vinthouse look as though the Sons trashed and robbed it, when actually the damage and loss is – '

'Superficial,' said I.

'Isn't it just? Yet it's all still on display. As for his niece and those other two women, how do you prove a woman's been raped? If someone has a sword stuck in them, that's visible enough. And how come the vineyards are in such splendid shape – when the Sons burnt and smashed other places, once they found they were losing the war?'

'Hmm, I see what you mean,' said Hasso. 'But how could we prove it? And if we could, what then?'

'Just that I wonder whether he would really report any runaways in the area – because if we caught them, they might tell us things about Beri's conduct. And if *he* won't tell us, you can bet nobody else in Tichini will. Not even a niece who's been offered to the Sons. They're all in it together. They take their cue from him.'

'We can hardly challenge him,' said Hasso.

'No, we can't. I might be totally wrong.'

I butted in. 'So do you reckon that old fellow with the rake actually lost his boy and his boy's boy? Or does he just stand on the road to waylay travellers with a tall tale about how much everyone suffered here?'

Martan shook his head. 'I don't know. It's possible. Maybe we could find out from those other places over the hills, Bruz and Little Rimo. And maybe we'd be wasting our time.'

46

The bouzouki music raced and thrummed. Feet stamped the flagstones of the courtyard. Beri presided over the revels, dispensing wisdom and vintage.

'We're wasting our time,' said Martan. 'Definitely so. After weeks of asking questions and suspecting lies, suspicion becomes a sickly way of life. Let's drink and sing and pretend that everything's right as rain. Dance with me, will you, Yaleen?'

So I did, because he'd asked. And then I danced with Hasso. But after a while the exertion began to tell on Hasso. He became breathless. He wasn't yet truly recovered from the siege.

Neither, perhaps, had Tichini recovered from what had befallen it during the war – namely, its own suspiciously prosperous survival.

The next day we returned to Verrino. On the way back I asked several 'jacks how they had fared in the homes of the villagers; but all had retired to bed late with a bellyful of wine, and had had the consequences to cloud their perceptions in the morning. Besides, they had all been on their best polite behaviour.

So: enigma unresolved. And perhaps, indeed, Beri had done well by his village; cunningly well. At least he had saved the future of the wine trade, though Tichini was, for the moment, lying low; and their old rakeman hadn't gone to repair the road just yet. Too much haste in that regard might have struck Beri as unwise.

The day after we got back I sailed at last for Pecawar, aboard – guess which brig? – the *Darling Dog*.

We drifted in past pale green cinnamon trees, and as we turned to shore the aroma of cloves greeted my nostrils – this, and the dead scent of dust. Even the water close to the bank wore a faint glaze of dust. I sneezed several times. My nose had grown unused to filtering out motes of desiccated soil and wind-blown desert. Maybe in my absence from Pecawar my nostril hairs had thinned out.

Dockside buildings and spice warehouses were all a dusty yellow, like long low sandcastles.

In town I stopped at a café for a glass of cinnamon coffee, to collect my thoughts. Really there were too many thoughts to gather into any neat bundle; so I watched the world go by instead: porters, dockers, factors, bakers' boys with trays of hot sesame rolls balanced on their heads. A lad selling chilled sherbet lemonade: he was quickly scooted away by a waiter.

And amongst the people passing by I spotted my father striding down the street. Riding high on his shoulders, a little girl.

'Dad!'

He stopped, he stared around.

I waved from the café verandah. 'It's me! Over here!'

He came at a run, to the wide steps. The little girl bobbed up and down as she hung on to the crinkly curls on the back of Dad's head, with her bunchy little fists. Dad was more bald than when I'd last seen him. Where before there had been some dark wiry sheep's wool on his crown, now there were just wisps; and I couldn't help wondering if this was Narya's fault. Did he so adore her that he had let her idly pluck and loosen his remaining locks? (It was from my mother that I received my own softer nutbrown hair.) The child seemed unbothered at the way Dad's gait suddenly broke into a gallop. She giggled gleefully, but then as he mounted the steps to my table she fell silent. He set her down on the dusty planking, and she just stood there unmoving, gazing . . . while we both lost interest in her temporarily.

Dad hugged me; I hugged him.

'So, so, *so*!' He laughed. 'The prodigal comes home. Or at least within a stone's throw of home . . .'

'That's where I was heading; never fear.'

'Oh, these have been terrible times! We were getting quite anxious. Still, with you safely down south . . .'

'Down south? Was I?'

'According to your last letter . . . goodness, that was long enough ago! What upheavals: Jangali men pouring into town. Arming themselves to the teeth! You *were* down south during the war?'

'Not really, Dad. Oh, I've such a lot to tell you. It's a blessing I met you here, actually. I was worried how you and Mum – '

'Worried?' He raised an eyebrow. 'We'd never have guessed.' But his tone was humorous, not harsh.

'That's why I stopped for a coffee. To give me a chance to find the words. I've some bad news.'

'About Capsi, is it?'

'You know!'

Dad shook his head. 'We guessed. Verrino, the Spire, the war. Well, we'd have been foolish to hope! Besides, Capsi made his own choice long ago, and it doesn't seem to have included us, or remembering us.' He sounded sad, but not bitter.

Of course! I could let them assume Capsi had been killed in the war . . . Then, in another half-year, they would read the truth in my book.

I chewed my lip. 'I'm afraid it wasn't the war . . .'

Dad held a finger to my lips. 'I'd rather rejoice at your return, yet a while. If there's mourning to be done, we'll tackle it later. Your mother and I have got used to the idea of not . . . seeing Capsi again.' Dad held his head high, surveying me. He wasn't a tall man, but he out-topped me by a good half-span. 'You look well, daughter.'

'Do I?'

'No. Actually, you don't. Not "well". You look as though you've suffered. But your heart has won through. You've grown up. You went as a girl, you come home as a woman.'

49

'Oh,' said I. 'Spare my blushes.' As yet Dad had no notion that it was *I* who had ridden the Worm downriver. The event was a matter of universal knowledge, but not the name of the heroine in question. Not yet. The guild was keeping mum till my book was published.

'Talking of girls,' said I, 'how's my new sister?' For the first time I really looked at Narya. She was hardly knee-high, and skinny, with lots of curly bistre hair like the knots in charcoalwood. In this respect she took after Dad. Her eyes were hazel, just like mine. I'd assumed she would seem a complete stranger to me, yet by virtue of those eyes it was as though, in her, I was inspecting a curious version of myself. She must have been watching me attentively all this while, since she hadn't moved from where Dad had set her down. Now she winked at me.

Some dust in her eye? Even as I thought of dust she started to rub her eye with a knuckle. She quit, grinned impishly and toddled towards the table, to clutch the edge.

'Oh, who's a big healthy girl?' asked Dad, tousling her curls. (She wasn't particularly big.) 'And so well behaved. Do you know, Yaleen, I've hardly heard her cry. Actually,' he whispered, 'I think she's almost too well behaved at times.'

'Not like me, eh?'

'Oh, she gets excited, does Narya. And she looks as if she's taking everything in, bright as a spark. But other times she just sits for hours like a broody hen. You'd hardly know she was there. Got a mind of her own, though, she has. She won't be overfed, even if your mother tries to pack it in. Just as well, or your Mum would have turned her into a roly-poly!'

'Hullo, Narya,' I said. 'My name's Yaleen. I'm your sister.'

Narya gazed up at me in silence.

'She's slow at speaking,' Dad confided.

'What about "wain"? When it rained. And all that. I thought you wrote saying – '

'She began speaking. A few words. Then she stopped – like someone who finds a whistle then throws it away again. Frankly, we're a bit bothered.'

'Oh, I expect it's that way with some kids. The ones who hold back are just damming it up. One day it'll all flood forth, then you won't know where you are for chatter.' I didn't know too much about this, apart from something I remembered Jambi saying about her own kid. However, it seemed a good idea to say so. What *I* was thinking to myself was that they oughtn't to have had another baby, so late on in life.

'Ah, she's my big darling, aren't you?' Dad hoisted Narya aloft. 'Let's step on home, Yaleen.'

Narya clung to Dad's scanty rigging as if sailing him from the top of a mast.

Alas for notions of dandling my little sister on my knee! Alas for the idea I'd got from those eyes of hers that she was some sort of soul-sister! As soon as Narya saw me take up residence at home, she did her level best to avoid me. I guess she was jealous. She must have felt I was butting in, out of nowhere, between her and her parents. But she didn't fuss or cry. She didn't hang around, or cling. Quite the opposite! She simply absented herself, in so far as it's possible for a very young child to do so. I thought this was weird, till I finally rumbled her game – cunning creature that she was. My mother and father were bothered because Narya was withdrawn and broody and couldn't talk. And now here was I intruding. Right! So Narya would withdraw *twice* as much, to force them to come to her and quit lavishing attention on this invading stranger.

Her ploy worked fairly well. Obviously she wasn't so much backward as plain devious. She was a little manipulator. She had already learned what is perhaps the most subtle trick in the game of life: to win by withholding oneself. To reign, by resigning. To triumph by taking cover; by not talking. She would only romp as a special gift, to be carefully rationed out. Since these little gifts of herself were so special, she'd convinced my parents that she was indeed their treasure, their joy.

That's how I saw it – in so far as I saw anything much of Narya during my stay.

Well, sod her!

By now I'd told Mum and Dad the tale of my travels – though I told them far less about my inner feelings during my adventures than I had written in my book. How odd that I felt free to broadcast my most intimate sentiments to all and sundry who might read the book, but couldn't confide these in my own mother and father! On second thoughts maybe this wasn't so curious. Those things which I'd experienced were right outside my parents' scope. I'd been in such extreme circumstances that their questions seemed impossibly banal – on the level of asking a starving man, 'Would you rather have mutton or fried fish for supper?' So during my account I stuck to the bare bones of events; and even then there were moments when I almost gave up. ('But what is this Godmind that comes from Eegen?' 'No, no, the name's *Eeden*. And the Godmind doesn't come from there; it's us who came from there originally.' 'So why did the Worm – ?' 'But I just told you that!' And so forth.)

Amongst events to be related was, of course, the fate of brother Capsi; tortured and burnt alive on a bonfire . . . This was the worst part to tell. One of the reasons why it was the worst, was that I was sure I was grinning idiotically as I told it. I simply couldn't find the right expression to wear on my face.

My parents took the news as nobly as could be expected. Afterwards Dad even declared, 'We should be grateful to the men of Jangali that there won't be any more horrors like that over here. The war was a good thing, don't you agree?'

No, the war had *not* been a good thing. It had poisoned too many people's lives. I myself had been on the brink of ordering another human being vilely tortured. And what of the west, where the same terrible existence went on as before? Except that now we knew about it. And what of a hundred other things – such as the cosmic war between Godmind and Worm? Loose ends were left hanging everywhere. The world after the war was more like a ball of wool a kitten has been ripping up, than like a garment well repaired! My parents couldn't see any of these loose ends; I could. I nodded and looked at the floor; they took my silence for consent.

And I wondered: who would look at me one day when I was older and would know that I couldn't possibly understand something; and then would lower their eyes, lose interest and give up?

I didn't tell Mum and Dad that I'd written a book. Their off-target comments might have annoyed me.

Maybe it was a reaction on my part to this failure of communication; maybe I thought that I could root out the cause by identifying myself with the mutton and fish of life, the ordinary mundane things. But I found myself wondering whether I ought to marry and settle down and raise a child of my own; a child who would of course, after a few years, be my friend and understand me.

Marry whom: someone who understood me? Or someone who would simply suck me down into the normal business of everyday life?

Should I return to Verrino and propose to Hasso? Ha! Or onward to Aladalia to propose to Tam (assuming that he could shed his mad infatuation)? Ho.

I dismissed this idea. Instead for a while I nursed fantasies of trekking into the interior to live as a hermit and write poetry; not that I had ever written any poems, but presumably that's true of all poets before they start out.

Probably what I *ought* to do (I decided next) was get back on board a boat and be a proper riverwoman. Ah, but wait! My book would soon be published, and might make me famous. In that case should I change my name and sign on a vessel anonymously, with the riverguild keeping this a close secret? Fat chance of that on our little river! (Our long, long river seemed to have shrunk a lot recently.)

Truth to tell, I was getting a bit scared of my book coming out. When I wrote the book, I hadn't really been thinking in terms of people reading it; so I could afford to tell the truth. But soon the truth would escape into the world on its own two legs – not that this ought to embarrass me, but other people mightn't see things exactly the way I saw them; or see me, exactly as *I* saw me.

In view of what was to happen I could have spared myself all these emotional squirmings in Pecawar. If I had put a single one of my fanciful schemes into action, though, I would have saved my life.

Two weeks after I returned home, my mother's cousin Chataly died unexpectedly. She vomited in her sleep and choked on some food. Chataly had lived on her own in a tiny spice-farming hamlet a couple of leagues out of town. A neighbour brought the news, so then of course my mother had to go to see about the funeral rites and clear up the house, she being the closest female relative. Mum would need to stay away one or two nights.

Dad offered to go along with her to help; and Mum quickly accepted. Then they both looked at me.

It was me who ought to have accompanied Mum. We all knew that perfectly well, and at first I couldn't fathom why my father had volunteered his services so eagerly; or why my mother had accepted. Unless (grotesque thought) my parents wanted to be alone together overnight in Chataly's house for some sort of second or third honeymoon without any nearby toddler to hamper them.

On second thoughts, maybe Dad felt that Mum wouldn't really want me with her? *I* wouldn't be much aid and comfort. That wasn't a very flattering interpretation.

On third thoughts, maybe they hoped that by leaving me alone with Narya this would force the little girl to come to terms with her big sister – something that my parents couldn't engineer by themselves. And then, of course, Narya mustn't be exposed to death, must she now? Shelter the little darling!

Fourth thoughts were rather like the third, with a twist. Mum and Dad wanted to show their love for me by trusting me to care for their treasure in their absence.

Aha, *fifth* thoughts! They wanted me to settle down and raise a family. Here was an ideal opportunity to show me the joys thereof.

But whether first, second or fifth thoughts were behind this, the upshot was that I must needs offer to look after the house for a day or two and nursemaid my little sister.

So Mum and Dad explained to Narya that they had to go away to visit someone for a couple of nights. Narya just stared at them, nodded once or twice and sucked her thumb. By then it was late afternoon, and within the hour they were gone. Nor did their actual departure seem to bother Narya one little bit. She even waved goodbye from the door with a certain panache.

I was left alone with her, well before any possible bedtime. What to do? Read her a story? Or ten stories? Play games? Stick her in a corner to mope? At least I didn't need to check whether she was wetting herself; Mum had said that Narya's bowel and bladder control were excellent.

'Shall we have something yummy to eat?' I suggested; and fled to the kitchen. Narya didn't follow me, so I pottered about inventing a new sort of spice pudding, all the while keeping one ear cocked for noises of breakage, screams or whatever. Silence reigned, except amongst the pots and pans.

After half an hour I got guilty and searched for *her*. Oh yes, that's the way she played her game; didn't I know it? Feeling like a fool I went looking. I hunted through the downstairs first, then checked the back stoop in case she'd slipped out through the screen doors into our little walled garden.

I loitered outside a while, pretending that I was looking for her.

Pecawar gardens tended to be mostly dry; and in ours we had a 'mountain range' consisting of shapely black boulders set around a white pebble 'lake'. Half a dozen large knobbly barrel-gourds occupied the sandy 'plains' on either side of this lake. These gourds were a glossy green, striped with bright orange and yellow zigzags. When I was a young girl I used to make believe that the gourds were bulbous cities banded with rows of windows aglow with light – cities somewhere out in the desert where nobody from the rivershore had ever been. The barrel-gourds were desert plants which grew very slowly; these ones might have been a century old. When I was even smaller I thought the guards were the heads of monster-people buried up to their necks in the garden; and when the sun went down I was a bit scared of stepping outside. As soon as I discovered the quayside and the river, of course, our garden became a totally boring place.

While I stood there pretending to look for Narya, I recalled my childish fancy, and I half expected to see my sister hunkered down by one of those monster-heads whispering to it; her only confidant, sole recipient of words from her. I fantasized how I might greet Mum and Dad on their return with the glad (or sick) tidings, 'She does talk, you know! She talks to the gourds in the garden.' Whereupon Mum and Dad could paint their faces green and orange to try to communicate with Narya by pretending to be vegetables . . . However, she wasn't lurking in the garden.

I went back indoors, bolting the screens behind me, and I mounted the stairs. When I was younger these had been of bare waxed planks, but now they were thickly carpeted, no doubt in case Narya took a tumble. I found her sitting on the floor of Capsi's old bedroom, which was now her room. Her head was cocked, listening to the breeze tinkle some wind-chimes by the open window. The night was warm so that there was no point in shutting the window in case she caught a chill, though the thought did cross my mind (worry, worry).

Capsi's pen-and-ink panorama of the opposite shore was still tacked to the wall. Someone (Dad, I presumed) had added lovable colourful baby animals romping here and there. Giant baby animals, dwarfing the terrain of that one-time never-never-land over in the west.

'You okay, Narya?'

Narya deigned to notice me; she nodded.

'Nice eats, soon,' I said encouragingly. 'Yum-yum.' I think it was myself I was encouraging.

Presently we ate the pudding, which wasn't too bad at all, and we drank some hot cocoa. Then I hunted out some kiddy tale for Narya to endure. I think 'endure' best describes the way in which Narya received this treat: with a mixture of stoic boredom and vague tension as to how soon the story would be finished.

By now it was deep dusk, so I announced, 'Off to dreamland with you!' and saw her to bed with a kiss on the brow.

I wondered what to do with myself. I tidied up a bit, then trimmed the oil lamp and settled with a book of poems by Gimmo of Melonby, who lived a few hundred years ago. Gimmo the Tramper, who wandered up and down our river shore singing his ballads for coins or a supper.

I must have dozed off. A noise woke me: creak, bump.

Narya must be up and wandering . . .

I was about to go and check, when in the doorway to the kitchen . . . stood a man.

A tall man with a freckly face and bald head. A few bunches of gingery hair were sprouting from the sides of it. Spectacles were perched upon his nose. I hoped I *hadn't* woken up at all, and was just dreaming.

Vain hope. Doctor Edrick was dressed in baggy trousers tucked into fork-toed boots, and wearing a scarlet jerkin. These were junglejack clothes, obviously looted from some dead soldier. In one big hairy fist he held a metal tube with a handle: a pistol, pointed at me.

Edrick had let his erstwhile toothbrush moustache sprout out into great drooping ginger horns.

'That's clever of you, Doctor Edrick,' I said, as steadily as I could. 'You haven't skulked. You haven't crawled. You've swaggered about in stolen clothes. You haven't shaved your moustache off – you've grown a dog's tail on your face, instead.'

He kept the pistol pointed at my chest. 'It's easier to travel, Yaleen, if you stride along the high road, and pay your way in coin of the country.'

His voice sounded altered. He'd shed the accent of the west, their funny broad way of pronouncing words. His accent still wasn't any of *our* accents, but it would serve to fool most people here in the middle reaches who would assume, by his clothes, that he was from Jangali.

'I've been watching this house for a while,' he said. 'And now you're alone. How timely. How lucky that your parents took a trip.'

'You didn't . . . kill Chataly, did you?'

'Ah, so someone died? No, there are certain limits to my energy and ingenuity. Whatever errand your parents went

58

on is none of my doing. "Lucky for your parents," is my meaning. Lucky not to be here, during what must come to pass.' He moved slowly into the room.

Suppose I hurled the book of Gimmo's poems at the lamp? Aye, and burned the house down with Narya asleep upstairs . . .

'Don't move,' warned Edrick. 'Or I'll shoot to cripple you. For a start.'

I didn't move.

'My dear Yaleen, I underestimated you once – and I shan't make that mistake twice. You were an agent of the Satan-Snake all along, weren't you?'

'What, me? Certainly not!'

'I suppose it let you ride downstream in its jaws as a favour pure and simple?' He snorted. 'Oh yes, you were spotted; and I knew at once. *Then*, how do we explain your oh-so-innocent revelation of a certain snake-poison we could use? Or how conveniently you stumbled upon *my* men – who would bring you to me, and not to some Brotherhood cellar where the truth could really have been squeezed out of you! You fooled me, Yaleen. I don't take kindly to being fooled.'

'I didn't! Honest.'

How much could I tell him? Without giving him valuable information about the current, the *Ka*-store, the Godmind?

'I'll grant,' he went on, 'that the Snake may well enter into compacts with its witches. If they serve it well, it will repay them with services in turn. In which case, my main problem would seem to be how to *motivate* the witch in question so that she'll really *beg* the Snake to do something for her, hmm? Beg the Snake, for instance, to quit the river once again? For a while?'

'Long enough for you to escape?'

'Long enough for whatever I have in mind.'

'You could have crossed the river easily enough if you'd walked north instead of south.'

'*How so?*'

'The head of the current halted at Aladalia. That's beyond – '

'I know where Aladalia is.'

'It didn't go all the way downstream.' No harm, surely, in telling him that? 'You needn't worry about your captured troops. When we've cleared up the mess they made, they'll be sent north then over to the other side. You could be repatriated too.'

'How very considerate. But maybe I want to make the Snake perform a few tricks, just as you did? I require a tool for this purpose; a key to unlock the Snake. *You*.'

'How did you know I'd be here in Pecawar?' I was playing for time. I guess people always play for time, even when it'll make not a scrap of difference.

'You described your home to me; you located it, remember? I decided that part of your tale wasn't a lie, since a dollop of truth always smooths the way. So where does someone head for after a dangerous secret mission and a war? Where but home, to rest? Fair gamble! It paid off. Let's move on to more important matters.'

I had to chance my hand. 'Look, Doctor, you're quite wrong about me. But I've learnt something about your so-called Satan-Snake that's pretty important. You ought to listen before you do anything rash.' (Why ever should I call him 'Doctor'? He was only a Doctor of Ignorance!)

'I've no doubt that you could spin me a fascinating yarn till the sun comes up again. We'll have hours and hours for it, later on. Right now you and I are going for a walk, to somewhere more secluded, out of earshot.'

Did he have any accomplices? Andri and Jothan would most likely have been involved in organizing the poison plot on the other shore. But Edrick might not have escaped from Verrino alone . . . though it would have been easier for one person to get away. Would Edrick have trusted others to be as clever as himself?

He kept the pistol aimed at me, while with his free hand he pulled a kerchief from his trouser pocket. To use as gag, what else? This he tucked into the neck of his jerkin. Next he drew out a length of cord – to bind my wrists. The cord dragged something else from his pocket, something half the size of a person's hand. This fell heavily to the floor, making a metallic clatter. Hastily Edrick scooped the thing up and stuffed it back in his pocket, though not before I got a look at it.

Part of a pistol? No, the tube was too fat and short. And what was that screw on top? The thing looked designed to be worn, to fit over finger and thumb. For punching with?

He hadn't wished me to see it.

Stick your finger inside the tube, turn the screw; and your finger, commencing with the fingernail, would be squeezed slowly till the flesh burst open like a squashed tomato . . .

Then another finger. Then another. There were plenty of fingers. Then your toes, one by one. I'd caught a finger in a door once. It hadn't bruised me much, let alone smashed anything, but the pain had been excruciating. Imagine that pain prolonged and multiplied.

When I was over in the west, to scare me Andri and Jothan had mentioned such devices, kept in the cellars of the Brotherhood. Later I'd heard tales in Verrino of the cruelties of the Occupation.

I doubted whether Edrick nursed scruples about torturing people, if he thought the gain was worth it. He wasn't me. He wanted to march me off to a quiet spot . . . where nobody could hear me screaming?

Before he could do that, he had to tie my hands and gag me. That isn't so easy to do one-handed – not unless he planned to knock me unconscious with the pistol butt and carry me.

I heard a faint rustle of noise. Ever so quickly, as if shaking my head, I flicked my gaze.

61

My bowels chilled. Narya was standing in the shadows outside the hall door. She was watching me. As yet the door jamb hid her from Edrick. If he could manage to tie me and march me away, he could carry Narya along under one arm. And torture her. The better to persuade me.

Go back, I thought at Narya. *Back back back. Hide!* I didn't dare look again.

In between Edrick recovering the fingerscrew and beginning to edge round the room, to get behind me, fifty thoughts seemed to have been packed into a few seconds.

Including: would Edrick actually *use* his pistol? What had Andri said about pistols? 'Pompous things. As soon explode in your hand, as harm your enemy.' Our army had been equipped with some pistols, crafted at Guineamoy. I gathered these weren't too popular compared with a bow. But Edrick probably had the very best.

I threw myself from my chair, rolled head over heels and bounced through the doorway, aiming to crash into Narya and carry her off. That was the idea. Not that I thought it out in detail. I just went.

It didn't work. I hit the doorway a glancing blow, knocking a good bit of wind out of me – but at least I ended up in the hall. Narya wasn't even there. She'd gone.

Where should *I* go? Out of the front door? Edrick *might* have a companion posted outside. Besides, I mightn't get time to unbolt the door. Upstairs and out through Capsi's open window? Climb up to the flat of the roof if I could manage it, and scream blue murder? Rouse the neighbourhood? I leapt up the stairs with Edrick right on my tail. His hand clutched my ankle. Swirling, I slashed flesh with my diamond ring like a cat clawing a dog behind it. He cursed; I wrenched free, and fairly threw myself the rest of the way upstairs. Narya might have fled to her room. I mustn't lead him to her. And my room had a key, hers didn't.

I slammed my bedroom door just a moment too late.

Edrick blocked it from closing completely. For a few moments I held him off with my back to the door and my feet braced against the bedstead. What a weird reprise of childhood years when a teasing Capsi used to chase me to my room, pretending to be a bogeyman. Now there was a real bogeyman loose in our home, with a machine in his pocket to crush my fingers. The key was in the lock but I couldn't for the life of me force the door home. Instead the door was forcing me back slowly but surely.

I couldn't hold it. My legs were packing up. A weapon: I needed a weapon!

Scissors! Sharp scissors of best Guineamoy metal were kept in the bedside cupboard. I could use those to stab in the dark. I could smash Edrick's glasses, blind his eyes! I mustn't be squeamish about where I stabbed him.

I let the door toss me right across the bed. I rolled to the floor beyond, dragged the cupboard door open, scrabbled inside, made a fist around those scissors. Staying low, I squinted over the covers.

Edrick bulked in the doorway as a vague silhouette. I made my breath leak in and out slowly so as not to betray myself by panting.

The silhouette announced quietly, 'If you try to get away again, I *will* shoot you.'

He would have to spot me first. As yet he wasn't venturing away from the door. He was waiting till his eyes adjusted. Already I could see grey outlines. Stars were bright outside the window; but apart from the leaflet up top the window was closed. The only way out would be to burst through wood, glass and all. The fall could cripple me on those ornamental boulders below.

I balanced, clutching my scissors, making believe I was a bouncy ball. Shutting the door behind him, Edrick took a few paces into the room. He didn't lock the door. Either he was unaware of the key, or he wanted to leave himself a quick exit.

'Though,' he whispered, 'I mightn't need to hurt you if you co-operate . . .'

I slithered under the bed and backed up against the wall. In this position he couldn't knock me senseless.

Footsteps; faint shape of feet.

'So: gone to ground, eh?'

He was kneeling down. He wouldn't be able to see me immediately in the deeper darkness where I lay, not if I kept still.

Shoulders . . . head . . . get ready!

Unaccountably the bedroom door began to open.

Edrick saw where I was crouched. 'Ah,' he said.

And past him I saw Narya faintly in the half-open doorway. The stupid, stupid child!

Edrick laid his pistol down and groped for my legs. He would expect me to kick, and would grip my ankle again.

What was Narya *doing*? She had crept around the door. The key! She was pulling the key from the lock!

Hold the scissors just so . . . Squirm – and stab!

'Aaah!' Edrick stifled a cry of pain. 'You filthy damn *witch*.'

Narya was backing out – and I was sure she had the key. Yes, I heard it scrape into the far side of the lock! Then I heard the key turn: the faintest click. That damn conniving brat was locking her unwanted sister in with the bogeyman! This bogeyman had obviously come in response to her secret desires to dispose of the stranger called Yaleen.

Edrick took up his pistol again in his wounded hand.

'This is your very last chance. You toss that knife out, or I'll kill you.'

'I really don't think you ought to shoot me,' I said. 'You've no idea what a mistake it'll be if you kill me.'

'Ha ha,' said tonelessly. But it was true.

'Just let me explain what'll happen.'

'I'll count to five.'

'No, *listen*.'

'One.'

'It isn't in your own best interests, Doctor Edrick.'

'Two. You *hurt* me.'

'The Worm – '

'Three.'

'That's to say, the Satan-Snake – '

'Four. Nobody hurts me.'

' – It told me it would – '

'Five. *Die*, Snake-daughter!'

A blinding crash, a punch in my chest as if I'd been impaled by a mast . . .

Your body is where the world begins and ends. Your body is the boundary. And when that boundary, of the body, is smashed, when it's stove in like a boat rammed on a rock, oddly it isn't you who sinks, it's the world. It's the world that disappears into the depths down a deep dark well of water.

The whole world sank right then.

I was in a blue void. I was aware of nothing except for that azure light. My body had vanished. So had everything else. Maybe I was spinning? I seemed to have nothing either to spin with or to be still with, but I did wonder whether I was spinning.

Maybe I was spinning so rapidly that nothing else was visible? I tried to slow myself down. I don't know *what* exactly I thought I was slowing, since I didn't have a body . . .

I seemed to be in this empty sky-space for a long time. Then:

Welcome back, Yaleen, said the Worm.

Damn it.

Edrick had had his revenge, all right. His revenge for dashed hopes, destroyed ambitions. His revenge for being diddled by a slip of a girl.

But what a hollow revenge this was, to be sure! If only

he'd known the truth, how zealously he would have fought to keep me alive!

Yet though he didn't know it, this was the best possible revenge he could have had. Because he had made me the Worm's own creature. I'd thought that event would be years and years in the future. It was soon, so very soon.

I said hullo, Yaleen.

I heard you. Hullo, Worm.

That's better. Maybe you're wondering where you are?

In the Ka-store, I suppose.

Not exactly. Do you recall how I was outlining my scheme to send a human agent back along the psylink to Eeden?

How could I forget? That's always been the great ambition of my life: to travel!

The great ambition of your death, surely?

Of course, my death. I forgot. How silly of me. Good joke, Worm. You always were a good sport.

Only since you became involved in my affairs, Yaleen!

How gallant.

Not at all. I owe you, my dear. Didn't I promise to inform you of Kas and Godminds, of stars and Eeden? How could I possibly break my word? I have my honour to uphold.

I'd be quite happy to overlook all that, Worm. Consider yourself absolved.

No, no, I insist. My treat. I shall now display how I intend to tackle this business. I'll show you what's about to happen, hmm?

Couldn't you send somebody else to Eeden? No, I suppose not. We're part of each other, aren't we? In that case, how awful to separate us!

Oh, you'll be back afterwards. I'm fairly sure I can manage that. With our affinity for each other, how could you doubt it? As you say, it's really quite touching, our relationship: a bit like Mum and daughter. Heigh-ho, a goddess and her girl!

Okay, so I'm touched. Except that there isn't anything

hereabouts to touch. I don't seem to have any hands. I suppose there's no chance of you changing your mind?

None at all.

I sighed. *Shall we get on with it?*

That's my girl!

All of a sudden there were images to see: and if I was spinning around, as I imagined, then those shapes must be spinning around too, keeping pace with me. This seemed to be so. Like the pattern on a child's top which wanders widdershins while the top spins the opposite way, the display slid slowly round me.

I drank those images greedily. I couldn't help myself. Absolutely *nothing* else existed, so those images were everything to me – and I guess this printed them pretty deep in me, the way that I'd printed my special image into the fabric of the Worm a while back.

If I'd had eyes to close, to shut those images out, maybe I could have avoided having to travel the psylink to Eeden as the cat's paw of the Worm. Maybe I could have become one of the ordinary river-dead, reliving my own life and other lives.

But I couldn't, so I didn't.

How to convey those images? They were shapes of power, if I can put it that way. They weren't pictures. Yet they conveyed knowledge, and this knowledge seemed to pop into my mind as if from nowhere. It was just as if the Worm knew exactly how my own thoughts were woven together, so it presented suitable patterns – and these immediately became garments of thought which I was wearing within me.

Stolen garments! The Worm had filched these from the line where they hung: that line linking Sons of Adam (now deceased) with the Godmind far away.

I began to understand the psylink. Somewhat. Perhaps 'understand' is too ambitious a term. Say rather that I knew how I would be using it in rather the same way that I knew how to talk, but couldn't for the life of me have said what went on in my mouth when I spoke.

I was aware, as if the knowledge had been born with me, of how the Godmind had sent out ships with seeds of life on board. When our parent ship arrived here, its seeds were adapted to our world. Out of the substance of the ship, bodies were bred, and minds were printed upon these bodies: minds which the Godmind could fish back to Eeden when the bodies died. The Godmind could fish back all natural descendants of those first 'artificial' colonists and replant their minds in artificial bodies, to live a second life back in Eeden: all, with the exception of those who were filtered out into the *Ka*-store of the Worm. And so the Godmind populated the universe with people, and brought back the knowledge thereof.

This was slightly at odds with what the Sons thought in their cruel and jumbled way. Andri had once told me that all of us were Eeden minds in puppet flesh. Not so! Only the first generation possessed manufactured bodies. Later generations were all genuine persons of *our* world. However, the psylink survived, and was passed down from generation to generation just like blue eyes or red hair.

Eeden must be getting kind of crowded by now, I remarked.

Ah, but those second-lives will also end, as soon as the bodies wear out.

What happens to their Kas after that? Do they just dissolve? Evaporate, what?

Maybe, the Worm said in jolly vein, *the Godmind eats them. But I'll get you back, I promise, then you can tell me what the Godmind really is – and why it bothers with human beings at all.*

Why it bothers: what do you mean?

Consider: the Godmind uses people as its tools on distant planets; as its eyes and ears. Why bother, when it can send out machines so clever that they can build people? What's the plan?

68

Where do people come into it? Who dreamed up the plan in the first place? And what about me? I was put here ages ago to stop intelligent life from blooming. Who put me here? Why? Okay, off you go, then!

Hey, I'm not ready! There are a zillion things I don't know.

Me neither. In at the deep end, say I.

Ho ho. That ought to have been *my* line. (With the caveat: 'Just so long as there aren't any stingers in the water!')

By now the shapes of power had melted back into the blue. I received the *Ka* equivalent of a pat on the back. Needless to say, the gentlest of touches on a spinning top will send it skittering wildly away . . .

I skittered; dizzyingly, a flutterbye blown by a storm.

A storm; oh yes, there *was* a storm in the vicinity. This was no storm of clouds and rain, of thunder and lightning. This was a turmoil in the blue nothingness; and thanks to those power-images, I knew the cause.

The psylink stretched away to Eeden like a long hawser mooring our world. Vibrations sped along this hawser. Where the hawser tethered our world, it splayed into a million separate fibres. A fair number of these hung loose. Tendrils of the black current, feelers of the Worm, blocked and parried many of these questing loose ends; there in what I now thought of as *Ka*-space. Others the Worm hung on to, knotting round them. This dance of thrust and riposte in *Ka*-space constituted the 'storm'. It caused a turbulence which hid any sight of far Eeden. I felt buffeted and battered.

What was the nature of these tendrils? Emptiness, nothingness. It seemed as if knots could be tied in nothingness; as though emptiness could be braided; as though strings could be formed by winding the void around itself – invisible strings as lengthy as thought itself.

Suddenly I was clear of the storm-front. I was a vibration travelling along the hawser. Actually, I felt I was two things at once. I was a wave; and I was a mote bobbing upon that wave. My bobbing (no, my *spin*) produced the wave whereon I travelled. Equally, what propelled me towards my destination was the twitching of the hawser, the fluid rhythm of the psylink.

A slim tendril of the black current had attached itself to me. This stretched out and out in my wake. By means of this I would find my way back to the *Ka*-store of the Worm . . . eventually, somehow, perhaps.

I wondered what Doctor Edrick was doing. Was he breaking open my bedroom door? Kidnapping Narya? Burning the house down in pique?

I would never know the answer. Not for a very long time, at least. Eventually I might re-live a life which could tell me, if I ever got back to the *Ka*-store. Eventually: that might as well be never.

Was Edrick doing any of these things *now*, at this moment? It might only be a short while since I'd died; equally it could be hours or days. No units of time meant anything any longer. In the blue void of death, with no sun shining nor stars, there was no way to tell the time or measure distance.

I sped. I wasn't cold, I wasn't hot. I wasn't hungry, or even lonely. I was just me.

I tried to recapture the sense of completeness I'd known once before in the *Ka*-store, when I'd taken passage aboard other finished lives. I tried to enjoy the luminosity that floods a life when it's over. But this balm wouldn't come. For although I was dead, things weren't over yet. I couldn't re-live my life. I could only remember my life ordinarily; which is to say: not very well.

I sped through the nothing. If nothing happened soon, how much longer could I go on being me?

* * *

I really ought to have borne in mind what Andri told me about all those *babies'* bodies lying in cold caverns under Eeden waiting for dead *Ka*s to return from the stars to occupy them. A full-blown artificial body awaiting me at journey's end wouldn't have been a bad exchange; but what happened next was downright humiliating.

The Worm had known what I was heading into. Obviously! And damn it, *I'd* known too, deep down. Yet I'd made believe that in my case things might be different, special. I was the secret agent of a junior god, wasn't I? A secret agent is a bold adventurer. She's competent. She's always on the move. She's able to look after herself.

All of a sudden I was in some other place. Bright lights were blinding me. *Things* were interfering with me. And I was feeble. And I was tiny.

I screamed.

Don't babies always scream?

PART TWO
Cherubs

I was racing through redwood forest as fast as my little girl's legs would carry me. The ground was scant of undergrowth, naked of boltholes or brakes where I could hide. Between each massive trunk was so much open space that it was easy to spot my fleeing shape from way behind. Even the lowest branches were far too high up for a little girl to leap and scramble into.

A metallic macaw watched me from a high perch.

'Help, they'll kill me!' I called to it raggedly.

The mech-bird bobbed its head, as much as to say, 'Message acknowledged!' but it did no more. Or, if the bird did speak to the Godmind, it didn't bother telling me so. I pounded on, although my legs were turning rapidly to jelly.

If only I could get out of line of sight! Then maybe I could slip behind a trunk and slide around it while the bloody-minded boys – Sons of the Truesoil, all of them – raced past . . . Well, *that* wouldn't work.

I glanced back.

The hunting pack of little boys had strung out, but that didn't mean I was outdistancing them. They were running relays now. As soon as those in the lead tired a bit, they dropped back to a quick trot, letting the former laggards sprint ahead. Me, I had no choice but to *race*, fit to burst my heart.

My glance excited them.

'Witchette!' taunted a voice. 'Wormy wormy witchette!'

Witchette, indeed! Not even a full-blown witch. They were really playing the part of small boys now. Maybe they thought if they kept up a pretence of fun and games, the

Godmind would condone their antics. But in those young bodies nestled evil, squalid, adult minds, bent on tearing me to pieces.

The Godmind couldn't be so dumb, even if this bunch of cherubs *were* Flawed Ones, from our own notoriously disadvantaged world. Maybe the Godmind wanted me ripped to shreds.

'River-bitch!'

'Water-witch!'

In another minute my heart would crack. My lungs would burst. My legs would flop. How far did this fucking forest stretch? Right the way across California? Where was the next service-hatch?

At least those squalid little boys couldn't possibly rape me before killing me – not unless they raped me with a stick.

Hey, wait a bit! If they did start in on torturing me instead of killing me straight off, and if they took their time over it, and if the Godmind did decide to butt in, then I could probably be patched together again. I simply couldn't let them kill me. I didn't know enough yet, to die.

Come to think of it, what better way to goad these Sons into tormenting me than by sneering at their prepubescent impotence? By taunting their lost manhood, their vanished virility? That ought to rankle.

Well, I'd been the one to think of rape; with a stick . . .

I saw a fallen stick, the size of my arm. (Which wasn't very large.) A cudgel, no less! Skidding to a halt, I hoisted the stick. I needed both hands to hold it. Stumbling to the nearest trunk, I backed up against the bark and waited for the boys to come, ready to swing my weapon.

A fair bit of wood was lying around hereabouts. Enough for a bonfire? Suppose I could incite them to burn me, the way they burned witches back home? That should set off a fire alarm and bring the Godmind's bits and pieces rushing to the rescue.

Oh hell and shit. Rape or the fire; or both.

One puzzle remained: *how* had they rumbled me? Or had I been set up?

The boys straggled to a halt in a half-circle. They were panting heavily.

'The Flawed Ones': that was how cherubs from our world were known, here in Eeden upon the planet Earth.

Earth was the name for this world of our origin; I knew that now. Eeden was merely the name of the reception area set aside for us millions on millions of reborn cherubs: roughly speaking, half of the North American land-mass (which is considerable).

In choosing the name Eeden, the Godmind had been 'mobilizing a precognitive myth'. So I'd been told by my Cyclopedia.

Precog myths were tales dreamed up by our primitive ancestors on Earth which forecast the far future – in other words the present time, the now – and which were used as guidelines to bring it into being.

One such myth concerned a God who would be born of flesh. And lo, the Godmind had evolved out of the thinking-machines conceived by human brains, built by human hands.

Another myth concerned Eeden: the paradise which lay ahead in time. The ancient spinners of precog myth back in the past were exiled from paradise by the span of years yawning between then and now. Yet one day, they dreamed, paradise would become a reality on Earth; and now it was so.

Precog myth also foresaw how the spirits of the dead would take up residence in another world, as cherubs. And so it came to pass, with the slight difference that it was the star-dead from other worlds in the galaxy who flocked home along the psylink to Eeden to be born again.

'Unless ye become as little children,' declared the myth.

Also: 'And in the resurrection they shall neither marry nor bear babies.' Our growth from babyhood was enormously speeded up compared with normal development, but our bodies quit growing short of puberty. We born-again cherubs all retained children's bodies lifelong, till we died our second deaths. Such was the nature of this new flesh given us by the Godmind.

Outside of Eeden in the rest of Earth, people grew up normally to womanhood and manhood. Yet it was we cherubs who brought those ordinary mortals wisdom – by going out amongst them as the little aliens in their midst, the harvest of the galaxy, the perpetual children of the stars. 'Out of the mouths of babes . . .' There in the outside world we cherubs were adored, protected, cherished.

In another week's time I too was due to go outside. So this was the Sons' last chance to clobber me.

Maybe the Godmind had been watching me all this while, wondering what my plan was; and now it had decided to have me snuffed. Again, maybe not.

But I'm running ahead of myself – would that I could have equally outstripped my pursuers!

I'm running way ahead . . .

When I first came out of *Ka*-space and became a baby, I was pretty confused. I was lying flappy, floppy and feeble on soft fabric in a low glass cradle. I was blinded by bright lights, I was assaulted by machines.

And these machines were most unlike any we had back home. These ones had as many soft parts as hard parts. What's more, they acted of their own accord, like living creatures.

I soon calmed down. A machine saw to that. It squirted a blue fog at me, and panic went away.

'Rejoice!' proclaimed a voice. 'You are safe in the bosom of Eeden, as promised. Your new brain is programmed with Panglos, in which I'm speaking to you. You'll need to exercise your voice for fluency. For the present kindly blink thrice to signify yes, twice for no. Do you understand me?'

I blinked three times.

'*Ex*-cellent. Now: are you fully aware of your situation?'

Ah, they didn't know who I was, or where I came from!

This was a ticklish moment – and I don't just mean because of the tubes and other things tickling me, or the peculiar squirmy in-sucking sensation down in my crotch region. What sort of new arrivals *wouldn't* be fully aware of their situation? Presumably those from a world such as mine. How would the machines go about disposing of undesirable babies? Would knives descend? I felt like a fish hauled ashore, flopping helplessly, about to be gutted. But I had to chance my hand; I needed information.

So I blinked twice, for no.

'Acknowledged.' This was a new voice. A crisper voice, as though there was a different type of mind behind it. 'It's highly probable that you're from a flawed world where the Satan-Snake foretold by precog myth has confused or corrupted my people, correct?'

Deciding to go along with the voice, I blinked: yes.

'Since you agree with that analysis, I can assume that my heritage still remains intact on your world. So: do you struggle to defeat the Snake?'

Yes, I lied. (Well, that was true of half of my world. The nasty half.)

'Are you from a waterworld of islands?'

No.

'Are you from the western shore of a long river bounded by wild ocean, precipice and desert?'

Yes.

I wasn't born in the west, but surely I could pass for a westerner . . .

'Identified: World 37.'

The next question really caught me off balance. (In so far as any baby lying supine can be caught off balance!)

'Nearest large town?' And the voice started to reel off a list of western towns. The Godmind knew more about our world than I'd expected. Yet of course that figured: it had been receiving new arrivals for centuries. Luckily for me the string of names began in the north. This gave me a few seconds to decide which foul hole in the south (which I knew at first hand) to plump for.

' . . . Adamopolis?'

' . . . Dominy?'

'Pleasegod?'

I blinked yes.

'Acknowledged.' And at once a different voice commenced my orientation. This last voice belonged to my Cyclopedia.

Cyclopedia! Once again I'm running ahead!

At this point I think I'd be well advised to capsule the set-up on Earth quickly so that I can get on with my story. (By the end of *The Book of the River* I flatter myself that I'd learned a few of what the Ajelobo critics call 'narrative techniques'.)

So I'll allow a couple of pages for *your* orientation, gentle reader; then it's right on to my meeting with Yorp the Exotic and his gang. And if you think I'm being stingy about facts you might need to know if you go to Eeden when you die, believe me, by the time I've finished gabbing on you'll know all you need to know, for what the information's worth. If Eeden's where you're headed – and of course you might not be – you'll arrive so wised-up compared with the majority of cherubs that you might be well advised to act dumb; otherwise the Godmind may just grow suspicious of your motives.

* * *

We aliens were all reborn in baby bodies at one or other of numerous crèches scattered throughout Eeden. The host bodies were continuously being produced in underground bio-vats by machines of the Godmind, like pie crusts in a giant bakery awaiting the filling to be popped into them. After manufacture, these bodies 'lived' in a state of 'ego-suspension', awaiting our influx down the psylinks from wherever. On being 'activated' the new bodies grew greedily and rapidly – such was the nature of our new flesh – till within about eight weeks we were toddling competently and within a couple of years we were fully-fledged boys and girls of apparent age eight or nine years. At that apparent age we would stay.

We all spoke Panglos, the polyglot world tongue of Earth designed by the Godmind long ago before the seedship that settled our world even set off. Even today our own native language isn't too different from Panglos. Panglos isn't a language that drifts easily, and our own speech certainly hasn't drifted far at all compared with the home languages of the Exotics.

(Exotics: there I go again. Getting ahead of myself.)

As soon as we grew into toddlers, we were shunted out of the ever-busy crèches to one of many minivilles. These were miniature towns, under weather domes, all built to toddler size and copied from various ancient cities of Earth. (Cities which themselves had been rebuilt by the Godmind, life-size, on their original sites for the ordinary Earth folk to live in.) I myself spent this period of adjustment in Little Italia, first in Classical Roma, then in adjacent Renaissance Roma. All this time I was accompanied by my personal Cyclopedia, a mobile fact-machine and nursemaid on which I could ride, a-saddle, whenever my sprouting young limbs grew weary.

Then it was goodbye to the minivilles, and out into Nature: a nature which was wild yet benign and well supervised. No Cyclopedia accompanied me now. Scattered

81

across the surface of Eeden, instead, were large numbers of service-hatches providing nourishment and knowledge and most anything we wanted, including transport through underground tubes to any other part of Eeden. Assorted beasts and birds, which were actually machines (called Graces, Loving Graces) kept an eye on the land and on us.

Out in Nature, roaming, we young aliens got to know the smell and touch of the Earth – and oh, the marvel (for me) of the waxing and waning of the giant Moon in the sky! We also got to know each other better; and got to know ourselves, discovering what sort of little boy or girl we were each growing up to be.

Our host bodies were made in vats, as I say, by bio-machines. But they were all different. Thus I was the only one in my particular crèche group with almond eyes, and on my head grew straight, jet-black hair. (Though no darkling hair would ever grace the rest of my anatomy.) My skin was cinnamon in hue, and I was inclined to be plump if I didn't watch my diet. On the other hand I was fairly tall for a child, which compensated for this. Though I would never be a woman, at least I was female.

I suppose we cherubs could as easily have been sexless. But the Godmind liked the idea of us being little boys and girls, just as it liked the idea of the ancient cities of Earth. On first arrival in Eeden our *Ka* triggered the host body's anatomy into a male or female shape – which was the reason for that uncomfortable squirming sensation I'd felt early on. Obviously this permitted us cherubs a certain limited amount of eroticism, between friends, if we felt so inclined. But not very much. The mind might be willing; the body wasn't quite up to it. Especially not in the case of boys.

I'd *liked* my old body; I'd been at home in it! Yet I didn't feel that this new body of mine was unbearably strange. Definitely it was the same sort as we had back home. However, for some of us cherubs – the Exotics – a body of this kind was weird. Which brings me to Yorp and his gang, whom I met while I was wandering through California.

I'd spent the previous night on a beach, unable to tear myself away from my first sight of the moonlit Pacific Ocean. How much calmer and warmer a sea this seemed than our own wild northerly waters back home! When I had laid me down to sleep on a raised bar of that wide soft strand – edged by sculpted turrets and jagged crests of rock – the ocean had lain, too, flat as a silken sheet.

When I woke to the half-light before dawn, I was soaking wet and spluttering. A flood of water was pouring around my sandy hammock, trying to drown me. A breeze had sprung up. Waves were rolling in. Worse, most of the beach had vanished. It was just as if the world had tilted, sloshing the water towards me. All of a sudden I was in the midst of the sea. How could a breeze push the water so? Maybe great monsters of the deep could reach me now! Big brothers to the little scuttling crabs I'd been watching a few hours earlier . . .

Plodging and stumbling, I fled to what was left of the beach and found shelter by a spur of rock. I stripped off my shorts and blouse and hung them up. At least the wind was warm.

I was pacing about waiting for my clothes to dry and for the light to brighten a bit; my stomach was starting to grumble and I was wondering which way it was to the nearest service-hatch for breakfast – when I noticed this shape approaching along the strip of sand. It moved through the half-light in quick darts and dashes and crouches. It looked like a giant crab, carrying its home on its back.

'Hey!' I called, alarmed, and the crab tossed back a hood.

Visualize a seven-year-old boy. He was on the skinny

side, with blue eyes and a cotton-top of blond hair. The boy wore a flappy brown burnous, so that the hood enclosed his head in a dark cave, and his sandalled feet stuck out of the bottom of the cloak like scrawny claws.

The boy scuttled closer. He hunkered down, pulled in his head, drew up his feet and disappeared inside the hooded cloak entirely.

'Hullo. Been for a swim?' said his voice from within.

'Not likely! I was sleeping, and the wind shoved the sea right up the sand.'

'It did what? Oh, I get it! You're from a world without a moon. Without a big one, anyhow.'

'We didn't have any moon at all back home.'

Somewhere inside his big hood he chuckled. His chuckle sounded like one of our croakers around the Bayou back home, vibrating its throat pouch. 'A big moon drags a bulge of ocean round the world with it. It's called a tide. That's why you got wet.'

'Tide.' I recognized the word. Of course; my brain knew it. Alas, I hadn't thought of applying this knowledge when I lay down on that dry and mellow beach with the sea decently distant. 'Damn.' I felt stupid.

'I'm Yorp,' said the boy. He poked his head out.

'Yaleen,' said I.

We got on fine together. I soon told him I was a Flawed One. 'I've met a few of those,' he said. 'But not *nice* ones, like you . . .'

Maybe that was why we got on so well. I was crippled and flawed on arrival in Eeden because the Worm had scrambled up our heritage. I did my best to act deprived, which gave me a good excuse to quiz my Cyclopedia about things I might otherwise have been expected to know in advance; though I never pushed my luck.

Yorp, on the other hand, had always expected to wind up here. His people possessed the heritage of Earth unbrokenly, and here was his goal. But I could fit into my new body without any undue awkwardness. The heritage of Earth – the foreknowledge – hadn't helped *Yorp* any, when it came to donning an earthly form so very different from his former body. He was hamstrung.

Yorp had run into other cherubs from his world, but they had all adjusted far more easily. This only made matters worse and more poignant for Yorp; he felt doubly a stranger. Perhaps the root trouble was that those others from his world had always been humans at heart. Yorp hadn't; he had been truly Other.

Till now Yorp had been hanging out entirely with Exotics from various worlds, who felt the same way. So I was a sort of psychological bridge for him; I was an abnormal normal.

This all spilled out as we talked.

'Mine was a heavy world,' sighed Yorp. 'Here I feel just like a puff of dandelion-down about to float away.

'Mine was a darkly cloudy world, with the thickest storming gases. Here, there just doesn't seem to be anything to breathe! Though of course I do breathe easily . . .

'And now I've only two legs! I feel as if at any moment I'll fall over!'

We were making our way together to the service-hatch. And a crab-like sideways way it was too! The sun was up in the sky by now, shining from the same inland direction as we were heading. To my eyes there seemed nothing unduly bright about the sun of Earth. But Yorp flinched from it. His cherub eyes were adapted to it, just like mine. He never acted as if they were. He was a crepuscular person, a person of the dusk and the pre-dawn – happiest then. If his new eyes could have seen in the dark, he might have lived nocturnally. But they couldn't; so he didn't.

On Yorp's world, the parent seedship made huge changes in those multi-million-letter words of life, the genes. The resulting bodies were squat, bulky and armoured with two

85

arms and four legs; the tough hide was beautifully marbled in distinctive pastel shades. The leathery bellows-lungs breathed poison gases under pressure. The crystalline eyes saw heat as well as light. The genitals were hidden in a horny slot. Oh yes, Yorp was exotic. Now he was just a shadow of his former self, a crab robbed of its shell, with two legs broken off. (I hadn't at this stage seen the animal called a 'tortoise', which could pull its head right inside its shell!)

When we got to the service-hatch I met his gang: Marl and Ambroz, Leehallee and Sweets. All of them felt equally out of step in different ways.

Leehallee and Sweets had been merpeople of a shallow water world. Now, as though the plug had been pulled on them, they were exiled on dry land. They grieved that they could no longer breathe water and swim with the fish, like fishes. The swimming ability of the human body seemed a joke to them; and the need to keep an earthly body dry for comfort went against their basic instincts. Nor could they now echo-locate, and see (quite literally) through each other. Now they could only see surfaces. When they spoke they heard no echoes from within. For them a screen had come down, isolating them inside their new bodies. (In this respect their sadness was the opposite of Yorp's; he felt terribly exposed.) These two girls went naked. Even bare flesh was too much clothing of the inner person.

Marl, on the other hand, was *grounded* on the Earth. He and his kind had been fliers: hollow-boned, hugely airy-chested, with great wings sprouting above their skinny arms.

They lived in eyries in honeycombed mountains high above a wind-whipped marshy world whose surface was plagued by vicious little beasties swarming and slaughtering each other.

To the tune of the winds blowing through the organ

pipes of porous cliffs they warbled songs. On the treasured bone-flutes of the dead they piped the music of their ancestors. From one cliffy minaret to the next they whistled messages.

And now Marl the airy flier was a heavy little runt. He'd been condensed. His voice had sunk way down the scale. High-pitched back home, his name had been a bird's mewing cry. These days it sounded more like a clod of soil. Yet Marl still clad himself in a coat of bright feathers: borrowed plumes.

And Ambroz? Ambroz was the most exotic of all.

His world was as flat as a platter. Only huge, deep-rooting vegetables broke the monotony; and in the atmosphere of his world there existed a curious form of energy-life – which was attracted, devastatingly, to any motion faster than a snail's pace or the growth of a plant. Ambroz's people surmised that the surface of the planet itself, over millions of years, had been rubbed down by the action of these energy-beasts. They surmised, too, that this energy life was somehow related to the giant local vegetables, or even generated by them. If a cabbage can have a free-ranging *Ka*! Perhaps the energies had been born aeons earlier as a defence against grazing animals. Of which none now remained. This wasn't proven, nor was there any communication with these energies, if indeed they were alive at all.

A world where there was no way to move without being blasted – and not much point in moving, since everywhere was just as flat! The decision to colonize such a place with plant-people – who would stay rooted and immobile most of their lives, only occasionally uprooting and waddling very slowly indeed – might have seemed a cruel joke on the part of the Godmind. Yet the inner lives of Ambroz and his kin had been vastly rich and contemplative. Besides, there was always the promise of an afterlife when they would all be able, at last, to move freely about . . . The plant-people communicated with each other by means of 'radio waves', a sort of heliograph signal employing not light but other invisible vibrations.

Now that he was in Eeden Ambroz could walk wherever he wished, through a world full of ups and downs, and ins and outs; and he was disenchanted. For no journey brought him any closer to himself. Ambroz's cherub body was tubby and brown-skinned, his hair was curly black, the pupils of his eyes were chips of coal; and he wore a grubby blue dhoti.

Over the next few weeks we all wandered about together, mostly on foot, occasionally taking capsules through the tubes from one service-hatch to another chosen at random. Generally we avoided other cherubs. We visited mountain and seacoast, desert and forest.

And we talked, of course. I told them about my world, though without betraying myself. They told me more about theirs. Marl and Yorp and the two mergirls talked most. Ambroz was inclined to be taciturn, verging on surly. Besides, there wasn't much to tell about a flat platter of vegetables; and his inner life and musings remained his own.

I did manage to coax Yorp out of his shell once or twice. He even skinny-dipped with me in a lonely lake.

I learned from him (what I could have asked my Cyclopedia or any service-hatch, if I'd been a bolder spy) that the Godmind didn't have any precise location. The Godmind was a whole set of communicating systems buried all over the planet. There was no single centre, no headquarters. So much for one half-baked idea, of breaking into its den clutching a hammer. (But why should I try to smash it? The Godmind didn't seem particularly malign, in the way the Worm had pictured it. Did it?)

I also learned from Yorp that the whole colonization programme had been – and possibly *still* was being – launched not from the Earth itself but from the huge Moon out in space. Thereafter I used to stare up at the Moon even more avidly, when it was in the sky and when the sky was clear, hoping to see some fire or flash of light; but I never did.

'How do you get to visit the Moon?' I asked Yorp.

He cringed. 'Visit it? There isn't any air on the Moon! The Moon isn't heavy enough to hold air – it's even worse than here!' He retreated inside his burnous; I'd undone my good work.

One afternoon we were camping on the edge of redwood forest when Ambroz broke a broody silence which had lasted for the best part of two days.

'There doesn't seem very much *direction*,' he groused. I assumed he was grumbling about our aimless wanderings. But no.

He went on: 'What a huge purposive *thrust* there has to be behind this colonization project! Yet what's it all for, Yaleen? So that we cherubs can eat lotuses a while in Eeden, then dispense our alien wisdom out among the Earthfolk – who are all living in a huge *museum*! Is that the only way to unify and conquer the cosmos? By turning people into toys on strings?'

'Conquer?' I asked. 'Who's conquering?' This was getting interesting.

'The Governor. The Godmind. It's using people as von Neumann machines to fill as many worlds as it can.'

'As what?'

He bulled right on. 'Why doesn't it use machines pure and simple?'

This was something that the Worm had wondered.

'What's the point in cluttering up the universe with junk?' asked Yorp.

'I suppose we shouldn't complain,' said Sweets. 'If there hadn't been any colonies, we wouldn't have been alive!'

Ambroz was really worked up after his long silence. He was like a constipated hen, nerving itself to lay an egg.

'The clue is *Ka*-space,' he said. 'People die. And people have *Ka*s. *Ka*s can come back here very quickly to spill the beans on how it's all going out there. Radio messages would take hundreds of years. Thousands! *Ka*-space is a way of keeping in touch.'

'One-way only,' said Marl. 'The Godmind doesn't talk back to its family of worlds.'

'I've thought about this a lot,' said Ambroz. 'Half my life, it seems! So have a group of us on my world. Perhaps it's because we couldn't move about, and because of the way we communicated . . . but we suspect that when *we* were made, we were made as a sort of model of the colonies. Each of us a separate world unto ourselves, but able to project ourselves – and thus try to plumb all sorts of philosophical depths. Old Harvaz the Cognizer came up with this theory, and I was working on it till I died. Some of us swore we would keep this secret till we could walk about freely and find an answer.'

'Go on,' said I. 'You can walk about now.'

'Well, the colony programme seems like . . . like the building of a very big radio telescope – made of *minds*! Like a giant array with an enormous base-line spanning hundreds of light years.'

'What's a radio telescope?' Leehallee wanted to know.

'It's a machine for listening to things very far away and very long ago. If you have two of those a good distance apart but slaved to each other, you get much sharper reception. Suppose you had a hundred of them whole star-distances apart . . . they'd be too far apart to keep in touch or act in concert using radio waves. But suppose you could build your machine of *minds* linked through *Ka*-space, and then switch it on – '

'Wouldn't you have to kill everybody on all the worlds, to do that? So that they'd all be dead?' asked Sweets.

'Would you?' cried Ambroz. 'Would you indeed? A star which explodes lights up the whole galaxy for a day. Does a species dwelling on a hundred worlds, all of whose minds explode at once, light *something else*? Something far vaster? Universal?'

'Go on,' I encouraged him.

'Well, I suspect – in fact I'm sure – that when the Godmind has all its colony pieces in place, when it has *enough* of them – '

We were interrupted by the noisy arrival of a party of boys. Six or seven boys rushed out of the forest towards our impromptu camp, whooping and shouting. They were naked to the waist, above buckskin breeches, and their chests and cheeks were daubed with slashes of pigment. They wore sweatbands with feathers stuck in them round their foreheads.

The leader ran directly up to Marl, tore a plume loose from his bird costume and jammed the trophy into his headband. He pranced around us, stamping his feet and hollering in triumph. His followers capered after him.

'Hey!' cried Marl, springing up as if to take flight into the sky.

Leehallee shrieked a little. Yorp shrank into his burnous. Ambroz went rigid.

I jumped up. 'What's with you guys? Cut it out!'

The boys straggled to a halt. Their leader squared up to me. He had fair hair, keen blue eyes in a thin pinched face. Those eyes looked rather mad. He was tall and gangly but I thought I could take him if I had to, given the edge on weight.

Of course I couldn't take all of them, and most of Yorp's gang weren't going to be much help in a fight. Though why the hell should it come to a fight? We cherubs were all grown-ups. This was the first sign of trouble I'd come across in Eeden.

'Okay,' the leader said evenly, 'just a bit of *fun*. By way of saying hullo.' I didn't care for the way he said 'fun'; he fairly snarled the word.

91

He gazed at me hard. 'Should we not all enjoy bliss in Eeden? The bliss that the Godmind promised us! How better to bless the Godmind than by being perfectly the children He has made us? Until our serious mission of sainthood starts!'

Oh dear. He *was* nuts.

He returned the stolen feather to Marl, with a sardonic bow and a sneer on his face. Marl managed to grasp the feather, but only just. The other lads applauded and hooted until their leader clapped his hands for silence; which he got.

'Eeden is the promised Truesoil!' the boy shouted. And my heart sank further. I knew all too well what sort of people talked about Truesoil. None other than my old friends, the obsessed and vicious Sons of Adam!

'Are we not the Godmind's best beloveds?' the boy harangued his team. 'Those who struggled, while most other worlds dwelled easy in his bosom?'

There was, I decided, something horribly familiar about this *particular* boy . . .

. . . whipping up fervour, to win followers – and thus win approval of the Godmind? Or to persuade himself that Eeden really matched his zealous expectations, when in fact he had suddenly become a minnow in an ocean?

'If I was as heavy as I *used* to be,' I heard Yorp growl from his burnous. His head emerged. 'And if I had my armour on, and all four legs to bear me . . .' He adopted a crouching stance. '*You!*' he bellowed. 'How dare you talk about other worlds having it easy! How dare you burst in on us! What do you know, you painted savage?' He was really incensed. This was a new side to him; but believe me, did I welcome it!

The leader of the boys pursed his lips. 'Savages? Ah, I see. Here we have a sophisticate. So what if we're savages?' he snarled. 'We'll wear our savagery with pride in the service of the Godmind! As His true soldiers!'

'What does the Godmind need soldiers for?' asked Sweets.

'Why don't you just go away?' sighed Ambroz.

'Are we not all true Sons and Daughters of the Godmind here?' the boy demanded, staring at each of us in turn.

I was beginning to wonder whether it was pure chance that this band of Sons had turned up at our camp. I fervently hoped that none of Yorp's gang would utter my name . . .

'I wasn't aware,' drawled Ambroz, 'that the Godmind is greatly bothered what we think of it. Unless you lot happen to be its special buddies, and can advise me otherwise?'

'You: what's your name?'

Don't anybody say my name!

'Not that it's any of your business, but I'm called Ambroz.' Weak, weak! You should never answer the questions of a bully. 'Go fry your face' is the best reply. Maybe Ambroz realized this, a little late, since he added, 'What's *yours*?'

Proudly the boy said, 'Edrick.' His followers all nodded, as though that name said everything.

Which to me, it did.

If Edrick was here, then he hadn't survived my murder by too long; which was nice news. Less nice, to run across him again light years away from home. Since there were millions of us cherubs bumming around Eeden, this roused my deepest suspicions. Still, coincidences happen. Sometimes our lives are chockful of that delightful ingredient. I kept a pan-face.

'And you? What's *your* name?' Edrick was addressing me now.

My heart thumped. (Never mind, he couldn't hear it thumping.) 'Go fry your face,' said I.

Yorp glanced at me oddly; and I realized that I'd spoken deeper and rougher than usual. I'd altered my voice in case Edrick somehow recognized it.

For a moment I thought Edrick was going to assault me then and there; or order his troops to thrash me. Instead, he sucked in his breath.

'Not very friendly, are we? The Godmind wishes us all to live together as little brothers and sisters, doesn't He? Let's try again.'

'How do you know what it wants?' I retorted. 'Did it tell you to come here and proclaim all over us?'

'Yeah, how do *you* know?' Sweets sang out; and from the speed with which Edrick swung to confront her, I decided a few things.

I'd told the Cyclopedia my real name. And why not? As far as Cyclopedia or Godmind were concerned I hailed from Pleasegod in the west. The only way Edrick could have come hunting for me personally was if he'd told his own Cyclopedia a hell of a lot about me and how I was such an agent of evil, and if the Godmind's bits and pieces had done some checking, and sent him. In that case, he should have known what I looked like, right off. *My* Cyclopedia had always been able to recognize me without any bother. Probably I was safe. Edrick's arrival was an unfortunate coincidence. Edrick just wanted to browbeat anyone; Sweets would fit the bill.

Yet . . . could Edrick and I possibly have some sort of affinity for one another? Not a pleasant kind of affinity, I hasten to add! Maybe this sort of thing happens when you murder someone, or when you think long enough and hard enough about killing them. This perverse affinity had guided him here, without his being aware of it.

Edrick glared at Sweets, but he didn't answer her. I'm sure he would have done so, if he'd had some special commission from the Godmind to fulfil. His troops would expect it of him – all six of them. (How were the mighty fallen!)

At this point one of the other boys chipped in.

'I've figured it out, Ed . . . . I bet they're Exotics, right?

They think they're better than us. That's why they won't tell you their exotic names – 'cept for fatso in the blue sheet there. Bet you can't get a human tongue around their names.' He spat a gob of saliva on the soil.

Edrick looked pained at the coarseness of his follower. Or did he? Spitting their juices at the Truesoil seemed to be a bit of a habit with Sons. Edrick knit his brows. Was he trying to connect something, remember something? Slowly he turned back towards me.

I chose my words carefully in the hope that my companions would realize I was giving them a message, about *me*. 'That's true, we're *all* Exotics here. All of us, aren't we, Gang? And proud of it.'

Alas, things went downhill from there.

Yorp had said how his people grew body-armour on their heavy world. He hadn't said why exactly . . . I'd associated these two facts as though one explained the other. Heavy worlds, heavy bodies.

Yet if everything weighed heavier, armour was the last thing you would want to haul around. You would only do that if you *needed* to, because of vicious beasts you might have to fight. You would only wear armour if rough-houses tended to happen . . .

And Yorp was a true native of his world.

He gave vent to the sort of battlecry a giant male croaker might utter if in dispute over a lady monstrosity of that ilk. 'Yup! Yup! Yup!' Lowering his head, and almost running on all fours, Yorp charged at Edrick.

Edrick was taken by surprise. Yorp knocked the wind right out of him and bowled him over.

But Yorp was of slight build here on Earth. The next boy he rushed at was forewarned, and easily clinched with him. A third boy began to thump Yorp viciously.

With a cry of, 'Come on, Gang!' I jumped to Yorp's rescue. A few flurrying moments later the whole lot of us were tangling with Edrick's troops, with greater or lesser success. Ambroz surprised me with his speed and vigour. In the midst of tripping someone, he flashed me a grin: 'Here's a *reason* for moving!'

But Leehallee was squirming on the ground, nursing a bloody nose; and Marl wasn't doing much except flap his arms frantically. Perhaps he feared they might snap in half if he actually hit anyone.

Edrick was up, recovering his wind.

He jabbed a finger across the mêlée. 'That one! Catch her, hold her! She's from *our* world! She's a witch!'

I took off as fast as I could for the woods. This wasn't an act of cowardice. The odds on our gang winning the fight were lousy. At least this way – I told myself – I would lead trouble away from Leehallee and the others. Maybe they would be able to summon help.

Supposing Edrick's arrival *was* a coincidence, how on Earth had he rumbled me?

I sprinted.

Backed up against the tree, I swung my club slowly to and fro.

'So who's first?' I sang out to the surrounding Sons. 'Come along, little boys! Can't kiss me, so you'd better kick me, eh? Truesoil is, you can't do nothing that *real* men can do. Can't shove your precious squirters anywhere, no more. 'Cos they're soft as worms, for ever and ever. You must be *burning* with frustration!'

Enraged, one Son rushed me. I swung. Rather to my surprise my club caught him full in the mouth. Wailing and clasping his face, dribbling blood and bits of tooth (I think), he stumbled back.

I jeered: 'Ya! Ya!'

'*Ya*leen, you mean!' snapped Edrick. 'That's who you are! Why don't you use your full name as your warcry, Yaleen?'

'Who's she?' I retorted.

'She's you. Knew you were of our world, soon as you sneered at me *proclaiming*.' Edrick was still panting. 'Nobody else would have used that word. Only in a *Ka*-theodral does one proclaim.' (So that was it! Me and my mouth.) 'Why pretend you're an Exotic, unless you're really a witch of the east? And who's the witch of the east most likely not to want me to know her?'

'Why would you be chasing after witches, whatever they are?' I swished my cudgel. Another Son had tensed up to spring – he untensed again. 'Is the Godmind holding a witch-hunt?'

If so, I'd be well advised to get myself killed as quickly as possible; and goodbye to any fancy notions of being nursed back to health by Loving Graces . . . At least then I'd be on my way back home along the psylink to the *Ka*-store. Perhaps, maybe.

'I said, is the Godmind shitting bricks about witches?'

'Blasphemer! Why should the Godmind worry about the mildew on a single leaf? Yet His dutiful gardeners will strip that leaf for Him!' (Ah, so the Godmind wasn't behind this. Back to Plan A, alas: slow torture.) 'I know verily which witch you are, to speak so vilely! The Godmind will reward us, Brothers. She was an agent of the Satan-Snake until I stopped her tricks! But she evaded my questioning; and maybe those questions are still worth asking!'

Edrick couldn't possibly suspect that I was here on Earth as an agent of the Worm. Would I be likely to babble that under torture?

'Reward you?' I hooted. 'The Godmind doesn't care a shit about you. Or about the rest of the human race!'

Edrick spread his hands wide in appeal. 'How can you call all this we see about us here in Eeden, *not caring*? This fulfilment of the Godmind's promises! This blessèd land!'

If only these wretched boys hadn't burst in on our brainstorming session. Ambroz had spent half his life

97

arriving at his conclusion: the telescope theory, the construction of a *Ka*-lens of galactic size. But could he ever prove it? Perhaps only the black current was equal to that task . . .

Where were my friends, anyway? Where was help?

'How *can* you?' Edrick cried again and again. He seemed genuinely dismayed. Maybe he was just being rhetorical, to work himself up. 'What do you mean, the Godmind doesn't *care*?'

Maybe I shouldn't have mentioned the matter.

'Oh, Eeden's *tidy*,' I said quickly, putting a sneer into my voice. 'It's a lot tidier than your *minds*, you bunch of . . .' And I said a rude word.

They rushed me.

They got on with their fun. Pretty soon I was screaming and finding how very difficult it is to faint when you really want to.

The fact that this was only a host body they were wrecking was, believe me, no consolation. All nerve endings functioned very nicely, thank you. Nor was it of much comfort that on this occasion Edrick lacked equipment such as a fingerscrew. I won't go into what they did to me. I've no wish to relive it. Suffice it to say that what seemed like a week later ingenious new pains stopped happening, leaving only the ones already in residence to carry on. But I hadn't spoken . . . I'd only screeched. When the symphony of pain changed key, I thought maybe it was bonfire time. I rather hoped it was.

A hawser squeals and groans when a boat tries to snap it in a gale. Then the gale drops and the hawser goes slack. So it was with my mind. With the decrease in the force of agony, my mind went slack at last. I faded out.

To awaken in a bath of fire!

No actual flames were dancing about me. The fire was

inside. The fire was me, my body. The slightest movement hurt me so much I tried not to breathe; but that was impossible.

Above: tiers of branches and blue sky. Then something bulky got in the way. A bristly muzzle dipped. Crystal mech-eyes looked into mine. A mech-deer? A mech-bear? A Loving Grace, at any rate!

'They've gone,' it said. 'I sent them away. It is over. You will be well.'

A puff of green smoke issued from its nostrils. This time I actually felt pleasant as I conked out.

I spent the next three or four weeks – I wasn't sure exactly how long – lying in a tub of jelly in some underground service-chamber being repaired. Soft machines attended me. Latterly one of these asked me questions about the assault. These questions seemed aimed more at working out the hang-ups of the Sons, than in trying to uncover perfidy in me. I lied through my teeth.

They were still the same teeth as before. I vaguely recalled that Edrick had left my mouth intact so that he could question me; the Sons had concentrated on other targets.

Towards the end of my convalescence, Yorp and gang visited me. With the mother-hen machines present, I couldn't say much of importance. But I managed a bit, as if in private code.

'Shame they interrupted,' I said. 'It was getting interesting. Telescopes, eh?'

Ambroz, bless him, understood. 'To light the darkness.'

'And see *what*?'

'To the end, and start, of everything. Why it all *is*. People are a way of seeing things. If you stare at the sun, you burn your eyes out; though you *do* see, for a little while. What if you stare at a billion billion suns at once? It's said on my world that a moment of illumination outweighs an eternity of blind ignorance. It's also said that people are the eyes of God.' Ambroz grinned crookedly. 'We're His pupils. Yet we taught Him to exist in the first place.'

'Excuse me,' interrupted a machine. 'Please clarify.'

Ambroz shrugged. 'Enough said. Time to go. Mustn't tire the invalid. But first, a kiss seems to be the custom hereabouts. Oh these soft and sloppy lips!' He bent over my jelly-tub and his mouth brushed my cheek. Quickly, very quietly, he whispered, 'Forget it. It doesn't matter. If our friend needs the whole galaxy as its eye, it'll take a thousand centuries yet.'

He straighened up. 'Let's go,' he said to Yorp.

The cotton-head Exotic wrapped his burnous about him. 'Come along, Gang.' I didn't see them again.

A week later I was hale and hearty, up and about.

A machine told me that I should take a tube to a certain service-hatch down south, to be sped from there to commence my cherubic duties. To be a starchild apostle, a focus of adoration. As many had been before me; so very many. I was to be routed by deep-tube under continent and ocean, to Venezia in Italia.

A few mouths later, like any good espionage agent, I was in deep with the rebel 'Underground'.

Such as it was.

Venezia is a city built in the sea. The city had drowned a millennium or more ago, but the Godmind had raised and rebuilt it. Indeed, so long ago had this happened that once again, where the tideline lapped, the city's stones were worn away like diseased teeth. Palace walls, balconies and turrets were fretted by brine spray. Before long, from the looks of it, the city would fall to pieces and sink for the second time. Though meanwhile, this vein of rot running through the fabric of Venezia seemed to make the place not moribund, but somehow more alive – like some ancient beast whose senses have sharpened amidst infirmity, who has grown subtle and tricky, and even entered on a second childhood of playfulness. And always within Venezia's sloshing foamy veins – reviving even as it destroyed – flowed the living sea.

At least that's what I *thought*, to start with! It took me a while to discover the truth about all this decadent decay: which was that the Godmind had rebuilt and embalmed the whole city in exactly this latterday condition – the way some people bore phony worm-holes in a piece of new furniture. Most other ancient cities had been rebuilt pristine and brand-new; not Venezia. It was rebuilt with worm-holes; with a skin disease grafted on to its walls.

It was one windswept early evening on the Zattere when I met Bernardino. Spray was whipping up on to that quay-road, slicking the worn stones. Clouds like enormous purple fists were punching each other landwards, over the sombre choppy waters. Blue lightning flickered out to sea. A skinny scruffy cat slunk for shelter.

(The Zattere: I shall mention the place-names of quays and canals, arching bridges and alleys and piazzas just as though you know as much about Venezia as you know of Aladalia or Guineamoy. Venezia *exists*, upon the planet Earth; be assured of that.)

Thunder growled. The Zattere was deserted . . . until a man came sneaking out of shadows. He was wearing soft shoes called sneakers, slacks, a blue jersey, a beret. Perhaps he was one of those who rowed the gondola canal-boats, stirring the water with a single oar from the stern, like a cook mixing a pudding. He had a ruddy jolly face.

I wasn't too worried about his furtive manner. What harm could come to us starchildren? Old black-shawled women called us 'little angels'. Gondoliers gave us free rides to wherever, whenever we wanted. Restaurant proprietors rushed to serve us the pick of their menus. All because our eyes had seen the sunlight of another star.

In return, we cherubs talked of our home worlds in the many 'churches' of the Godmind: ornate buildings, these, full of paintings of cherubs and visions of *Ka*s flying to and fro in the heavens, and other stuff from precog myth. We had lodgings in grand hotels, and mingled and mixed as we chose.

In Venezia when a starchild died, he or she always received a fine send-off to the Isle of the Dead reserved for us out in the lagoon, San Michele by name. And his or her *Ka* flew away to the bosom of the Godmind, so it was said.

When a starchild died – of old age, after twenty or twenty-five years of extended childhood . . .

That's right. Our new bodies weren't very long-lasting. The Godmind hadn't bothered to include that piece of information in the heritage of Earth; I only found this out from another cherub in the hotel where I was staying, *à propos* a death and a funeral. But said cherub wasn't bothered about it. 'We go home to the Godmind.'

I didn't believe it.

Oh, the twenty years bit I believed all right! But not the other.

'Excuse, Starchild,' said the man. 'May I speak? I heard *you* speak of your world in La Salute today.'

'Oh did you? Have you been following me?'

He grinned. 'But of course! How else do we meet? Don't worry, though.'

'Why should I worry?'

He waved an idle hand. 'Oh, it's such a dingy evening! Nobody about, not even an eye of the Godmind. A storm rises. A small body might be swept off this quay.'

'Thanks a lot! I feel totally reassured.'

My curiosity was teased; and surely that was his intention. The man wasn't behaving in an unfriendly manner, but he certainly wasn't adoring me, either.

'As a former sailor-woman,' he said, 'you must find life in our city very compatible, hmm? All these waterways!'

'Oh yes, wouldn't I make a fine gondolier? Lazing around the lagoon, ferrying artichokes and whatnot. Pity about my size.'

'Yes, what a shame you can't sail boats here . . . But you never were a sailor-woman, *were* you? You lived on the west bank of your river. You kept well away from the water because of that thing in it which is the enemy of the Godmind, hmm? That's what you told us in church. We all know that old habits die hard – so naturally here you are hugging the waterfront!'

Oh hell and damn it.

The fellow chuckled. 'You described your starhome in too paltry a way, you see. Not because you are poor at describing; oh no! The real reason is, you don't know *quite* enough about that west bank. And frankly you were more elegant in your account, poor as it was, than I could account for coming from a woman reared in such a sancti-monious pigsty. Then when you mentioned that river and the boats far away across it, your eyes lit up; though you pretended ignorance. So I followed you out of La Salute and saw you watch our boats plying the Grand Canal. You watched with delight – yet with a certain air of superiority, as though you had seen better boats; and sailed better boats yourself. Don't worry: no one but me would have noticed.'

'What do you want?'

'That's easy. I'd love to know the real tale of your world. I'd love to know of *your* side of the river; the side where you actually lived. Here in Venezia over the years we have hosted several boy-cherubs from your eastern shores. Yet they don't know any river secrets. Never once has a river-woman come here as a cherub – not till now – which is odd.'

No, it wasn't odd. When river-women died, they all went to the *Ka*-store of the black current. I said nothing, just looked at the man.

He said, 'My friends and I follow these things with care. We take notes. Allow me to surmise, admittedly on insufficient evidence, but – ' and he tapped his nose – 'on superlative instinct, that perhaps you are the first riverwoman ever to reach the Earth?'

'You're assuming a lot, Mister.'

'Bernardino is the name.'

Had he heard about our war back home? Undoubtedly not! It was too recent. Cherubs were routed to destinations all over the Earth; and the Earth was a big place, with a million times more land than our own riverbank.

'I'm betting,' said Bernardino, 'that you're a riverwoman who is concealing this fact. Now why should that be? My friends and I would be most intrigued to learn more of this current, which fights the Godmind.'

'Why would you be interested in something that's hostile to the Godmind?'

'Ah, I place myself in your hands! Perhaps, perhaps that's because my friends and I are opposed to the Godmind too? We've heard of the flaw in your world. We're hungry to learn more.'

'Haven't you ever . . . ?' 'Met anyone from a flawed world before?' was what I was going to say. I checked myself. Probably they would have seen a few flawed cherubs in church now and then; but could they ever have accosted one with any confidence? Hardly! Cherubs who arrived on Earth from flawed worlds wouldn't be very proud of the flaws back home; and probably would be pretty ignorant of the cause – they certainly wouldn't be intimate with it.

How many worlds had the Worm said were flawed (according to the Godmind)? Half a dozen, wasn't it? Myself, I hadn't run into Flawed Ones from any world other than mine – on that single unforgettable occasion! Six worlds (plus mine) wasn't a large number. Proportionately there must be fewer *Ka*s reaching Earth from such worlds than from unflawed ones. I hadn't exactly gone searching for flawed folk in Eeden; maybe I should have done . . . Oh yes indeed. Score one black mark against this secret agent, who had been a bit too secret! Now here I was in Venezia, where cherubs weren't nearly as thick on the ground. I could hardly buttonhole all my fellow cherubs at the hotel and ask each in turn, 'Psst, are you a Flawed One?' The only way to root one out would be to spend all my spare time in churches listening to others speak, waiting for the odds to pan out eventually. But as a rule we cherubs never attended each other's 'services'. Eeden had been the place to get to know each other. In Venezia sensible cherubs got on enjoying their earthly afterlife.

Hmm. I'd been deficient.

Don't blame me. Look what happened when I did run into some Flawed Ones, from my own world. Flawed Ones from other places might have been even worse.

'I'm hungry,' repeated Bernardino. 'Are you perhaps hungry too? May I invite you to dinner?'

'I can get a meal anywhere, any time I want.'

He kissed the tips of his fingers. 'Yet not such a meal as this! Nor such conversation, either.' His eyes twinkled. 'Come and discover a conspiracy.'

Without openly committing myself, I went with Bernardino. The promised conspiracy might give me a chance to stick my oar in and stir things.

We hurried through alleys across the narrow spit of land to the Accademia bridge; thence to the Piazza San Marco. Only a few old ladies were about in the Piazza, feeding flocks of pigeon-birds. A hundred or so pigeons clattered into the air at our approach. The majority of the birds wheeled around steeply to land again but a few peeled off and flapped up to perch on the Basilica where four galloping bronze horses pawed the sky. (A horse: imagine a goat as big as a cow. It's used for riding or racing.) Maybe one or two of those pigeons up there were eyes of the Godmind, mech-birds . . .

Some preliminary stinging raindrops overtook us as we sped along the Riva degli Schiavoni. Way out over the water, rain was already sheeting down upon the Lido.

'Not much further, little lady!' Bernardino assured me.

We turned up the Calle delle Rasse between the twin buildings of the Royal Danieli. The narrow lane took us to Giacomo Square. Down some other Calle we hurried, and just as the clouds really opened we dodged inside the Doge's Tavern. We puffed and shook ourselves, then Bernardino led me upstairs to a private room.

The window overlooking the narrow Calle was shuttered tight. Illumination came from glass bulbs in sconces, each with a tiny bright fork of lightning captive inside. A table was set with glasses and cutlery, the starched tablecloth white as snow. Above a sideboard hung a tapestry featuring an antique war fought by men wearing suits of metal, many on horseback. I recalled the tapestry in the cabin of that schooner at Spanglestream, far away and long ago. Three men and two women stood chattering by the sideboard; they hushed as we entered. Here was another sort of conclave entirely. The five regarded me.

Bernardino beamed. 'It's okay. I was right.'

He was right about the meal too. A smiling though silent waiter rushed in and out discreetly, dishing it up. Mounds of tasty seafood, lobster, clam, octopus, sprats in batter. The works.

He was also right about the conversation – just as soon as I had a bit of wine inside my young frame and decided that I *would* converse.

Thumbnail sketches of those present:

Tessa, otherwise known as 'The Contessa'. She was elderly, with lively sparkling eyes and a habit of darting her head to agree with something, like a pigeon-bird pecking seed. She wore jewels and rings galore.

Prof, 'The Professore', a dapper fellow in his forties; what he professed was science, though there wasn't much demand for this since machines of the Godmind did most of it.

Then there was Cesare, a burly fellow, a baritone singer at the Teatro della Fenice.

Luigi, an art restorer; he seemed sly.

And finally: Patrizia, young, dark and fiery. She described herself as their theoretician.

I soon gathered that there were several dozen others of like heart in Venezia, organized into separate self-contained 'cells'. Elsewhere too, in cities all across Europa, similar cells existed. This particular one was the 'Doge's Tavern cell'. (Oh, and a 'doge' is the name for a chief magistrate of old, a city boss; no connection with four-legged barking beasts.)

Presently Luigi said to me, 'Not everyone is so sure that you cherubs are aliens at all.'

'That's dumb.'

'Is it? It's a minority view – I don't hold it personally. I'm sure no one here does. I merely mention it. But consider: maybe the Godmind manufactures you all in its private province over in America, and fills your heads with false memories?'

I gaped at him. 'Whatever for?'

'Why, to give us tame idiots the illusion that human history is still happening – if not here, then somewhere in the galaxy! Thus we won't lose heart and die out from lack of stimulus. Lack of events; lack of *change*.'

'Huh. Nothing much changed on my world for long enough. When something big did happen, I don't know that it was such a boon!'

Bernardino said, 'You must tell us how your world

107

changed, hmm? And what part *you* played in that momentous event?'

'Did I say I did?' I clammed up; and ate a few clams.

'No, you didn't say.' He chuckled. 'But you showed it. Whatever Luigi says, I believe in you, my little visiting alien.'

'And I too!' exclaimed Tessa.

A little later Prof began to profess.

He said this: 'The Godmind is well known to be the end product of intelligent intuitive self-directing machines built by our ancestors. But alas, our ancestors themselves weren't too bright when it came to organizing the world. They brawled like brats, and they were on the verge of destroying this planet with incredible weapons. It's small wonder that the Godmind decrees a quiet static world. Small wonder, either, that it ranks children above us.'

'Children in appearance only,' I reminded him.

'Yet appearances *count*, Yaleen! Centuries of admiring you starchildren has bred in us a certain humility, a meekness. Which suits the Godmind perfectly. In the beginning – before it got its own act together – the Godmind must have inherited some inbuilt directives, though; just as people have behavioural instincts wired into them by evolution. Now what would its directives be? I've done research amongst the data still on access, from which I conclude that our Godmind's "instincts" were twofold: to preserve humanity, and to enhance it. Yet there's a huge difference between preserving – and enhancing.'

'There's practically a contradiction,' chipped in Patrizia. 'You can't simply preserve a living system in stasis, or else it dies out. Look at us: refugees in our own world, dispossessed of our initiative!'

'Hence,' said Prof, 'the role of you starchildren: continually to top up the psychic energy pool of a time-locked Earth. It's you who do the enhancing, by returning from the stars. If you didn't return, humanity would wither.

108

The discovery of *Ka*-space and the psylink allowed the Godmind to enhance and to preserve, at once; but at a cost to us. We consider that cost too high.'

I shovelled some Fritto Misto dell'Adriatico into my mouth and chewed the crispy lovelies. 'Is life on Earth so bad?' I asked, still munching.

'It's a question of dignity,' replied Tessa.

'Of liberty,' Patrizia corrected her. 'We wish to decide our own destinies. And we don't. We can't even make our own mistakes. We built a God for ourselves, and now we have to carry out its oh-so-benign will.'

'A God as foretold by precog myth?' I mumbled.

'Pah!' snapped Cesare. 'There's no such thing as "precog". I don't believe that our ancestors in the deep past intuited all this stuff happening. I say the Godmind just used a lot of myths and symbols to play a tune on us.'

'Long ago,' said Prof, 'an age of religion gave way to an age of science. Yet the psychic forces of the previous age remained extremely powerful. We aren't particularly rational creatures, Yaleen – and as an aside, if the Godmind was *obliged* to preserve us, it would need to preserve our irrationalities too! So it kept the form, but it dumped the earlier content. Deep down, as Cesare says, humans think symbolically. Now we are just the living symbols of the past. Nothing new occurs here. Whatever is new comes from the stars, where at least you aren't ruled directly by the Godmind on account of the sheer distance. But it can still haul you home through *Ka*-space, like fish in a net; then serve you up for our mental feast.'

'From which we depart,' concluded Patrizia, 'with our bellies forever empty. Those of us who still care deeply enough about human independence.'

'So you see,' said Bernardino, 'it excites us to meet somebody who is hiding important knowledge about an enemy of the Godmind. Any enemy of the Godmind is a friend of ours.'

They all looked at me expectantly.

It must have been the wine. Or else a need for allies.

I told them: of our river and our way of life. Of the black current, and the war against the Sons. Of the Worm's head and how I had ridden it. And of how I had died.

The only major thing I held back was that I was supposed to be here on Earth as an agent of the Worm.

This narrative took some while, and it was interrupted as much by crashes of thunder as by questions. By the time I'd finished, the Doge's Tavern was closed for the night; the waiter and proprietor both joined us. My throat was as rough as an old boot in spite of many cups of cappuccino coffee and glasses of aqua minerale.

'That's all,' I growled at last.

'Bravo, well sung!' Cesare applauded.

'Dear child,' exclaimed Tessa. 'Dear cherub, a thousand blessings!'

Bernardino grinned. 'That's all? Apart from the one little secret that you're keeping to yourself?'

'What secret?'

'I'd hazard a guess that it has to do with your presence here on Earth. Hmm?'

'No comment.'

Prof rubbed his hands gleefully. 'Ah, this is excellent. Far better than I hoped! So this Worm of yours was placed on a number of worlds long ago, as a destroyer of intelligence? An aborter of native life which might evolve? That would be very much in keeping with a mission to enhance the human race out amongst the stars. How better to pursue this mission than by strangling the competition in advance, before it even got going? Think of the destroyers that way, rather than as a set of ambushes laid for the Godmind's seedships! Maybe worms were planted on *all* suitable worlds – but most duly expired when their work was done!

'This would certainly explain something which has always rather puzzled me: namely why no intelligent life evolved on any of the colony worlds.

'But if this is true, two startling facts emerge. Fact number one: The Godmind is a master of time, able to send those worm creations back into the distant past of our galaxy. And fact number two: the Godmind doesn't know this.'

'Eh?' said I. 'How could it be a master of time and not know it?'

'Easily. Either it has *not yet* done this deed, nor even foreseen the doing of it . . . that's one possibility. Or else the Godmind isn't as united as we thought. Parts of it operate independently, unknown to the rest of it – just as the workings of our own subconscious mind are mostly hidden from our waking consciousness. If so, potentially it is a house divided against itself.'

'That,' I said, 'is like adding two and two together and getting twenty-two.'

'Sometimes twenty-two might be the right answer. You have to learn to see things from a new perspective. A new perspective sometimes reveals the *true* picture, as Luigi can tell you.'

'Can I?' said Luigi.

'Yes, yes, that painting of the skull and the carpet you told me of! Look at it ordinarily, and you just see a carpet. But if you tilt the picture and look at it askance the carpet becomes a human skull.'

'Oh, Holbein's *Ambassadors*. Right.'

The worms could have been sent *backwards in time* by the Godmind? But the Godmind didn't even know this? And most worms had done their duty, nipping competition in the bud then faithfully expiring? But a few had survived and awoken when the seedships arrived? My brain buzzed. It made a crazy kind of sense, if the end result of colonization was to be as Ambroz and his mentor Harvaz the

Cognizer suspected. Death at the starting line, death at the finish!

I hadn't mentioned to my new friends what Ambroz had said. I'd been busy talking about my own world and the war and the Worm. Now I told them hoarsely of Ambroz the Exotic and of the telescope the size of the whole galaxy.

When I'd done, Prof got so excited that he knocked a glass of water over. It's remarkable how much liquid a glass holds . . . when you knock it over. A pool spread. 'So, so, so,' he exclaimed, thumping his fist into the palm. Everyone ignored the spillage.

Bernardino frowned. 'What, kill everyone just to use their *Ka*s for a few moments? That makes as much sense as burning down a pigsty to get a plate of pork.'

'No, it does make sense,' said Prof. 'The Godmind can cast its fishing net in *Ka*-space, but essentially, it's a thing of the physical universe, our Godmind. It doesn't control *Ka*-space; it doesn't understand it. It just uses it. I'll wager it can't have a *Ka*-store like Yaleen's Worm. Our Godmind's bosom is empty.'

'Perhaps,' said Cesare, 'that's what it wants to see with its telescope; if indeed it *does* have its eye set on building this lens, whatever the cost. It wants to see how to own *Ka*-space.'

'Well, it *would*,' said Prof, 'if ka-space is the clue to what the universe is, and why there's one. *Ka*-space certainly seems to be the domain of the dead. Maybe the dead are like a sort of . . . subconscious of the cosmos? Life evolves in the universe through the aeons. *Ka*-space fills with more and more dead souls. So does the subconscious grow richer and deeper? If so, the real key to action may lie with the dead. Yet how can the dead ever act?'

'You're becoming metaphysical,' Patrizia chided him. 'Fascinatingly so, perhaps! But I say we should discuss possible action in the here and now. Yaleen has given us a lovely tool to subvert the Godmind and seize our freedom again: this threat that the Godmind means to snuff us all one day.'

'One day,' agreed Luigi. 'One day a thousand centuries hence. How many people care about such a time-span?'

'They ought to!'

'Ought to. But do they? Do revellers worry about the hangover the next day? Or the state of their liver in twenty years' time?'

'We needn't *mention* the time-span. If we spread this rumour, and alert our contacts throughout Europa to spread it too, and then if a starchild should publicly denounce the Godmind – '

'Don't look at me.' But of course Patrizia already was.

'Who was it who said they could shift the Earth if they had a lever long enough?' she asked.

'And somewhere to stand,' Prof reminded her. 'Archimedes said that.'

'Maybe we have such a lever here – a lever as long as the distance from the Sun to Yaleen's star!'

'What about the Godmind controlling time?' I objected hastily. 'If what Prof says about the origin of my Worm is true – '

'*Your* Worm?' Bernardino seized on this avidly. 'Why not come completely clean with us, Yaleen?'

'Because, well . . .' (His grin broadened.) I tried to recoup. 'If the Godmind controls *time*, damn it, what hope is there?'

'Look at it this way,' said Prof. 'A new perspective! If you introduce things into the past, albeit far away in space, maybe something has to vanish from the present – or change – to compensate. To preserve cause and effect. That something may well be the *knowledge* of what you have done. Anyway, dear cherub, you too have tricked time already. So have all starchildren who have died and been reborn here.'

'How do you work that out?'

'You arrive here through *Ka*-space much faster than the ordinary universe permits anyone to travel. So the dead travel through time.'

I yawned. I just couldn't stop myself. I was dead beat. After all, I was only a little girl.

'You shall have a room tonight here in the tavern,' Bernardino said amiably. 'Tomorrow, we'll all have lunch together, hmm? You can come as clean as this tablecloth – *was*, before we began.' (The pool had soaked in. Crumbs were scattered about, and a couple of purple rings marked where wine glasses had stood.) 'We shall decide; and act. That's why you came to Earth, isn't it?'

'Do you read minds?' I grumbled at him.

'No, only faces. And the language of the body. Right now I read that if you don't soon go to bed, you'll fall asleep in that chair.'

So over lunch next day (fish soup and liver risotto) I did come clean about the Worm and me, much to my new friends' delight. Tessa even presented me with her favourite chased-gold ring – she *said* it was her favourite, anyway. For had I not worn a fine ring when I triumphed, Worm-wise, once before? I accepted it as a fair substitute for my lovely diamond ring, lost forever.

Over the next few weeks the conspiracy thickened. The Underground contacted cells of comrades all around Europa, in Paris, Berlin, London, Petersburg, by 'phone' – the lightning speaking tube. Journals began to pick the rumour up. According to Prof, there used to be much quicker ways of spreading news around: by radio (which Ambroz had mentioned) and even by picture-radio. However, the governing Godmind had phased these methods out, as inappropriate to its design for order, calm and joy on planet Earth.

During those weeks I learned quite a bit of this-and-that: things which my Cyclopedia hadn't bothered to fill me in on. (Not that I'd asked. I hadn't *known* what to ask. And I hadn't wanted to alert it by too many leading questions.)

What particularly caught my attention was the system of justice on Earth – since I presumed that I would (to say the least) be committing an antisocial act by foul-mouthing the Godmind.

Patrizia explained all this to me. The name of the system was Social Grace; and its ultimate sanction against anyone who oppressed anybody else was permanent banishment to some distant place of exile, which was generally assumed to be an icecap or a desert. (Though *how*, Patrizia insisted, could my proposed misdeed be regarded as 'oppressive' of anyone, when it was clearly liberatory?) In contrast to directly-administered Eeden – God's own half-billion acres – law enforcers on the rest of the Earth were humans: Paxmen. These Paxmen advised and arbitrated, and soothed and smoothed out disputes and difficulties. Sometimes they were assisted by machines: a mech-bird or mech-hound.

Now, nobody knew of any family whose son had ever entered the Paxman Corps. Besides which, all Paxmen had a striking similarity of countenance which bespoke body-engineering. Either they were specially bred to their role, in vats; or else, as one whisper went, they were actually recruited from the ranks of ornery people who fell foul of the Paxmen: murderers, rapists, vandals, arsonists, insane devotees of weird imaginary gods, or whatever. According to the whisper, these criminals were made over in a body-vat, and had their minds changed too; *this* was their exile – an exile from themselves, poetic justice.

Patrizia thought this whisper unlikely to be true, since on Earth nowadays there was precious little murdering, raping, vandalizing or whatever. Luigi, who restored pictures, knew that things had been otherwise in the bad old days, back when 'life was Hell'. Many ancient paintings showed atrocities: burnings, lootings, butchery, rapes, people nailed up on wooden crossbars.

The pacifying hand of justice was, according to a saying, 'both light and dark'. It rested *lightly* on the world the majority of the time, caressing and gentling, barely even felt; but it could grip tightly and suddenly. And it was *dark*: hidden away until the moment when it popped into sight.

I myself hadn't even seen any Paxmen. I hadn't come across any of the 'fingers' of the Godmind. My schedule of talks in various churches – hardly a very punishing schedule – had been arranged by the hotel management.

According to Patrizia, Paxmen had never bothered very much with the Underground in the past. Why should they? So far as I could see, the Underground hadn't *done* very much till now, beyond gourmandizing and theorizing – and circulating leaflets which most decent citizens promptly tossed away, as nonsense. For did not the Godmind genuinely resurrect its starchildren to the glory of Humankind? Had it not brought Heaven to Earth? It delivered the goods (as foretold by precog myth).

So the Underground assumed that they could carry on playing treason games, and maybe play them so well that one day the Godmind would suddenly, to its surprise, find itself defeated.

I wasn't so sure. Maybe the activities of the Underground simply amused the Godmind – to the extent that they were wide of the mark, and ineffectual.

After several weeks of preparation, the Doge's Tavern cell decided that the time had come. I was due to appear in the Basilica of San Marco, the grandest church in Venezia. It was there that I should denounce the Godmind.

* * *

Came the day, I felt damn glad to be wearing that ring of Tessa's. It was *something* to set against the glittering splendour of that 'Church of Gold'. Oh the sensual glory of that Basilica, crusted with scintillant mosaics inside and out – and its golden altarpiece studded with two and a half thousand jewels! Oh the glory of the Godmind, dwarfing the rebel cherub: me.

When I arrived, a machine was playing a symphony from the gallery by way of warm-up. Long golden chord progressions soared and soared. The Pastor took me into an antechamber and supplied me with a white soutane and a square white biretta hat to wear for the occasion. Thus attired, I was escorted down the nave by the Pastor, a doting old codger dressed in the usual belted red frock. The symphony faded when I arrived at the altar-rail. I turned and stood near the speaking-tube, which would make my voice resound around the Basilica.

'Earth-mortals of Venezia,' the Pastor cried out through the tube. 'On this blessèd morning we mass together to hear from the cherub Yaleen, daughter of an alien sun, starchild of the Godmind. Let us praise her!'

The audience did so by clapping loudly and calling 'Bravo!' The Basilica was packed, and for a moment I thought that none of my friends were in the congregation. Then I spotted Bernardino near the front. He winked. With fingers crossed I rubbed my ring, and kissed it for good measure.

The Pastor departed back up the nave; silence fell. To me, this silence descended like a ton of feathers, suffocatingly. What the hell was I going to say? I'd made my mind up to speak simply and clearly, as in previous churches, but this building was so *ornate*. How could I match it? I licked my lips. Then I recalled the old fragment, *Julius Czar*.

'Mortals, Venezians, Earthfolk, lend me your ears,' I sang out. 'And keep them open please! Don't stick your

117

fingers in them. I come here to bury the Godmind, not to praise it. I come to bury it under a pile of accusations which are all too true! Why? Because it intends to bury us all, starfolk and Earthfolk alike. It means to light a bonfire with our minds, burning our brains out so that it can see to the end of the universe in one big flash – '

This was *awful*! Burials, bonfires, big flashes. I glanced at Bernardino; he grimaced. A rustling mutter of perplexity spread amongst my audience, like a scuttling rat. Or six rats.

'Look here,' I said, and proceeded much more simply.

Things went better from then on, for the next five or ten minutes. The rats of murmur didn't quit their scampering but now they mostly scurried to my tune. Or so I thought.

I was helped by my claque in the audience. At one point Tessa rose, dressed in black weeds – I hardly recognized her at first till I noticed all her rings. Wringing her hands, she wailed, 'It's true! The Godmind is a Devil. A Satan rules the Earth! The Demon of precog myth!' Quickly she subsided back into her seat.

Cesare and Patrizia and Bernardino also joined in briefly from seats far apart. What's more, members of other cells seemed to be scattered about in the congregation. Then Luigi spoiled the effect by appearing in the gallery and showering down leaflets. He hadn't said he was going to do this; Patrizia glared angrily. (Or *was* she angry? Her expression was weird.)

The Pastor, after flapping his hands at me for quite a while from the back, arrived at some decision and left.

I spoke on. Presently a drab little man leapt up. 'You insult us!' he cried. 'You insult our Basilica. You insult those robes you wear.'

'You insult us!' parroted the woman next to him.

'You aren't a real starchild!' another woman shrieked. 'You're an imposter!'

118

'No she isn't!' someone else shouted back. A member of the Underground? 'No normal child could speak that way. So she must be a cherub.'

'Nobody normal would talk that way!'

'Shut up! This may be true!'

And so on.

'Yes, hear me,' I called. I had the advantage of the speaking tube. 'Hear me – for the sake of the future! Listen, for the sake of life on all the worlds!'

At this point the speaking tube went dead. And just then two pigeons flew into the Basilica. They flapped up together to perch on the gallery.

'Here comes the proof,' I shouted, in my child's unaided voice. 'The Eyes of the Godmind! No doubt the Fingers will follow. But am I oppressing anybody? No! So why should I be silenced?'

Sure enough, two tall strapping men hove in sight. Both wore identical sky-blue uniforms. They could have been twins. Neither of their broad bland faces bore any hint of personality.

I crossed my arms and awaited them there at the altar-rail. The congregation had hushed; and so had I. I had no intention of being dragged shrilling from my podium. There was, as Tessa had observed, such a thing as dignity.

The pair of Paxmen halted a few spans away from me. And then, from the machine-mouths which had made music up in the gallery, spoke a voice: a rich, sonorous, sombre voice.

A voice which could only be the Godmind's own. (And in the audience: muted gasps, wide eyes. Somebody keeled over in a faint.)

The pigeons cocked their heads, and the Paxmen stood blankly before me.

'In precog myth,' said the voice, 'a child went into the Temple to argue with the Wise; and ended up nailed to a tree . . .'

119

'Really?' I croaked. I cleared my throat. 'Is that so?' I said, more boldly. 'There aren't too many trees in Venezia! So will you nail me up on the bell-tower? Nice view from up there.'

'Do not mock me, cherub.'

'Why don't you tell all these people the truth about what you're actually up to?'

'Why, cherub, the truth is that I am filling this galaxy of stars with human souls. Did you not know that?'

'Did *you* know that you sent black destroyers *back through time* to all sorts of worlds – so that you could stroll in later on and set up shop? But the scheme didn't pan out properly everywhere!'

Luigi raised a ragged solitary cheer. Which I suppose was quite brave, or stupid.

'*Silence*! You refer, cherub, to the precog myth of Satan-spirits expelled from God's bosom before the Earth was peopled? Why? That did not come to pass.'

'Oh didn't it? Where else do you think you got the idea for the black destroyers – on World 37 and elsewhere? You've cocked-up, and you don't even know it. If you mess around with time, you change what happened – and that includes knowing that you did it! You made your own enemy on seven worlds at least.'

'Interesting hypothesis,' said the voice, after a while. 'I shall think about this.'

'Of course,' I ploughed on, 'it's also possible that *part* of you knows this – and is hiding it from the rest of you!'

'Now you're trying to be *too* clever, cherub. You've had one bright idea. Yes indeed, I shall know the answer . . .'

'*When*? When you've filled the galaxy with human minds? And then set light to them, to see to the end of the universe through the biggest lens you can build?'

There was no reply to this. None. Soon the congregation began to whisper.

So I called out, 'It's the dead who will know the answer, Godmind – not you!'

'Then should not everyone die?' came the soft reply.

Now there was shock and consternation on many faces.

'If a God is immortal – ' began the voice.

I interrupted. 'Oh, so that's it! You want to preserve your own existence for ever, even though you're only a created thing, made by people? Let me tell you, you'll get goddamn bored with no people around to occupy your idle aeons. Everyone will have vanished into furthest *Ka*-space.'

'Be quiet, cherub. This is a holy moment. A moment of illumination. I see now that if an immortal God comes into existence at a particular point in space and time – it must become pre-existent too. Otherwise how could it be immortal?'

'Eh?'

'The God must be able to reach back into the past; and in the process it will cause precog myths of itself to be born. Yet the knowledge of how this can come to pass . . . may vanish in the very instant of its happening . . .'

The voice suddenly grew harsh. 'If Satan is the blindness of a God,' spake the Godmind, 'that blindness may yet be burnt out in a flash! You: I will put you somewhere safe while I think on these things.'

The pigeons took wing. The Paxmen advanced a step further.

It was at this point that a riot broke out in the Basilica of San Marco.

PART THREE
The Rose Show on The Moon

Black smoke billowed above the Basilica. Fountains had begun to blossom from the Piazza. Motor boats of the fire brigade clustered at the nearby quay like flies busy at a cowpat.

We were fleeing – not very fast – in a commandeered vaporetto, Bernardino at the helm.

Maybe we'd have done better to escape into the alleys of the city. But Paxmen had begun popping up all over. By the time we did decamp, slumbering bodies already littered the Piazza San Marco. The Paxmen were gassing everyone with their mercy-cans.

There may not have been any riot in Venezia for centuries; or anywhere else for that matter. But the ability to riot obviously hadn't been lost . . .

I wasn't too clear about the exact sequence of events, though I guess that's in the nature of riots, especially when they're being deliberately fomented. But anyway, the sudden eruption of brawling throughout the Basilica caught the two Paxmen off balance. Interrupted in their attempt to arrest me, they tried first to quell the congregation. Tough as those two servants of peace were, they were quickly overwhelmed and beaten senseless. Oh it was chaos in there; not least from the point of view of a little girl. All those big adult bodies crashing about. Then Bernardino appeared, picked me up bodily and forged through to the exit. When we got out into the Piazza, *that* was in turmoil too. But the fires of violence had already been lit out there. What spilled out of the Basilica was only extra oil to add to the flames.

Just as Bernardino set me down, Prof and Luigi happened by. 'They're ruffians!' Prof was shouting at Luigi. 'You've hired ruffians!'

'Hired? They're volunteers of the Underground, that's who! Well, most of them. So maybe some people have had a few drinks. But use your eyes, man! It's the normals who are berserking. The sheep have got their dander up at last.' Luigi danced aside to shove somebody into someone else. This someone-else swung round and punched his supposed attacker.

Prof grabbed Luigi by the arm to stop him from slipping away. 'There'll be a dire come-back for this!'

'It's worth it.' Even thus impeded, Luigi stuck out a foot to trip a careering youth, who cannoned into the two brawlers. 'Paxmen can't arrest a thousand people. Won't! This thousand will remember. Think of the news value. Journals pick this up all over Europa. After we phone 'em.' Shaking loose, Luigi kicked a stout matron in the butt. She plunged screaming and flailing, claws out. Bernardino sheltered me.

Luigi cried, 'It's a huge spontaneous explosion of protest at Yaleen's revelations! Needn't have happened if those Paxmen hadn't tried to shut her up. That's what angered everyone.'

'They'll find our *leaflets* in there, you idiot!'

'Will they? Will they? Don't count on it! Anyway, we've drawn the Godmind into the open. We've called its bluff!'

Just then Patrizia, fiery and radiant, came wading through the mêlée with Tessa in tow. A woman was lying on the ground, bleeding and moaning, and feet were trampling her heedlessly. A fat man was stamping around, grunting like an angry pig as he nursed a broken finger. Tessa was cackling with glee, and for a moment it seemed to me that these people were totally childish. They were the children, not me. They knew *nothing*. They'd never been in a real conflict, or seen Verrino trashed. They didn't

126

even understand pain – till they got hurt. (But did that mean it was *mature* to go through a war?)

That was when three crackling bangs came from within the Basilica one after another. Heat gusted out.

'What in the name of – !'

'Firebombs, Prof,' bragged Patrizia – as the congregation began flooding out, everyone fighting to be first. 'Come on, Lui, *action*! But always from the rear.'

'Don't I know it!'

'Down with the Godmind!' she shouted. The two of them melted away into the mob.

I grabbed at Bernardino. 'You set me up! You really fooled me!'

'Not me. I'm as astonished as you are. Oh, we had a plan to save you from the Paxmen; to spirit you away safely. But not all *this*! Pat and Lui must have cooked it up between them.'

'If you're so damn clever at reading people's faces, how come you never suspected?'

'I didn't read Pat's intentions – because I already *knew* her so well. I never thought to!'

Smoke began drifting out of the Basilica. Some hideous cries still came from inside.

Bernardino looked sick. 'I didn't know her!' It was hard to say what anguished him more: the agony inside the burning building, or his own failure of insight.

Tessa directed a ringed finger towards the south end of the Piazza. 'The Paxmen cometh,' she said whimsically. Me, I couldn't see a thing, down where I was.

'He's not the only Paxman,' Prof cried. 'Look, look.'

Rioting may not have been in fashion for ages, but the Godmind's response time was speedy enough; its officers were armed with mercy-cans, as used by medics. They mowed the rioters down with smoke.

★ ★ ★

Looking back on it, Bernardino didn't quite have his wits about him. Or else he was determined to prove his own good faith to me, in recklessly chivalrous style.

For him, Prof, and Tessa the obvious way out would have been to let themselves get gassed in amongst the milling crowd and take their chances. I, of course, would have been arrested. I was far more identifiable: a child in a white soutane.

Instead of letting the confusion be his cloak, Bernardino acted on one of those impulses which seem like a good idea at the time. He hustled us down to the waterfront ahead of the advancing Paxmen. Bellowing something about evacuating victims – as though that was *his* job – he boarded a waiting vaporetto. The pilot didn't argue too much at the change of command; not after Bernardino pitched him into the water. Then Bernardino ordered panicked refugees on to the boat – enough refugees to confuse things – and we promptly took off, while more people were still trying to board. A couple of men joined the pilot in the water. We headed out and away, on the regular route towards the Lido. Like any ordinary bus-boat.

Naturally, this way of escape isolated us conspicuously on a huge expanse of water where any mech-gull could spot us.

Even so, we almost got away.

From somewhere along the Lido, an absurd contraption arose. It tilted, and headed in our direction.

It was a balloon the size of a sloop, striped in red and white, with a basket dangling below. This basket was being hauled through the air by a flight of four great white birds in harness. The birds had necks as long as snakes. Their wide wings beat lazily but firmly, towing the wicker carriage, and the air-bag that held it aloft, towards us apace. Two Paxmen in sky-blue clutched the ropes of the basket, staring our way.

I couldn't help wondering if this crazy form of transport was meant to *say* something to me. Was this some precog myth, specially staged for my benefit?

'Oh, the swans! The swans!' exclaimed Tessa. She sounded more enchanted than scared.

'They're mech-swans,' Prof told me. 'They – and that balloon – were at the festival of the marriage of Venezia with the sea.'

'Yes, when a ring is thrown overboard to wed the city to the ocean!' Tessa promptly stripped off a ring (the one with her family seal embossed) and tossed the ring far out. 'A signet for a swan, sirs!' she cried. Obviously she had gone bananas. She laughed gaily. Then she leapt overboard.

I shouted, 'Bernardino, stop the boat!' But we had already left Tessa behind. 'No, *don't* stop! Circle round!'

Tessa was bobbing in our wake, supported by her outspread skirts. She appeared to be wearing several white petticoats under the black weeds. She was making no effort to stay afloat, yet the air trapped in the layers of her garments prevented her from submerging. Angrily she began punching at her costume to beat it down; to no avail.

Prof clapped his hands. 'She would rather drown than be exiled from Venezia! How romantic.'

'Don't be stupid. We can't let her drown!'

Our boat's engine was roaring at full thrust, though oddly we didn't seem to be moving so fast. 'Bernardino, I told you to circle!'

'I just reversed the engine!' Bernardino shouted back at me. 'We'll be going backwards in a moment.' (And meanwhile our passengers milled and pointed and protested.)

'Oh . . . So who's going to jump in?'

'Alas,' confessed Prof, 'I cannot swim. But why should anyone jump in? This is the Contessa's own free choice – to preserve her honour and dignity.'

I jerked my thumb towards the wallowing, flapping woman. 'You call *that* dignified?'

It was all an academic question. The swans were already upon us. The *swish-swish* of their wings beat overhead. Both Paxmen leaned out, to drop green glass globes resembling fishing floats. Several of these burst on our deck, disgorging clouds of green smoke . . .

For a brief moment after I awoke I thought that I'd died and was back in *Ka*-space without a body; I simply had no weight at all. Then I opened my eyes and discovered that I was strapped to a seat inside a travel-capsule of some sort. Slouching figures lolled in other seats. Arms floated in midair. Hair stood up like waterweed.

No windows, no sense of motion, *no weight*. I let my hand lift itself with hardly any impulse of the will. Where the hell was I?

Ah: I spied Prof slumbering open-mouthed two seats away.

I squirmed round, though the straps clung tight. Tessa slept in the seat just behind. Her clothes were bone dry; so time had passed by, but how much? All the other faces I could see so far were unfamiliar, and some looked quite exotic, for Venezia. Black, brown, yellow. Were we anywhere near Venezia at all?

Then a door slid open. A Paxman stood . . . No he didn't. He floated. His feet were half a span off the floor.

As soon as everyone was awake, the Paxman made an announcement. We were all criminals who had seriously violated Social Grace. Therefore we were being sent into exile.

On the Moon.

On the Moon: Tessa had a feeble fit of hysterics at this; but she calmed down quickly, and thereafter sniffed superciliously at everything the Paxman said.

Concerning how to unfasten our seat-belts.

And how to move around the 'shuttle' without bashing ourselves.

How to use the toilet in back. How to vomit without filling the air with a cloud of spew. (But anti-nausea medicine had been pumped into us while we were asleep, he assured me.) How to eat our food-blocks and drink our squeezy-juice. Concerning the pills we should take to avoid farting.

Give me *Ka*-travel any time!

Our journey would take three days. During this time we were sternly warned against brawling, riot, mutiny, vandalism, or spitting at the crew. Any of that, and we would all be gassed again; and this would cancel the effect of the anti-farting pills. So saying, the Paxman departed. He ignored all anxious queries about the moon.

Out of the twenty criminals on board, only four of us were former members of the Venezia Underground: me, Prof, Tessa, and Bernardino. I hadn't spotted Bernardino when I first woke up. He looked wretched. Prof, on the other hand, appeared chirpy and alert; he busied himself with little experiments in weightlessness.

No sign of Luigi or Patrizia. Or any of the real stirrers of the riot. How damned unfair.

Most of the other criminals weren't even from Italia, and no one knew where our ship had sailed up into the sky from; we'd all been asleep.

In our group were two brown-skinned Indians from India, woman and man; a black African, an Arab, a Chinese . . . there were people from all over Earth. Amongst our crimes we numbered: murder, banditry, fanatic worship of 'Allah', drug peddling, not to mention vandalism and arson. This all emerged courtesy of the Indian bandit-woman, Kalima, who floated about demanding answers and getting them. (A 'bandit', by the way, is an armed

131

robber who waylays wayfarers and attacks lonely farms; they're not unknown on the west bank of our own world.) But it was Tessa who averted what might have become a schism between the ordinary criminals and us members of the Underground. Since we were in the minority, such a schism wouldn't have been a good idea.

Loosening her seat-belt, she rose up, holding on to the back of the seat with one hand, and declared penetratingly, 'No matter why we are here, we must all now support each other in adversity. The Earth is gone from us forever. So are our former lives. The past is erased.' She floated across the aisle and held out her hand to the Chinese 'opium-man'; who clasped it. Kalima regarded Tessa sharply, then nodded and smiled faintly.

The Bandit-woman drifted over to me. Her hair was a long black braided rope. 'Why is a child here?'

'I'm a starchild,' said I. 'The Godmind decided I wasn't its favourite cherub.'

'*I* kidnapped a starchild for ransom,' announced Kalima. 'I did so because a bandit is courageous! And because you cherubs are set above us like little rajahs and princesses.'

'Don't pick on her,' said Tessa. 'We must all support each other.'

'Don't presume *too* much, old lady!' our bandit warned.

'Nor you,' growled our black African. 'We want no leaders.'

Kalima swung around, as a result of which she floated away from me. 'You may not *want*,' she told the African, 'but you will get.'

On that score, alas, Kalima was to prove perfectly correct.

By the time we landed, three days later, inevitably hierarch-ies and alliances had formed amongst us; whatever use, or otherwise, these might prove at journey's end. Kalima emerged as top card of the pack, with Tessa playing a grandmotherly role in the background.

What had prompted Kalima to become a bandit, of all things, back on the peaceful orderly Earth? Despite Tessa's dismissal of the past, curiosity finally overcame her and she asked Kalima this. The answer snapped back:

'My ancestress was a bandit, long ago. I am her, come round again on the Wheel of Years. Perhaps!'

Later, Kalima added, 'My family hoped I might become a *pandit*. That's our name for a wise person. I must have misheard them! Who needs pandits on the Godmind's Earth?'

'*I* was a pandit,' said Prof. 'Not,' he hastened to add, when Tessa frowned, 'that I'm bragging about it.'

Kalima laughed. 'Being a bandit was more fun! I earned my ride to the Moon.'

Other vignettes from the journey:

Muhammed Ibrahim, the worshipper of Allah (which was an ancient name for a God), kneeling and bowing in weightlessness, facing the rear door that led to the toilet on the assumption that the Earth lay in that direction.

Chu Po's mockery: 'Where there's no religion, opium's what the people need!'

Max the murderer looming over me: 'I killed two star-brats. Two!' He dragged a finger across his throat. 'Me! I killed . . .' He sounded dim-witted. But was he scary! Kalima swam through the air: 'Do you want both arms broken, or your back?' 'Uh? Do I want . . .?' Max's brain tussled with the choice. 'Never mind!' snapped Kalima. 'Get back in your seat. Strap in and stay there.'

On the whole, though, we all got on together and sorted ourselves out. Eventually the Paxman came to tell us to strap in for landing. Shortly after that our weight returned in surges, accompanied by a roaring which went on and on. I felt crushingly heavy. When the roaring died I was left feeling much lighter than I ought to be.

* * *

133

We didn't see the surface of the Moon. Nor did we even see the outside of the ship. A long metal corridor led directly from the door through which we disembarked. The shipside end was linked to the shuttle by massive rubber seals; and the corridor, lit by glowing strips, terminated in a largish metal chamber some way away. We had to walk carefully in case we bounded off the floor.

Once we were inside that chamber, a thick door sighed shut behind us. Bright violet light pulsed from glass tubes on the ceiling. Stinging misty vapour filled the air, then was quickly sucked away. At the same time I could feel the entire chamber starting to sink slowly. Down it travelled for several hundred heartbeats before the door slid open again, and a harsh but more natural light flooded in. Out we all filed gingerly, into the belly of the Moon.

Imagine a vast pit roofed with rock. Up on the ceiling, lights too bright to look at burned like little suns. The pit was a cone-shape, with the apex at the bottom.

Imagine this; and now carve a road spiralling round and round, descending. Then hack out one grand staircase, for speedier descent. Quarry caves and galleries, grottos, cells and tunnel-mouths so that the rockface becomes a stony honeycomb, with people as the bees. Let there be terraces for green crops, and irrigation ditches, as well as a long cascade of water feeding these ditches, before emptying into a lake at the very bottom of the cone.

'Why, here is Hell,' exclaimed Prof, enthralled. 'We've been sent to Hell.' The metal door clanged shut behind us.

We were on a broad platform up near the roof of the pit. Because we were close to the suns, it was very hot. Six or eight scruffy, burly fellows lounged about awaiting us. They were stripped to the waist, well-tanned and bearded. A bushel of beards! Black. Ginger. Shaggy. Bunchy.

The neatest of the Beards produced a notebook.

'Names?' he demanded.

We told our names one by one. When Kalima gave hers,

she added, 'I'm the leader of this group. We remain together – except for him.' She jerked a thumb at Max. 'Him, we expel. The rest of us are to be housed together.'

The man laughed nastily for a while.

'Ah yes, madame? In a suite of luxury apartments? Now you listen to me. All new arrivals are assigned billets where I choose, and wherever's convenient. Don't expect to sit around sunbathing and dabbling your toes in the streams, either. You'll work. At cultivating, tunnelling – '

'Are you trying to escape?' broke in Muhammed Ibrahim eagerly. 'In which direction? Which way is the Earth?'

'Are we trying to escape? Did you hear that, boys? Shall we dig a tunnel through hard vacuum? And if the vacuum's hard enough, crawl through it? Brilliant idea!' He rounded on Kalima. 'Every new intake needs to be taught a damn lesson, one way or another. Right! So you spoke of expelling that one, did you?' He indicated Max, who stood lumpishly. 'Obviously he deserves it. So be it. You shall see someone expelled. It's a while since we've expelled anybody. High time we did! Couple of hundred metres along this way is the exit tube for rubbish, with an inspection screen showing pretty pictures so you can check it's clear. It's our vacuum cleaner, you might say. Bring him!' he told his men. 'You lot follow me.'

Two Beards glided smoothly forward and pinioned Max with some sort of thumb-lock. They shifted him by the simple expedient of lifting him bodily off his feet. He didn't weigh much here. Max protested feebly, grunting and shaking his head.

Tight-lipped, Kalima stepped in the way. 'Wait! This is unnecessary.'

'You just expelled him from your group, remember? Any trouble, and you're next. I can call on forty men for assistance. Don't try to play the saint suddenly.'

Fury in her eyes, Kalima yielded.

'Follow!'

135

They went. We followed.

A straggly line of scantily-clad, sweaty men and women was portering wicker baskets up the grand stairway, towards our destination, which was a cave mouth. Some baskets contained dead chopped vegetation. Others had broken stone in them. Porters carried their burdens into the cave. Others emerged with empty baskets and rubbed sweat from their eyes before descending the stairway.

'But how inefficient!' complained Prof. 'Where are the machines?'

'Keeps people busy, don't it?' said one of the Beards. 'Toughens 'em up.'

'For what? Toughens them for what?'

There was no reply. We had reached the cave by now. Our host shouted for the work to cease. All the ascending porters unhitched their baskets and sat down. One woman, whose basket had already been emptied, sat down too. Our host promptly kicked her in the butt, knocking her down several stairs. The woman might have tumbled all the way if she hadn't fetched up against another porter sitting on a basket of rocks. The basket toppled over, tipping its contents a long, slow way down the stairs. Cursing, the man laid into the woman, who scrabbled to pick up his debris. Our host laughed.

The cave was as big as the main hold of a schooner. Within we found the contrivance which got rid of rubbish. This was an enormous metal cauldron resting in a deep hole cut in the cave floor. The cauldron was attached to rails running up at a steep angle through an open hatch in the roof. It was about a quarter full.

The two Beards threw Max unceremoniously over the side into this cauldron. Our host stepped smartly to a panel set in the wall and pressed a button. Immediately a see-through lid sprang up and closed the cauldron, imprisoning Max. Next to the panel there hung a large glass picture. This showed the cauldron in a miniature, with us all standing about. It was a picture that moved and represented real life as it was happening.

Max had gathered his wits by now, and decided that something was amiss. He scrambled up on the rubble and other refuse and thrust in vain at the lid. He hoisted a hunk of stone and began to batter. With no result; obviously the lid wasn't made of glass.

Our host pressed another button and the cauldron began to rise smoothly up the rails. Max's efforts redoubled. The cauldron was above us now, but we could still see Max inside it on the picture-screen; its vantage point was changing to match the progress of the cauldron. Once the cauldron had cleared the roof, a metal door sighed shut above.

Now, side by side, the picture-screen was showing two separate scenes. One was of cauldron and contents rising up the rails, as seen from above. The other was of the empty rails ahead of it. The rails seemed to lead to a blank metal wall, but then another door slid aside. We saw points of light, stars. None of them were winking.

Then there was only one picture again: of a dead, harshly sunlit landscape – grey hummocks, craters, boulders casting jet-black shadows. A ramp towered up, supported by struts and pillars. A mobile machine with a scoop on the front was shifting debris away from underneath. Then the cauldron emerged from a hole in the ground and slid up the ramp.

When the cauldron reached the top, the lid sprang back into the metal body. The whole container tipped, dumping its load – and Max.

He fell. So did the stones and other scruff. But that wasn't what killed Max. He leapt when he hit the ground, missing most of the avalanche. He took two giant steps. Then he seemed to shrivel up. He hunched. At the same time he threw his arms out, fingers clawing. His mouth gaped so wide he could have dislocated his jaw. Blood bubbled. His eyes bulged. He fell over. He writhed a while, scratching the dust. Soon he was still.

Above, the cauldron righted itself. It slid back down into the Moon.

'Doesn't the Godmind *care* if you kill?' cried our other Indian. 'Why don't the Paxmen stop you?'

'Because,' bellowed our host, 'the Moon is not your soft and pampered Earth! That's lesson number one. The Godmind has other ambitions here. Lesson number two is that I've just done your ex-companion a favour by freeing him from this hole.'

'In that case,' murmured Tessa, 'spare me your kind favours, sir.'

The ceiling hatch re-opened. The cauldron slid down the rails into its previous berth. We regarded its empty belly warily. It seemed to catch my breath away.

'The third lesson is that we only have so much space, and so much air and food. We get some rations from Earth, but space we have to hack out for ourselves.'

'I'm surprised,' said Bernardino lightly, 'that you don't just kill everyone new who arrives.' In the circumstances I thought he was taking an almighty risk. But he looked relaxed. He must have read something on our host's face that reassured him. Perhaps we had all passed over some emotional hump. Or maybe Bernardino was so sick at heart, he didn't care.

'The Godmind wouldn't like *that*, friend! It makes use of us; and it likes a lot of variety. Your next lesson is: when the Paxmen call on you to serve, you go with them tame as a lamb.'

'Serve?' I asked. 'How?'

'By donating part of yourself for the seedships. The Godmind builds 'em in another cavern – it uses tissue samples from us. The scum of the Earth are here on the Moon, girl, and that scum is a powerful brew. Strong and ornery and bold. That's how new colonies got going on

138

Earth in the old days, I'm told. Our Godmind's got a long memory. Now *you* tell me what a little girl's doing here.'

'That's simple,' said I. 'I'm a starchild, and I think the Godmind sucks. I said so in the biggest church in Venezia, then we burnt it to the ground.' (Not quite true, but never mind.) 'I'm fairly ornery too! But I don't need to toss people out with the trash to prove it! That isn't very bold. Real boldness would be messing up the Godmind's ship-building plan.'

'Oh, would it? You listen to me, tiny tot. We're stuck in a stinking hole on a dead world. No way can we upset the Paxmen or the Godmind. And why should we? This way at least a bit of us escapes and gets back to Earth eventually, transfigured. Here's where *your* stock came from originally: the bowels of the Moon. So don't be smug.'

'A bit of you gets back to Earth eventually: that's your consolation prize?'

He swooped and open-handed me across the mouth. The blow knocked me right off my feet. I didn't crash too heavily, though. Through tears I saw Kalima square up to our host.

'So you hit children too?' (Kalima was a fine one to talk. She kidnapped children.)

'Lady, I was hitting an *adult*. That's what she is.' (Still, he sounded . . . distressed.)

'What you just hit is your so-called salvation: starchildren.'

'Shut up!'

I thought he was going to hit Kalima too – which could have ended up with her in the cauldron. I struggled up. Wiped some blood from my lips.

'Sod all starchildren!' I said. 'Do you know what the colonies are all about? They're about the murder of the whole human race – everywhere.'

'What do you mean by that? Explain!'

139

I explained as briefly as I could. Even so, he soon interrupted. 'Rubbish. I don't believe a word of it.'

'He can't believe it,' said Bernardino. 'He *daren't*. Therefore he won't.'

Surprisingly our host let this pass. 'Okay,' he said grimly, 'if we've all *quite* got over our teething troubles, play time is ended. Unless you want me to vacuum someone else. My name's Jean-Paul, and I'm your boss – '

And.

And.

One of the poets of Earth was once of the opinion that 'The best lack all conviction, while the worst are full of passionate intensity.' Chu Po, our drug peddler, told me that. I suppose the poet must have been Chinese.

The Best were all on Earth. They were the sheep whose only conviction was a dumb faith in the glory of the Godmind and the wonder of its cherubs. Here in this hell below the surface of the Moon, the Worst had their abode. Here the offenders against Social Grace were simmering away in a nasty stew; this was being spooned out by the Godmind into its seedships.

And the stew had to be stirred and kept on the boil. Hence the hardships. Hence the rock-hewing and toilsome agriculture. Hence the arbitrary punishments and random acts of violence. All these added savour and spice to the stew.

Prof poured scorn on this idea that human tissue-samples could be tempered and toughened through the struggles and suffering of those who owned the flesh in question. But obviously the Godmind found life in this pit poetically appealing. The Moon-Hell was fulfilment of yet another precog myth, was it not? Heaven on Earth, Hell on the Moon. And here in Hell the Godmind used the wicked to bring about eventual Good: namely the winging homeward to Eeden of starchildren.

Generally the Paxmen kept out of our way. They let us exiles bully and harass each other and fight to be top dog or run with the pack in charge.

Generally. But if Hell showed signs of becoming too comfortable, the Paxmen would reduce the quality of life for a while by switching off the water-cascade or raising or lowering the temperature so that the exiles cooked or froze. They'd done this before; they would do it again, if we ever looked to be having it easy.

Now, once you got used to the assorted rigours and cruelties, life was rather better than it *appeared* to be – to those who weren't themselves living it, namely the Paxmen whose abode was way off in another cavern. So after a while I realized that Jean-Paul's regime was almost benevolent. He'd been boss for half a dozen years, and he was a more complex tyrant than at first he seemed. Looking back, the sudden arbitrary murder of Max had been done to prove how savagely Jean-Paul ran the shop, but without actually killing anyone's dear friend in the process. Likewise, his other outbursts of violence. Booting that porteress. Slapping me so hard.

We were allocated billets around the various circles of this spiral Hell. Tessa and I were assigned to a nook close to Jean-Paul's own king-pin cave. Only later did I cotton on that this was so that Jean-Paul could keep a semi-kindly eye on the two of us: the old woman and the child. To begin with, I would never have believed it. My mouth was still stinging from his blow and my teeth felt loose (though they weren't), so I hated him.

Ours was a tiny little cave. A tatty curtain hung over the entrance, and inside there was barely room enough for two sleeping pallets. ('Farewell, my lost palazzo!' mourned Tessa when she first saw inside.) On the other hand, we had no possessions to clutter the cave with. All hygiene and cooking was communal, carried out nearby. Unlike some other new arrivals, we were well away from the worst heat of the suns.

The suns: these dimmed but did not die by night, which was twilit throughout. Someone told Tessa that not once during Jean-Paul's reign had the Paxmen quenched the lamps of Hell to chasten its inhabitants. On several prior occasions the whole Hell-pit had been plunged into darkness for days on end. People had fallen to their deaths. A few had gone mad.

Tessa was set to work as a cook; and indeed she showed such an ingenious flair for improving the cuisine that one day Jean-Paul felt obliged to stop by specially to kick over one of her best creations. Tessa took this in her stride as a compliment to the chef. She had cottoned on to his real motives a bit ahead of me.

I was set to work as her assistant peeler and washer-up. Shades of my stay with Doctor Edrick!

Of Bernardino and Prof we saw little. They were labouring over on the other side of Hell. Of Kalima we saw a lot more, since Jean-Paul had ordered her to his own billet, beaten her a bit, and taken her as mistress. Personally I wouldn't have trusted Kalima in bed with me in case I got knifed in the ribs while I was snoring. But obviously I'm not always a brilliant judge of character. She seemed to acquiesce happily in her new role. She put on queenly airs. Now she was Jean-Paul's 'secretary'.

There were no kids, except for me. Apparently the water contained a drug very like our own Safe back home. An exile's only offspring was whatever they contributed to the Godmind's seedships.

Thus life proceeded, after a fashion.

For me, this was a routine of peel, peel, fetch and carry, scrub, scrub. Now and then the monotony was interrupted by the spectacle of fights or beatings administered by the swaggering Beards. As punctuation we heard the occasional muffled bang as new galleries were blasted in the rock. I began to appreciate another reason for the arduous chores hereabouts: there was nothing else to while away the years.

Nothing at all?

Oh, with one exception! Every now and then a couple of Paxmen would appear, locate somebody and lead them off in the direction of the great enterprise, to donate of themselves. The donors departed from a distant cave housing a transport tube. They always returned, none the worse for wear.

The Paxmen had no difficulty in locating whoever they wanted, because we were all under surveillance in the pit. Powerful glass eyes watched us from the roof, hidden amongst the suns. So when Jean-Paul had kicked Tessa's vegetarian lasagne over, he'd expected this to be noted on high with approval.

One day a couple of Paxmen came for me.

'Accompany us,' said one of them.

'I'm not donating so much as a flake of dandruff to your wretched seedships!' said I.

'No,' he agreed blandly, 'you aren't. The Godmind wishes to converse with you privately in His garden.'

'In its *what*?' Incredulous, I took in the terraces of cabbages, bean-sprouts, watercress, whatever.

'Not here. Elsewhere. Hurry up.'

The Paxmen escorted me to the cave I've mentioned. This was bare, apart from several glass eyes scanning the interior. The travel-tube itself was sealed off by a metal door, to which one of the Paxmen had a key. He only used this when a green light glowed to show that a capsule was waiting on the other side.

We boarded. With the exception of a number of seats bolted to the floor, the capsule was almost entirely blank metal inside. No windows at all. A fan-machine purred behind a grille, creating a draught.

One Paxman sat in the nose where there was a tiny control panel. The capsule door shut. We sighed way.

The other Paxman sat opposite me, watching, barely blinking.

'Hey, you guys,' I said, 'when you're off duty what do you do for fun?'

'A Paxman is never off duty,' my escort replied. Ah, here was progress indeed! No one had ever got very far trying to chat up a Paxman. If the Godmind had decided to talk to me, maybe their tongues were loosened too.

'Don't you have desires, ambitions?'

'We desire to do our duty; that's our ambition.'

Hmm. Did I say progress? Maybe not.

I tried: 'Were you born, or made?'

'Which were you?' he countered.

'Born, of course!'

'Wrong. Your body was vat-made in Eeden.'

'Oh, I know that! But I was born: the original me. How about you?'

'Made to measure. To suit the Godmind.'

'Hey, are you trying to be witty? Well gosh, witty folk like you must do something to amuse themselves!'

The Paxman regarded me levelly, then said, 'I garden.'

'You do *what*?'

'I garden roses.'

Roses: you know the name? 'The Queen of Flowers', so-called. You'll never have seen any roses, of course. To us, they're just a myth.

I first saw roses in palazzo gardens in Venezia. Roses come in different colours and styles. Some are big, some are tiny. Some are flat and simple, others densely petalled. Some are climbers, others bushes. Many are perfumed. Roses have nasty thorns to prick your flesh.

So where, inside the rocky Moon, did my Paxman garden

roses? Or was that just a conversation stopper? It certainly put a stop to my chatter!

Our capsule soon soughed to a halt. The door opened upon an empty, well-lit platform with a wall mosaic announcing: *Rosaluna Station*. The other Paxman stayed inside when we two stepped out. Behind us, the capsule itself was hidden by a second wall, of metal.

A corridor curved away. We went along this, passing through a couple of metal doors intended to keep the air in, in case of moonquakes.

The third door opened upon . . .

. . . masses of foliage and blooms under a sunlit, cloud-dappled blue sky! There were beds and thickets and mazes of roses. There were arbours, pergolas and archways all clad with leaf and flower. There were trellises, screens, tubs, hedges, brick walls a-blossom! Extending how far? Three thousand spans in length, and as much in breadth? I don't know which sight was the more amazing; the garden or the view of the sky above!

About one hundred spans above. I could tell that the sky was artificial. The real sun shone down through it from beyond, but the white clouds floating about were flat. They were squeezed between two giant panes of glass the size of the garden itself; and were adrift in some blue liquid. Since the clouds changed shape slowly as they drifted, they must be like blobs of oil in water: of a different substance from the blue medium they floated in. The false sky filtered and diffused the sunlight which would otherwise, perhaps, be too fierce – as there was no air between the Moon and the Sun.

The sky surely couldn't be made of ordinary glass, else it would have snapped under its own weight, not to mention the weight of the liquid sandwiched between. Anyway, didn't little rocks rain down on the Moon all the time, according to what I'd heard? That was why Hell was underground.

Yet here was a sky! So why couldn't Hell have a sky? Presumably because Hell was Hell . . .

A number of Paxmen were browsing, here and there, snipping off overblown blooms and wiring up stray new growth.

We descended a broad brick stairway between trusses of fluffy white blossoms, on to an earthen avenue. This avenue was flanked by large bushes bearing vermilion and creamy-buff flowers alternately, and led towards a metal gazebo set upon a low mound in the very centre of the garden: the gazebo roof was ringed with glass eyes.

We were only part of the way towards that gazebo, which I guessed was our destination, when my Paxman turned aside to lead me around by pebbled paths on a guided detour.

He stopped by a trellis tangled with branches bearing pinky carmine blooms. 'This is *Zepherine Drouhin*. Uniquely, as you'll see, it has no thorns. It's a climbing Bourbon rose, with semi-double blooms. Please smell the fragrance.'

To oblige him, I sniffed. 'Nice,' I said.

'We have to watch out for spindly growth. That's on account of the lower gravity. Equally, there's the plus of bigger blossoms and a longer flowering season.'

'Oh really?'

'And here we have *Picasso*, the first Floribunda rose to be described as "hand-painted" – though of course we don't literally paint it by hand.'

Next he pointed out a blood-red specimen. 'Ah, *Park-direktor Riggers*. It's vulnerable to mildew and blackspot, but of course we don't have any of that on the Moon.'

He pinched off a couple of flowers which were nearly finished. It occurred to me that Edrick would have felt beautifully at home here, stripping off mildewed leaves to the glory of the Godmind, though of course there weren't any such diseased leaves, said my guide.

146

'Now here's *Pink Grootendorst*, a rugosa shrub. Observe the frilled petals. The bush itself isn't much to look at. But the flowers are excellent for displaying at our annual rose show.'

A rose show? And practically next door we had to grub around in our wretched pit painfully growing vegetables!

'Are you mad?' I said.

Ignoring my jibe, he indicated a bush of silvery lilac flowers which looked like thin porcelain. 'Here's *Blue Moon*. It's as close as you can ever breed to a true blue rose. Why? Because the rose family doesn't anywhere include the blue pigment Delphinine.'

'I shouldn't have thought the Godmind would have too much trouble making a blue rose! Not when it can turn people into alien birds and merfolk at long distance.'

'Ah, but that would be cheating.'

'I give up.'

I oughtn't to give up, though. Not if the Godmind cared so much about this crazy lovely garden. How, I wondered, did one go about introducing mildew and black spot into it? Was that why we had been sprayed when we first landed on the Moon?

Why the hell did the garden *exist*? What did it all *mean*? Could the Godmind's glass eyes really perceive beauty? Could these robotic Paxmen?

Aha. If the Godmind tried its hand (a mech-hand) at painting or pottery to prove to itself what an artist it was – just like real human beings! – it might have made a fool of itself. But flowers were safe. Flowers were already dipped in beauty.

Our route led us back presently to the metal gazebo.

'You go on up, Yaleen. I'll be dead-heading nearby.' My Paxman gave me a little push in the right direction.

I mounted the metal steps and entered. 'I'm here, Godmind,' I said to the air. 'Why roses?'

After a wee pause the same rich sombre voice as I'd

heard in the Basilica spoke from the roof. (If I remember aright. It was a catchy little verse):

> 'Gather ye rosebuds while ye may,
>   'Time is still a-flying:
> 'This same flower that smiles today
>   'Tomorrow will be dying . . .

'You're lucky to be here while so many are coming into bloom, Yaleen. Roses are transitory. Humans too.'

'So you *do* admit it!'

Pause. 'Admit what?'

'Admit that you plan to burn the brains of everyone alive in another thousand centuries or so!'

Pause. 'Well, aren't you going to answer?' I demanded.

'Please note that our conversation will inevitably suffer from brief delays. That's because I am on the Earth, which is some distance away. You can see it, if you look at the sky above the entrance.'

I hastened to look, and spotted a swirly blue and white ghost of a disc beyond the blue of the false sky . . .

'I shall say "finish" when I finish speaking,' the voice went on. 'You will kindly do the same, otherwise we may get tangled up. I've been considering in depth your idea that I have had, or have, or will have mastery of time. I've been mulling your theory that I myself planted – or will plant – the black destroyers, yet do not know this. Alternatively, that such creatures exist as a result of my past or future effort to reach back through time. You sparked an interesting speculation, and I'd be interested to learn exactly how you arrived at it. Finish.'

I was just about to say that I was a whole lot more interested in the fate of the whole human race, finish, goddamn finish. But then I had an inspiration.

'Don't get me wrong!' I assured the voice, in a tone which I hoped sounded fervent and sincere. 'I've changed my mind a lot recently. I think your plan to build a lens is a super, fabulous one. It's a stroke of Godly genius. It's far beyond the sort of thing that *people* could dream up, which is how I had trouble adjusting to it.' My brain was zipping along nineteen to the dozen. 'I want in on your plan. I want to know what the universe is all about. I want to know what time is, and what *Ka*-space is, and why anything exists. That's what I really want. But *you* need someone on your side who understands you, and who isn't just a puppet. I'm sure you do, or you wouldn't be talking to me now! . . . er, finish,' I concluded breathlessly.

Pause.

'You've changed your tune, Yaleen. It isn't long since you abused me bitterly. And set fire to my Basilica.'

'Oh *that*! I had to draw attention to myself. In any case, I didn't personally burn the Basilica.'

'. . . a spell in Hell is salutary, perhaps? Please don't interrupt.'

'Sorry! Oops.'

'. . . but how can I know if this is a true seeing-of-the-light upon the Damask road, as in precog myth? Finish.'

Whatever was the Damask Road? I visualized a bolt of rose-red silk rolling out along a highway.

'Oh precog, tree-frog!' said I. But this hardly squared with my new demeanour. 'No, wait! What I mean is: precog myths mightn't be precog at all. They might be the proof that you influenced time past – that's how they got planted there in the past. But anyway: about my change of heart. People often oppose things because they secretly want in on them! Didn't you know that? The closer folk come to seeing the light, the more bitterly and blindly they oppose it. Till all of a sudden, flip. That's human nature. Finish.'

One thing stood out for sure. The Godmind didn't really know me. The Worm had strolled around my mind nonchalantly, whether I liked it or not. The Worm really knew the *Ka*s in its *Ka*-store. But the Godmind could only use the psylink to shift *Ka*s around: back to Eeden to inhabit new bodies.

Maybe it could build a lens with the *Ka*s of all the dead, but they certainly wouldn't inhabit its bosom afterwards. Not unless the view through its lens showed it how.

Whatever its limitations, the Worm had *insight*. The Godmind didn't. Yet. So the Worm was like the blind spot in its eye: an entry point to awareness, where nothing could actually be seen by it.

'Conversion is a behavioural jump, as in Catastrophe Theory?' The voice seemed to be asking itself, not me. 'Perhaps – ' and this definitely was addressed to me – 'you're just fed up with peeling carrots and washing dishes? Finish.'

'Oh no, that isn't it! It's all on account of this fabulous garden. Here's my damask rose. Road, I mean. I'm overwhelmed. I've fallen in love with it. I mean, just look around! Here in this garden you're searching for order and beauty – for the roots of existence! And the blossoms. Anyone who can fix up a garden like this just *has* to be on the ball. Finish.'

The Godmind was obviously proud (as Hell) of its garden. Maybe, when it had solved the secret of existence and wiped out the human race in the process, here it could walk in the afternoon warmth of the lunar sun, alone and content.

'Walk'? If the Paxmen all went 'poof' at the same time as everyone else, it could always jolly up some mech-gardeners with glass eyes . . .

'Ah yes indeed. This is probably the leading rose collection anywhere in the universe. It far outrivals the Empress Josephine's Malmaison. It can definitely hold a candle to the Parc de la Tête d'Or, the Westfalenpark or the Hershey Rose Garden. You still haven't said how you arrived at your other conclusions. Finish.'

'I *intuited* them, Godmind. Because . . . because I guess I must have been born with a freak gene for intuition! I can guess right, and I usually do.' (What a lovely lie. If only it were true!) 'Here's an example. This is just on account, as a goodwill gesture. I'll tell you how you'll be able to zap your enemy the black current, and any others of its ilk that are lurking about. I'll tell you how to wipe that cataract from your vision, that blot from your plan, that warp from the lens of your telescope!' Nice rhetoric, huh? 'When your lens is ready,' I said, 'why should it only receive? Why shouldn't it also transmit? And focus? and . . .' I left my clue dangling.

A tasty bait for my prospective partner, if I say so myself! I'd thought of it on the spur of the moment.

Even though I hadn't said 'finish', the voice purred at me: 'And *burn*. Oh yes, Destroy the snake which partly masks your world from me! And so I shall connect you all to me without exception in that climactic moment when I carry out so many billion operations!'

Aye, while many billion patients die.

The Godmind was definitely going a bit over the top, I thought. Though maybe when you've hatched such a megascheme you're entitled to go over the top? and who was I to criticize – me, who had just claimed impeccable intuition?

'I shall tell you a secret, Yaleen. My plan doesn't require as great a time as you thought. By no means do I need a whole galaxy to build my lens. I only need part of the galaxy, quite a small part. Finish.'

I felt such a chill in me as though the sky had cracked and space rushed in.

'You're still building new seedships and launching them, though? Finish.' (Spoken casually.)

'The second-last seedship is approaching completion right now. It will fly away within twelve Earth-weeks. Only

151

one more to go after that.' (I'll skip the finishes from now on. You've got the idea.)

'Maybe they'll both get an attack of the Worms at journey's end!'

'I doubt it, statistically. Besides, that direction has been safe so far.'

Obviously the new-style Yaleen had to pretend massive commitment. 'Oh dear! When they arrive, it'll take lots more years to establish colonies!'

'Not really. A few years will ensure a size that's adequate for the purpose. A presence is what counts. It's more a question of the topology of connexions in *Ka*-space.'

'Oh. But it'll still take those last two ships simply *thousands* of years to get to the far frontiers. I'll never live to see the outcome!'

Something resembling a chuckle issued from the gazebo roof. 'When I plan, Yaleen, I plan ahead. The earliest seedships travelled to the far frontiers. These last two ships are heading for the *nearest* stars with usable worlds. They'll arrive quite soon. It'll seem ever sooner to anyone on board. Accommodation can be added for a passenger.'

'What do you mean?'

'You wish to be in on the, ahem, *kill*? If you stay here, you may miss out. But if you travel as a passenger on this ship that's about to depart, you'll enjoy the boon of time-squeeze. You'll arrive in good time to be around when the final colony blossoms. You'll live to see the light. This shall be my gift to you, on account of all you have suggested. My ship will be programmed to amuse you *en route*.'

Oh no. No, no and no.

'Meanwhile, as an immediate reward you shall judge the rose show this year.'

'I'll *what*?'

'From amongst my new varieties, plus the older established specimens, you will select the Supreme Rose; and award it a gold medal.'

'Er, just where do I find a gold medal?'

'You're wearing a gold ring on your finger. That will do excellently. You can slip it on to a stem of the victorious rose.'

'I don't know how to judge roses! There weren't any roses on my home world.'

'That's because I didn't send roses anywhere else.' (*That* figured. In alien soil, under alien light, we aliens might have built up better rose gardens!) 'My Paxman will bring you here often, to instruct you on the relevant criteria. Fear not: You'll have time enough to learn. Then after the show your ship will fly to a nearby star. *Paxman to the gazebo*!' the voice blared out.

My escort came running.

'So what happened?' asked Tessa when I got back to our Hell's kitchen. (Incidentally, it took the capsule at least twice as long to return, as to go to Rosaluna Station.)

'I'm going to judge a flower show,' I told her. 'Then I'm going to zoom off to another star. What else did you expect?'

'Dear child, once I have swallowed the elephant of Hell, should I strain at a gnat? Tell me all.'

I did; and as she listened, her head pecked away like a pigeon's at every grain of detail. At the end she said firmly, 'You must speak to Jean-Paul.'

'What for? What's he got to do with it?'

'Ask yourself this, child: what will the Godmind do about Hell, and about us who live here, when the final ship flies away? Maybe it'll still require a Hell for its exiles. But what if it doesn't? It won't need tissue samples any more. What if it just turns off the heat and light and water?'

'I hadn't thought of that.'

'No. You will be going; so you didn't think. Such is human nature. But *we* will all be staying.'

'Oh Tessa!'

'Ah, I tell the truth – and I hurt your feelings.'

'No, it's you who's hurt! Isn't it? Because I'll be giving your favourite ring away, to a rose! And I'll be leaving you with all the washing up.'

She laughed; and I laughed too. Then she said, 'Do go and see Jean-Paul. If he kicks you, that's the fate of messengers who bring bad news. No, wait! The eyes in the roof will see you going to his cave. No doubt they're keeping a special eye on you. I'll go instead.'

'And get kicked?'

'I'll take him some cannelloni.'

'Don't make it too tasty, then.'

At breakfast time next morning Kalima came to see me, ostensibly to grouse about the rubbish we'd been dishing up. She slapped me about, smashed a plate or two, then hauled me roughly into the nook where we stored the victuals which the boss's men doled out.

'Tell me, but speak softly,' she whispered.

I told.

Afterwards, she brooded.

'So you will learn how to judge roses,' she decided. 'And you'll keep your eyes and ears open for me.'

'For you, or for Jean-Paul?'

She smiled, twistedly. 'You'll report to me, when I collect meals. Confide in no one else.'

'Maybe,' I suggested, 'you should bring Prof into this? Remember the pandit from Venezia? He knows science, and he was a member of the Underground.'

'We're all underground here, little girl.'

'Do tell Prof – and Bernardino. Please.'

'Are you seeking privileges for your friends? Beware you don't double their burdens.'

Carefully I said, 'They're good at . . . organizing.'

'So,' snapped Kalima, 'was I.'

Soon after, my Paxman collected me to return to Rosaluna Station and the rose garden.

During the next several weeks I began to get the hang of roses. Assiduously I studied the difference between Hybrid Teas, Floribundas and Polyanthas; between Rugosas and Hybrid Musks. I mastered the distinction between flowers that were high-centred, open-cupped and pompon. I learnt all the criteria for showing at exhibition: blooms should be pointed, without a split centre, not blown, free from blemish . . . I memorized strings of strange names, such as *Napoleon's Hat, Little Buckaroo,* and *Thrilled Nymph's Thigh.*

Meanwhile the ghostly Earth went through phases in the false sky, but the Sun sank out of sight. In its place sun-lamps blazed from the four corners of the enormous skylight. I wondered why I hadn't seen this huge lighted window on the Moon when I was watching from California, but maybe it didn't look so big and bright from Earth.

I also asked my Paxman questions such as, 'Don't the roses get too much light with the Sun shining non-stop for two weeks?' (The sky, it turned out, could be dimmed to imitate night.) 'Oh, how's that? What's the sky made of? What happens if a rock from space smashes into it?' (Not to worry, Yaleen. 'Radar-controlled laser-zappers' were watching out for any stray rocks zooming in from the void.)

And most importantly: 'How many Paxmen will be at the rose show? What, all of you? Gosh, how many's that?'

One day the Godmind summoned me to the gazebo.

'How's it going, Yaleen?'

'Well, it's absolutely fascinating. Intoxicating! Gosh, am I grateful to you!' (In fact, it *was* quite interesting. Definitely a lot more interesting than scrubbing dishes.)

'Good. Now, on the topic of time . . . it seems to me that when my lens is complete, and when I annihilate the black current through *Ka*-space, that will also be the moment when I discover how to send those destroyers back through time to reserve habitable worlds for my seedships. I shall tear the blindfold off, and hurl it into the past; as it were. The circle will be complete, and causally closed. I shall proceed onwards.'

'That's really neat, Godmind! Could I see the ship I'll fly in? Please?'

'Does your intuition tell you that I'm right, Yaleen?'

'Oh absolutely. Well, that's to say: *almost* absolutely. I'm a bit fuzzy about this because, because . . . because if you foresee something *too* clearly, then it can't happen exactly so. It'll happen, but in a slightly different way. If you follow me.' (I certainly didn't!) 'But getting back to my ship . . . what a huge explosive force it must take to chuck a ship at the stars! Could I take a peek at it? Please.'

'I have to plumb time itself, Yaleen! *Ka*-space is non-spatial. Yet it is analogous with actual spatial locations existing in the here-and-now. Maybe an implosive event such as the sudden death of all conscious beings can deform *Ka*-space along a time-axis, thus opening a paradox channel into the distant past of the universe . . .

'The ship? Ah, the ship. Yes, you may see it provided you can answer a couple of questions successfully.'

Questions about *Ka*-space, paradox channels to the past, and my intuition? I suppressed a groan.

'Ask away.'

'My first question is: Which was the first serious challenger to *Allgold* for the crown of top yellow Floribunda?'

I did groan. 'Er . . . *Sunsprite*.'

'Correct. And now a harder one: What is the pedigree of *Pink Perpetuity*?'

'Um, by *Danse de Feu* . . . out of *New Dawn*.'

'Well done. Your Paxman will take you to view your seedship.'

* * *

So my Paxman and I returned to Rosaluna Station earlier than usual that day. Once there, I discovered that I hadn't taken off my gardening pinafore as I usually did before quitting the garden for the day. Such is the interruption of routine.

I'd decided a while since that the tube line must run in a large circle, with traffic travelling in one direction only; but on no previous return journey to Hell had the capsule stopped at any other intermediate station, and unless it did, and the door opened, there was no way to see out.

'From Hell to Rosaluna, from Rosaluna to where?' I quizzed my guide.

'To our Pax barracks. Then to the Navy yard. Then to Hell.'

Four stops in all.

'So the Navy yard is quite close to Hell?'

He nodded.

'And the ship I came in landed between the two?'

'Correct.'

'Do you know?' I said, 'in all this time you've been my teacher, you've never once told me your name. Do you have a name?'

'Of course. I'm Pedro Dot.'

Pedro Dot: he had been one of the great rose breeders of the distant past, from the part of the Earth called Spain, home of the fabled Parque de Oeste rose gardens . . . Well, well.

Just then a green light lit, announcing that our capsule had arrived.

This isn't a discourse on how to build seedships. That would fill a whole tome by itself, and I'm certainly not the one to write it. Most of what I saw in the huge crammed hall of the Navy yard, I couldn't fathom. Still less could I plumb the workshops and flesh-vats adjacent. Nor, since most of the work was being done by soft machines, with only a handful of Paxman technicians in attendance, was it always easy to distinguish the makers from what was being made.

What I *did* understand well enough, and what curdled me, was my proposed accommodation aboard the seedship.

To reach this we rode up a gantry. Up top within the hull the 'pod' – to use Pedro's word – lay open for inspection. Air-and-water-machines were being fitted round it.

It wouldn't be quite fair to call the pod a tomb. It was a bit bigger than that, with a window-dome on top, for journey's end; but much of the space inside was taken up with exercise machinery including a treadmill – so that I could march to infinity, getting nowhere, on magnetized shoes. Pedro showed how.

After this, in there, we tried out a snack of food-bars produced by a machine which, Pedro assured me, would turn my shit back into food with added goodness. Great, delightful. *Go eat shit yourself, Godmind,* I thought.

So much for my bodily comfort. How about my mind?

I had a library of machine-music and another library of thousands of picture-radio stories from the ancient days which I could summon up on a screen. I flipped through a few of these: men in funny hats rode horses and shot each other with pistols; men drove four-wheeled metal machines which crashed and burned; a man in a loin-cloth swung from tree to tree . . . Thus would I while away my idle hours when I wasn't busy treading, rowing, pulling and pushing.

Just *how many* idle hours?

And lo, it transpired that whereas I would be First Lady of the world I arrived on, I wouldn't – couldn't – myself be modified to fit the alien planet. I would have to stay indefinitely inside my pod,which would be deposited on some hilltop with a nice scenic view from the dome if I was lucky. Or if I wasn't, maybe it would be deep in some swamp or jungle.

That was the bad news.

The good news was that when the colony came to life I could set up – still stuck in my pod – as a wise oracle and source of advice. I would be the respository of the heritage of Earth; until such time as the whole colony and every other colony in the galaxy had its mind blown out.

Shit, with knobs on.

So much for the pod. Of rather more urgent concern to me was the matter of how the ship was powered.

Pedro had already satisfied my seemingly innocent curiosity on this point. On our way to the gantry he had indicated a hopper which was excreting orange 'fuel-balls' on to a moving belt. Each fuel-ball was the size of a marble. I had no idea what sort of fuel this was, but it surely had to pack a lot of power. Further along the belt a machine was inspecting the balls and plucking out the occasional one with a suction tentacle, to toss down a chute.

As I say, I was still wearing my gardening pinny with a pair of secateurs in the pouch. This, over my soutane, with its generous sleeves which were practically pockets in their own right. When we were coming out of the pod on to the gantry again, I tugged Tessa's ring off my finger and dropped it into my pinny. Rings can be quite useful sometimes.

As soon as the hoist-platform was descending I jerked my hand up. 'My ring!' I babbled. 'It's gone! I've lost it! I knew something felt queer – it must have slipped off. The Godmind will be so upset! He wants me to present that ring to the champion rose, you know. We'll have to find it, Pedro!'

The platform reached the ground. 'Inside the pod: is that where you dropped it?' he asked.

'I must have. Yet I'm not sure! I think I may have lost it earlier. It might be up there, though! Will you go and look? I'll search around down here. We have to find it, or the rose show will be ruined!'

He nodded. 'I'll go back up and look. You stay here. You can search around a bit, but don't get in the way of any machines – they wouldn't notice you.' (That was nice to know.)

While he was riding up again I made a show of hunting about in the immediate vicinity for my mislaid treasure. As soon as he was out of sight I took the ring from my pinny and hid it under one of several crates which were standing about. Then I sprinted tippy-toe back to the hopper. Snitching several fuel-balls, I hid them in my sleeves. I returned just a few seconds before Pedro emerged, on high. 'Not inside!' he called down.

'Oh dear!' I wrung my hands. (I'd always wanted to wring my hands ever since I read *The Cabin Girl and the Cannibal*.)

Once he'd returned to the ground I made a big and frantic show of casting around – then finding the ring. Actually, this *was* quite a frantic show, since I couldn't find the damn thing when I did descend on the crate in question. At last I spotted it and hooked it out. 'Phew!'

When we got back to Hell station later, I had the bright idea of insisting that Pedro return my pinny with its nice big pouch to its rightful place in the garden. Should any machine count balls and come up short, *that* ought to allay suspicion.

I asked Tessa to go immediately to Jean-Paul to arrange a meeting between him and me. And never mind about his supposed orders to the contrary, as relayed by Kalima! I sent one fuel-ball to Jean-Paul, care of Tessa, and kept the rest up my sleeve.

A couple of hours later the man himself hove in sight.

He jabbed a finger at me. 'Hey, you! Yes, you, what's

160

your name! We have a sneaky swine of a crack that needs widening. You're just the right size to place the charge.'

Grabbing my arm, he hustled me away down the grand staircase then along a spiral path past a procession of rock-porters. We came to a narrow crevice which ran back a dozen spans or so. Jean-Paul stuffed me inside then rammed his body into the gap behind me, plugging it. I managed to squirm round but couldn't see his face too clearly, what with the way he was corking the entrance, blocking most of the light. But I saw his raised fist. He opened his fist; in his palm nestled the fuel-ball.

'How many more have you got?' he murmured.

'Five. Know how they work?'

'No.'

'Prof might be able to tell you.'

'Who?'

'Prof. He arrived on the same shuttle as me. He knows science; he was in the Underground. Didn't Kalima *tell* you?'

'No.'

'Didn't think she would. I told her you ought to have a talk with Prof. And you must!'

'Must I?'

'Yes! The last two seedships will fly soon. No more need for Hell after that, eh?'

'What? The Godmind wouldn't trash us!'

'Want to bet on it? Well, do you?'

'No.'

'Listen, there are one hundred and fifty-three Paxmen on the Moon, and they'll all be at the rose show. All standing tamely underneath a sky that isn't solid rock. Suppose they all happen to meet with an accident, do you think you could run the Moon yourself?'

'Go on.'

'With them out of the way, you can seize the Pax barracks and the Navy yard. You'll have much more space.

You'll have machines and food. I've seen one machine that'll turn any old crap into meals. Build more of those, and you're laughing. You've got yourself a treasure cave next door. You'll survive. And you'll be *free*. You won't have any more people cramming in, either, not unless you ungimmick the water supply and start having kids yourself.'

Jean-Paul licked his lips. I could see his face more clearly now. He was sweating.

'Who knows how to build more food machines?'

'Prof could work it out.' (Could he? Maybe, maybe not.)

'The Godmind wouldn't like it.'

'The Godmind's planning to murder everybody sooner or later. It told me so! If the last two ships can't fly, maybe it'll have to think twice.'

'It'll send more shuttles full of Paxmen to the Moon to quell us.'

'So then you can burn them out of the sky. There are laser-zappers for shooting down stray rocks. Prof can fix them so that they'll shoot shuttles too. He'll have time enough. The Godmind will be in a right old state of shock and sorrow when all its lovely blooms get blown away.' (Would it be? Maybe.)

'Just what are you proposing, Yaleen?'

I told him, and he whistled long and low.

'You do understand what'll happen to you?'

'All too well. I saw Max vacuumed, remember?'

'Okay. Rather you than me.' Jean-Paul pocketed the fuel-ball. In its place he produced a thin stick resembling a pencil. 'You came here to blast rock supposedly, so you'd better blast some. Crawl in as deep as you can, stick this in some crack then snap it where the wire's wrapped round. You'll have three minutes to get clear. If you're stuck I'll haul you out by the heels. Oh . . . but first of all hand over those other fuel-balls.'

'Right,' I surrendered them promptly.

A few minutes later we were both safely outside the

crevice. I'd got out without having to be hauled. The blasting stick went *krump*, and dust gushed out.

'So!'

I was grabbed by the hair. I dropped a plate, which smashed on the rock. My head was twisted round – to face Kalima.

I gritted my teeth. 'Shut up!' I hissed. 'Or you'll spoil things. If you do, Jean-Paul'll expel you.'

'You got me into trouble, over your precious Prof.' Kalima did look a bit bruised. 'Me, his secretary!'

'He'll get over it. Play your cards sensibly and you'll be queen – of a lot more space.'

'Do leave her be,' said Tessa. 'Surely there's no reason to be *jealous* of Yaleen? Bit on the small side, isn't she?'

'You caused me a spot of unpleasantness.' Kalima touched a purple patch on the dark skin of her cheek. But her other hand did relax its grip.

'A beating a day keeps the Paxmen at bay,' said I. 'Jean-Paul will change, afterwards. He'll become gentler.'

'He'd better not!'

'Oh, you like that sort of thing, do you? How screwed up can you get! You ought to be thanking me, then!'

'What I *meant*, Yaleen, is that if all goes well – with the venture – people will wish to relax, and that would be dangerous. Jean-Paul will have to carry on bossing them. But how?'

'He'll need a subtle diplomat at his side. You, Kalima, eh? Better start being subtle. Get some practice in now.'

She looked daggers, only for a moment. She controlled herself. She even managed a smile. 'Yes, you're right. Jean-Paul admires you, Yaleen. I mustn't resent that, must I? Because you're no competition.'

'Exactly what I said,' muttered Tessa.

'Especially not afterwards.'

Tessa raised a quizzical eyebrow. I hadn't told Tessa the plan. Kalima obviously knew it, though.

'Afterwards?' said Tessa. 'After *what*?'

'After Yaleen here – '

'Be quiet,' I snapped. 'Be quiet.'

And Kalima indeed was quiet. She nodded thoughtfully. Before departing she actually stroked my hair, smoothing the yanked strands back into place.

Prof turned up to work nearby with light duties only. Bernardino, also. Jean-Paul was discreetly assembling his team for the aftermath of the Plan. Just as I'd recommended.

Meanwhile I continued to be escorted to Rosaluna by Pedro Dot, to learn how to judge the finest rose show in the universe.

I felt quite jolly about the way things were proceeding, so I fairly threw myself into rose appreciation, much to Pedro's satisfaction.

One day I had another interview with the Godmind, who was suddenly bothered as to whether my famous intuition mightn't prejudice me when it came to deciding upon the champion rose. I mustn't on any account try to foreguess the winner. That would be a lazy short cut. I must put my wild talent on one side – that wouldn't be difficult! – and abide solely by the rules of the game of roses.

I promised faithfully so to abide.

One thing which amused me almightily was that two new varieties of rose recently bred by the Godmind and for which it had high hopes had been given the names of *Bombe Glacée* and *Bombe Surprise*. Both of these were fine white roses, with *Iceberg* somewhere in their parentage. Both boasted high-centred inner cones and the insides of the petals were neatly striped: nearly blue in the case of *Glacée*, crimson in the case of *Surprise*. These two 'bombe' roses were named after ice cream puddings. 'Surprise Bomb': there's my baby! I thought.

Prof dropped by one evening, to confirm in a whisper that he had put together what he insisted on calling an 'infernal device', using the rock-blasting pencils as detonators for the fuel-balls.

That was a relief. I hadn't been entirely sure that he could make a bomb even if he put his mind to it. Unlike Luigi.

'It should work okay,' he said. 'I scraped a tiny flake off one ball and got it to flare wildly. It's just a matter of concentrating and maximizing the bang.' He pulled a flat can of fish – sardines – out of his pocket. 'A present for you. Same size, same weight. Try it out.'

'Shall I toss it high in the air, as if in glee?'

'Better not. The Paxmen might think you were trying to knock out one of their glass eyes. Just get used to it. Imagine chucking it.'

I passed the can from hand to hand a few times, weighing it.

'Even with a kid's strength behind it, it'll hurl high enough here on the Moon,' he murmured. 'It'll go the distance. I'll stick a tuna label round the real thing, so you won't get your cans mixed up.' (A tuna is another kind of Earth fish.) 'Before you throw the real one, you should shake it roughly. The instant it stops going up and starts descending, it'll explode.'

'We hope.'

'We shouldn't have any trouble hot-wiring the tube trains. But we won't be able to recover any, um, bodies. From that garden, I mean.'

'That doesn't bother me. This is only my second-best body.'

'I'll deliver the tuna the day before the show.'

'Oh no you won't. What if they change the day? I want

165

my *bombe* with me up my sleeve the whole time from now on. And will you get me some more sardine cans too? I'll take one to work with me from time to time. I'll produce it out of my sleeve, rip the tab off and eat the fish for lunch. Pedro'll get used to seeing me with a can of fish. Just now and then, though. So he doesn't wonder if I've cornered the market.'

'I'll ask Jean-Paul.'

'No. You'll *tell* him.'

The day of the show was drawing closer when something new cropped up. Another spaceship-load of exiles arrived.

Pedro was late collecting me that morning, so I had time to spot Jean-Paul and his bearded brigade toiling up the grand staircase. Shortly after, Kalima stopped by and murmured, 'Paxman told the boss to get upstairs. There's a new batch due in an hour or three.'

'Don't they know the exact time a ship's due?'

'Paxmen do, but if they told Jean-Paul that would be convenient, wouldn't it?'

'Oh, and he wouldn't be in such a bad mood by the time the new lot arrive.'

'He isn't in a very jovial mood right now.' And she told me how the impending arrival had thrown Jean-Paul's resolve somewhat. True, one last seedship was still scheduled to be built and stocked with snipped, sliced rebel-flesh. But surely there was enough rebel-flesh on the Moon already? Why continue sending people into exile if the idea was to close down Hell in another two or three years? Maybe the status quo was safer, after all? Maybe it would be better to wait.

'I shall work on him,' she promised. 'I'll keep him staunch and courageous, never fear! There's only one golden opportunity: yours.' She reached out and stroked my head. 'Yet who am I to tell *you* not to fear?' She was really behaving far more nicely.

'So long as my little plan works,' I reminded her. 'Don't count too many chickens.'

'If it does work, then you'll go to the bosom of the Godmind, won't you? The Godmind isn't going to be very fond of you. Maybe this Hell will be nothing compared with a Hell in the Godmind's heart.'

'I'll go *where*?'

'If it's true about the bosom of the Godmind . . .'

Of course! She didn't know that I had a lifeline (or rather deathline) stretching way back to the *Ka*-store of the black current . . . Assuming that I *did* still have.

'That's just a rumour, Kalima. I don't believe it. In fact I'm sure it's a lie.'

'Let's hope you're right, for your sake.'

Oh, I was right, and no mistaking. Final proof: if the Godmind could operate a *Ka*-store it wouldn't have needed to reincarnate us all as cherubs, to keep tabs on the fortunes of its colonies. Though admittedly cherubs were a neat way of keeping old Earth from dying of boredom . . .

'I assure you, Kalima, *anything's* better than spending the rest of my days locked up in a pod eating shit!'

'Which reminds me, I'd better rush. I have to tidy *our* pod. Jean-Paul messed it up a bit this morning.'

'Wait: ask him if there's anyone called Luigi among the new arrivals. Luigi, or Patrizia. They understand . . . you-know-what.'

'Will do.'

I watched her go, then for a while I stared across this disgusting slave-pit buried in the Moon. I realized that I was becoming very homesick: for Pecawar and Spangle-stream, for Aladalia and Verrino. Then I saw Pedro striding my way and hurried to meet him.

Neither Luigi nor Patrizia were amongst the new intake. Tessa passed the message on that evening after I got 'home' from a hard day's rose appreciation.

167

Tessa told me that Jean-Paul had spent hours up at the top of Hell with his men before the new people stepped through the door. When he came back down to his cave he looked boiling and furious. But Kalima must have worked on him (or under him) well. The next time Tessa saw Jean-Paul outside the cave, he looked loose and easy. Kalima had stopped by later on, unbruised, to pass the news: no Luigi, no Patrizia.

Why did I want them, anyway? Luigi had only been involved in making fire-bombs, which might just have been wine bottles refilled with oil with a wick stuck in them. Or something of the sort. Besides, both he and Patrizia had acted irresponsibly without regard for the innocent or even for old comrades. We could do without them. Anyway it was too late to involve confused new Moon-virgins in the plan. The Event was nigh. Event with a big 'E': for explosion, which I hoped would also be big.

On the great day of the rose show Pedro Dot collected me as ever, and we rode to Rosaluna. By now I was so accustomed to carrying that phony tuna can up my sleeve that for one ghastly moment on the tube-train I thought the *bombe* wasn't there! A quick squeeze reassured me.

When we arrived at the garden, Pedro stuck close by; much closer than usual. When I tried to hang back at the top of the brick stairway, where I was closest to the sky, he draped a comforting arm around me. This effectively scuppered any chance of tossing the can then and there at the very outset.

He couldn't imagine, could he, that the prospect of being supreme rose judge of the cosmos awed me? Or that I was daunted by the massed phalanx of Paxmen awaiting me below? Oh yes: all one hundred and fifty-two of them (minus Pedro) – or what looked like that many – were drawn up to attention in two long columns lining the avenue between the foot of the stairs and the Godmind's gazebo. The rose show was the event of the lunar year: the big treat, not to be missed. Attendance compulsory. Every twenty spans or so on either side stood a Paxman. Faced with such an assembly, how could I possibly haul out a can of tuna for a supposed quick tuck-in?

'It's *okay*,' I muttered. But Pedro officiously led me all the way down the stairs betwixt white trusses into the dappled sunlight. (It was daytime again on the Moon.) Never mind – maybe the false sky was more vulnerable in the *middle* than round the edges. Maybe it was thinner there.

Each Paxman I passed wore a tiny vermilion rose in the buttonhole of his sky-blue tunic; and I had no difficulty in identifying this as *Starina*, queen of the miniatures. I felt tawdry beside these immaculate troopers. I was wearing the same old soutane as ever; and as we adanced at a slow and stately pace through their ranks I panicked a bit in case I might be asked to slip into something more elegant. Something without big sleeves.

Sensing my flutter, Pedro hugged me even closer.

'It's *okay*!' I shook myself brusquely to disengage him. He finally got the message and I stepped out ahead, leaving Pedro a pace behind. Meanwhile the Paxmen fell in behind, two by two, as escort.

The entire area around the gazebo was crowded with benches loaded with vases, bowls and boxes of cut blooms. I halted, and tried to look snooty.

'Welcome!' the Godmind's voice boomed out. 'Welcome to the annual universal rose show. As judge this year we are privileged to welcome the cherub Yaleen . . .'

The Paxmen crowding the end of the avenue applauded.

'. . . who will open our show officially, then select the category winners, and finally choose the supreme champion rose!'

'So what do I do now?' I muttered to Pedro, who was breathing down my neck.

'You should make a little speech from the gazebo steps. A few words will do. Then declare the show open.'

'Right. I can handle it. You stay here.' He did.

I mounted the steps. I turned and confronted my audience: of Paxman faces and of roses. I was on my own at last.

This, of course, was the right time. There mightn't be another.

I swallowed. I nudged the can in my sleeve.

Why not make a little speech? I wouldn't want the Godmind to think I'd rather blow myself up than say a few words.

'Godmind . . . and Gentlemen,' I called out. 'And when I say "gentlemen", what gentle men you are indeed! Such preservers of peace – and of course *Peace* is a beautiful rose, is it not? And what a mind our Godmind has, to breed such beauty amidst all his other cosmic duties!'

More applause. This was going down quite well.

I held my hand up modestly for silence. 'I have here a golden ring to present to the grand champion rose of my choice: the prime rose of the Earth and the Moon, the best rose in all the galaxy.

'But first, by way of appreciation of the honour done me, here's a little personal trophy of my own.'

I yanked out the can of tuna, shook it violently, flexed my knees, and leapt – sending the can soaring skywards.

'Sucks to you, Godmind!' I shouted.

I had a few seconds left in which to reflect that vandalism was getting to be a way of life. First the Basilica of San Marco; now the premier rose garden in the galaxy.

I didn't look up to follow the progress of the can. Most of my audience did.

Then the bomb exploded.

Oh indeed. Shock and heat beat down, sending me sprawling back inside the pergola, though the roof had sheltered me from the worst of the blast.

Tough as they were, many of the Paxmen sagged. A lot of them were clutching their eyes. Petals rained off roses by the thousand. The show tables were particularly devastated.

I rolled to where I could peek out and up. Globs of cloud-ichor were oozing from a shattered sky.

With a ripping thunderous crack, the upper layer of the sky also parted.

It seemed then, when all the air howled out into the void, that the garden itself screamed. Leaves, flowers, branches from all over, all the cut blooms and even small bushes flew upward.

Along with the air from my lungs. Along with the heat from my body. Along with sound itself. Oh the lancing pain of my eardrums bursting! (But that was the least of it.) Oh the sudden empty silence!

For a while – which seemed too long to me – my body was flopping and clawing for life where there was nothing to sustain life. Like Max, when Jean-Paul had ejected him, I was hollowed out inside; and the hollow collapsed into itself, all my inner surfaces sticking together.

Stars burst behind my eyes. I tasted blood which froze.

Okay, Worm! I screamed within me – no other place left to scream than in my bursting skull. *Do your stuff! I'm counting on you!*

PART FOUR
Narya's Narrative

Thank goodness, I was dead!

Once more I was in the blue void. Once more I was spinning, bodiless. With a difference this time: no storm was disturbing the weather of *Ka*-space.

I quickly became aware of a huge number of cords, of hawsers, converging from all over upon some place nearby. Upon Eeden, centre of the web of the psylink.

Myself, I felt no urge to fly there. Indeed I felt that I couldn't even if I wanted to. I wasn't riding back to Earth from a far world like a bead on a string; on the contrary a thin string stretched away from me to some far elsewhere. And besides, I was twice-dead.

If it weren't for my deathline, where would I go? I searched for clues.

The psylink extended through *Ka*-space; but did *Ka*-space itself have any pattern or texture? Any directions, any destinations?

I concentrated on this. After a while – which might have been a short while, or quite a long while – I began to grasp something of the essence of the blue void which was *Ka*-space.

My first impression was of timelessness. There seemed to be no way to measure any activity. Maybe a moment lasted for an aeon. Or maybe an aeon of events could be packed into a moment.

Yet that wasn't quite it.

Rather, it seemed as though time was bubbling up within this timelessness. The void *simmered*. Pockets of time occurred, expanded, vanished again. Bubbles fluctuated in and out of eternity, as if the void was breathing them in and out. Each of these bubbles could be an age, or no time at all; or both.

I strained to understand this.

Here was nothing; here was no-time. Yet something was occurring. Here in *Ka*-space, as in a river, floated the keel of the universe – of that I felt sure. And what shaped that keel, what caused its existence, what measured its progress was this bubbling up of time, this flow of the current of the void.

But how? Why?

Could the answer be: for no reason at all? Could the answer be: that the universe simply occurred, like a bubble containing whole aeons? Yet eventually it was nothing? Just a bubble?

There was only one of me. If I were many, would I see better? For a moment – or an age – I felt that I was on the brink of . . . some transformation, which would allow me to see.

Then I felt a tug on my line. Faint, feeble, insistent. I started to move through *Ka*-space. And as I moved, I lost touch with my source of inspiration.

I was soon aware of something else: namely that my Worm wasn't a particularly good angler! (How could you expect it of a worm? That's like expecting a sheep to herd dogs.) I speeded up crazily. Soon I was lurching and bumping along, fit to snap the line. This made me slip off my proper course. I started sliding sideways. And here's where things started to go wrong.

Think of a ball on the end of a long string. Imagine this ball being hauled at breakneck speed, quite without finesse, through an obstacle course consisting of, say, a number of logs. They're all just floating nowhere in particular; in a fluid with eddies in it.

The ball bumps and bounces. The string gets bent against one log. When the ball gets there, it doesn't zoom past the log. It wraps around it, clings a while – before unwrapping and flying free. And now though the final goal is still the same the ball is even further off course. Another log gets in the way. The ball wraps and clings; unwraps. And so on.

The ball was me. The string was my link to the *Ka*-space of the Worm. Those logs were: other worlds, full of *Ka*s.

It was only after the second such collision that I worked this out. And you'll have to bear in mind that this is simply a *picture* of what happened. I think I saw it this way because of my nightmare flight through the Californian redwoods. Of which I'd had dreams which were similar in style! Dreams of the trees reduced to stumps, of myself as a ball that the boys intended to kick about.

To begin with I was pretty confused. I thought everything had messed up.

Suddenly I was in a body.

When I say I was *in* a body, I don't mean this was like being reborn into a new body in Eeden. I'd *been* the body, then; the body had been me. Now was different. I was only along for the ride.

And that ride was through the air.

It was through gusting air high over blue and bile-green swamp bristly with tufted weeds and wafting sedges. Denser brakes of tangled pod-vines sprawled across sand-bars and isles of silt. My eyes were intent for signs of movement. Whenever these eyes of mine fastened upon something interesting, the whole central portion of my vision magnified it.

Down below, a dank pool suddenly erupted with a squirming mêlée of furry bodies, red eyes, teeth and claws. Strings of blood coiled in the water like purple toadspawn or thin sausages, so quickly did it coagulate. It was as if I were holding a lens over the landscape.

This wasn't what I wanted. I glanced briefly behind me

– and in that glance I discovered great broad-feathered wings, which were silver-blue, barred with ochre and gold. Skimpy arms were tucked up tight under these. A bony claw of a hand clutched the corpse of some finned snake-creature. I also caught a glimpse – a foggy one since I wasn't focusing there – of distant castellated cliffs soaring upward in tiers and towers. The sky above was streaked with high hairy dazzling clouds. My eyes wouldn't look at the sun.

And I knew where I was.

Why, it's Marl's World! I exclaimed to me.

In surprise my hand dropped the snake. Immediately my body veered, plummeted – and I had caught my prey again.

What are you? What are you doing in me?

Oops, pardon the intrusion. I'm just a Ka on my way to another star. I'm trying to get back home.

A Ka? The dead do not return.

No, but I tend to. Listen: I was good friends with one of you birdmen, back in Eeden. Name of Marl. He can't have died more than three or four years ago. If he and I got on, so can you and I.

Marl?

I rose a few octaves in pitch in my thoughts, to repeat the name.

My bird-host caught on. *Ah, Maaayyrrl! No, I never knew such a person. If you've really been to Eeden, stray spirit, sing me a song of Eeden! Sing it in my bones.*

A song? Well, I'll give it a go . . .

I was just about to – after which we might have got down to business, such as how to live together – when I was rudely torn away. Back to the blue void.

In the next world I collided with I was back on my own two feet again. Or rather I was on someone else's feet. Those feet were toiling up a steep stony track between tumbles of boulders and wiry bushes tipped with saffron fluff. It was hot. Mostly I stared down my bare, duskily-tanned legs at my ropy sandals. I seemed to be a woman. Black beetles with horns scuttled over the pebbles of the path; I trod indifferently on a few.

When exhaustion overcame me and I started staggering, I offloaded the burden I'd been toiling under. This was a huge block of yellow wood, slung in a cradle of rope. I subsided beside it, to rest.

Dully my eyes noted the distance I'd come – up amidst savage slopes of scree and scrub. Finding some sprigs of bitter herb in a pocket, I chewed, and stared at my toes. The nails were coarse and horny. Maybe they were meant to be. My hand strayed aside to the wood, which resembled a churnful of very stiff butter, and stroked it idly.

Excuse me, I thought, *but what's the wood for?*

My body jerked to a crouch. In my hand a bone-handled knife with short bronze blade had suddenly appeared. I stared about wildly, spying only harsh slopes, angles of stone, mauve sky. Drooling herb-spittle, my mouth cried out, 'Who speaks? Does the dead tree speak? Is that what a lurker wants me to think? To confuse me and steal?'

She surely believed in voicing her thoughts aloud! (Yes, I was sure I was a woman.)

'Aiieee!' cried my host. 'Aiieee! Aiieee!' I cocked my head to listen to the echoes. 'Aiieee!'

Was this to summon help from further up the track? Or to deafen the 'lurker' which didn't like loud noises? (But which could throw its voice in whispers?) It had been so very silent before. When the echoes faded it was still totally silent.

Please calm down, I thought. *I'm inside your head, sharing it. If you'll just listen, I'll explain –*

'The dead tree has entered me!' she howled. 'Through my backbone it has bored a hole!'

No it hasn't. Don't be hysterical.

179

'I only port heartwood to the Sculptor! The tree is bled dead! No offence!' (No offence to whom? To the tree? To the Sculptor? To the lurker amongst the rocks?)

No need to get upset! I don't think I'm going to stay here too long.

Never a truer word. Before I could work out what was going on, I was wrenched on my way.

Only to collide, next off, with a farming wench. She was wading knee-deep in a paddy field, with her skirts hitched bunchily up around her waist. Several large snails with opal shells were crawling on her thighs. In the distance a tall lizard-thing stood bolt upright. Her pet? Her guard? The creature looked totally dull and in a stupor. Two suns shone in the sky, one of them tiny but blinding bright.

Presently the wench that was me paused in my work. I plucked one of the snails from my wet flesh, cracked its shell and munched the contents . . .

Next I was gutting long black fish on a white marble worktop. I was an old crone blind in one eye. The fish-shed was lit by flaring torchlight. I spilled the guts into drums. I slid the flesh along to another crone, for her to chop into slices with a hatchet. I chanted over and over to myself an idiot ditty:

> 'Eelfish,
> 'Peel fish,
> 'Make a wish!'

These brief encounters were quite confusing. Not to mention the vertigo of plunging in and out of them. Even so I was almost beginning to relish these dips into other lives. Quite like being in the *Ka*-space of the Worm, it was! I might already be at journey's end, bouncing from one dead life to another . . . except that back home we had never lived such lives as these.

I was starting to feel like a child swapping seats on a wheeling carousel. Maybe I would carry on around the whole sphere of star colonies in similar style, bopping back into the void between whiles!

But then, en route from my eel-wife, the void bubbled up more bubbly than ever.

Ever?

Ever-never? ¿ɹǝʌǝ-ɹǝʌǝN I moved sharply otherwise, otherways. How can I put it? No words come close!

What happened now was to a moon as is the colour of blood in a pitch-dark room by night. It was to a fish as is the smell of a rose-bush in space. To a diamond as is the timelost instant of orgasm.

You see? No you don't.

All those things I've just mentioned connect, if you try hard enough. A diamond is an eternal kernel of light, outside of time. So also is ecstasy, the bright inner light. They can be related and make sense. Poetic sense. Ultimately in a poem almost anything can be related to anything else.

But if this happened ordinarily we would be drowning in a sea of chaos.

What was happening to me was a *relating* – a relating and a re-ordering along an unfamiliar axis: the name of which, for me, was 'never-ever'.

It was *ever*, and always. Yet also it was *never* because no happenings are unalterable. Nothing that happens in the universe is locked like an insect in amber. All is a shifting fluid – and this is as true of the past as of the future! What-had-been and what-might-be were both 'never-ever'. I felt very strongly that this was so.

Here was an answer to that old riddle which occurs in the *Alice* fragments supposedly written ages ago by the Artful Dodger's Son. I'd seen this discussed at length by savants in an Ajelobo newspaper.

The riddle: 'Why is a raven like a writing desk?'

(For those who don't read Ajelobo newspapers, a raven is an ancient flying creature with feathers, a sort of black chicken that likes to steal bright objects such as rings.)

I knew the answer now. And the right answer was: 'Why *shouldn't* it be?'

Please bear with me. Words divide things from other things. They box things into categories and classes. And so words make the world. They build reality. But words are also gluey, melty things. They leak. (If you say the word a hundred times over, it leaks all over the place.) So eventually any word can stick to any other word; and I guess poetry is all about the glueyness of words rather than their usual role as solid boxes.

In exceptional circumstances, reality can be leaky too. It can get glued together in a different way.

Or maybe I should say that there isn't just one single reality. There are many possible realities, out of which only one exists. Whilst it does so, it excludes the others.

Okay. Call one reality 'the raven'. Call the other 'the writing desk'. They're as far apart as any two things can be. Thus good old familiar reality exists. A raven is. A writing desk also is. Has been, and will be.

But glue *can* join them together. And when this happens in *Ka*-space, where the keel of the universe sails, things can change.

I was sure now that the void 'imagines' the shape of the universe which is sailing upon it. Yet the void is unaware of what it dreams. Awareness only exists inside the universe dreamt by the void.

Admittedly people possess imagination too, in a weaker form. But people keep ravens well clear of writing desks, because words say that ravens and writing desks are far apart. Only poets, madmen and riddlers ever say otherwise, and they're in a minority of one, besides being stuck in a universe where one individual can't alter things.

I sensed two forces at work upon the universe. There

was a dividing force, which was strong, which kept all classes and categories of things neatly organized. There was also a glueing force, which was weak and which could alter the way things were arranged in their various boxes. In the never-ever of *Ka*-space, where an aeon could be a moment, the weak force could beat the strong.

You might suppose that my own 'reality' was weird enough to start with! Here was I, zipping through *Ka*-space and bouncing off alien lives on other worlds. That was *nothing* compared with when the void bubbled; when I dived into ever-neverland, when I lost all familiar connexions.

One connexion which I lost right away was my deathline. The fibres parted; it snapped. Perhaps it was the snapping of my deathline which caused the bubbling of the never-ever? So thoroughly did the order of events collapse that I couldn't say for sure. Now and then, before and after: all melted.

And in this moment it seemed to me as if the void was bubbling out of itself a private time and private place for me alone, a tiny universe of mine own which would shrink back again into the void, with me contained inside it.

I wasn't having that.

That's when I cried out to my mother-world. I cried out to my home; to Pecawar; to the house where I was born and raised and murdered. And to my mother too. Oh yes, even though a mother can do nothing you still cry out to her!

That was when the never-ever twisted.

That was when the raven became the writing desk. When I cried.

Cried and cried.

I stopped crying.

I was feeble. I was tiny.

I knew what I was, and no mistake. It wasn't all that

long since I'd been a baby back in Eeden. This was altogether a wetter, stickier, messier experience. My hips hurt like a wash-leather wrung out by strong hands. My face felt squashed out of shape, clogged-up and mucky. Someone else's upside-down face swam before my eyes. Presently this other face flipped upright and stabilized. Hands held me firmly but gently. Arms cradled my body. My eyes were dabbed clean, my nostrils too.

And because I'd been in this selfsame predicament within recent memory I had the wit to shut up and not scream out in my baby voice . . .

. . . the name of Chataly, my mother's cousin who choked on some food in her sleep and died, yet who was now tending at my delivery into the world . . .

. . . from out of a woman who lay on a bed, sweaty, hair-slicked and weary, her legs still wide apart, leaking some blood and the long white cord which was my birth-string.

I didn't recognize my mother immediately; not looking like that.

When I did, I didn't want to. This may seem ungrateful in the circumstances, since she had just given birth to me, but the mother I knew wasn't this drenched exhausted naked suffering animal lying on the bed. Mother was cooler and neater.

Chataly set me down for a while, to cope with the cord sprouting from the midst of me.

That was what the string connecting me to the *Ka*-space of the Worm had become, when connexions changed! And the blue void had changed into the waters of the womb! Way back home, where I'd cried to be.

But I wasn't a baby *Yaleen*. I wasn't back at the time of my own original birth two decades earlier. I didn't make the mistake of supposing that! Mother was so bedraggled by the effort of giving birth that I couldn't have said what age she was. But I remembered full well what Chataly had looked like in her later years; and these definitely were Chataly's later years.

Taking me up, she laid me under my mother's breast. Mother's hands held me. Her heart thumped under me. She crooned. My lips tasted sweet milk bubbling. I squirmed my floppy head aside but then thought twice about refusal and suckled a bit. Obviously I would have to feed.

Chataly must have been tidying the afterbirth away into a pan, meanwhile; rearranging sheets and so forth. Next I heard her call to my father. A door opened. I heard Dad's voice, close by:

'She's lovely! Oh isn't she wonderful! Our own little Narya – oh doesn't she suit the name!' (*Do I, Dad?*)

I kept quiet while he fussed in my vicinity. Truth to tell, quite soon I fell asleep. That little body of mine was tired.

As you can perhaps appreciate, this was a difficult period in my lives!

Unlike in Eeden, here at home I wouldn't be growing up at high speed. I would be advancing at the same slow pace as any other baby born of woman. I would be suckling and pissing myself for ages. I'd be unable to walk, unable to do most anything till my body decided it was the right time to perform. I'd be a floppy doll. The prospect frustrated the hell out of me.

I think I could have managed to talk within a few days. It was entirely up to me what sort of noises I set my vocal cords to work on. But I didn't dare talk. I didn't dare be anything other than a baby. (Crying was a total waste of time; why bother?) I had to think, think, *think*. Ahead. Behind me, and all around.

I'd done what the Godmind couldn't do. Or couldn't yet do. I'd gone back in time. Right now, at this very moment, Yaleen – that's to say, *me* – was somewhere off along the river, up to her adventures. Those adventures were only about to happen, or in process of happening. And they must. Happen.

I'd lost any link with the Worm, of course. How could I be its bosom-buddy when I hadn't yet died into the *Ka*-space? Let alone boarded the Worm at Tambimatu, with diamond ring held high? Let alone dived headlong into the black current for the first time?

But *why* 'must' my adventures happen as before?

What if I spoke to Mum and Dad instead (shocking them silly)? What if they spoke to the Guild? What if the Guild knew in advance that there would be a war, and chaos, if Yaleen crossed the river? The Guild would surely believe me once one or two things started coming true.

Lying first in my crib, and latterly in a cot, I played endless variations upon the theme of 'What If?' Yet all variations seemed to come up with the same answer.

If I spilled the beans, then I wouldn't be murdered by Doctor Edrick. I wouldn't zoom off through *Ka*-space. I wouldn't return home again, reborn as the new baby me. In other words I wouldn't, couldn't, be here.

I remembered what Prof had said in Venezia (far away, but *not yet*) about how something might vanish from the present if the past was altered. I called to mind what I'd sensed in *Ka*-space about reality. And I nursed a dire suspicion that if I was indiscreet, then something might indeed vanish from the present. Namely *me* – plus chunks of history which were yet to happen. Yaleen's life would surely change as a consequence, and couldn't lead to me now.

Meanwhile oceans of time slopped slowly by: oceans which had flowed by once already.

I tried counting the nights (they're more distinctive than days) but I soon lost count.

And I still couldn't come to any conclusion other than: *keep silent*! Keep mum. Whilst Mum kept me.

One day she lifted me on to a rug to practise rolling and

crawling and holding my head up. Other highlights: I started to eat mash and hash and broth and custards. Presently I was given rusks to suck and grind my gums on.

Oh but wasn't I just a cute child! Hardly any bother at all. And oh shit, wasn't I bored! But I sure as hell wasn't going to liven things up prematurely.

After goodness knows how long, the stairs got carpeted in my honour.

One night I seemed fretful. I was, too. So Mum carried me out into the garden to see the stars. 'Look, Narya: little lights all over! They're called *stars*. Can you say stars? Stars, darling, stars.' She was worried because I wasn't yet babbling or lisping. I stayed mute. I knew what my first word had to be.

Swaddled in her arms I gazed straight up, wondering which of those little lights I had visited personally. Which was the sun of the world where the birdpeople flew? Which, the suns that shone on the wench with snails on her legs? Oh the ludicrous indignity of it, when I'd been to those goddamn stars myself! I definitely deserved a star – a gold one – for patience.

Fearing a chill, Mum took me back inside and tucked me in, to dream sweet dreams.

Hi there, Yaleen: where have you got to by now? My older, younger sister; my self. As far as Edrick's house at Manhome South, is it? Or as far as the conclave at Spanglestream?

Edrick! Well, at least I wouldn't have to bother with that sod ever again; he was dead.

Oh *no* he wasn't. Must keep events in their proper order, mustn't I? Edrick would have to pop up in my life once again like a bad fin-coin.

I was losing touch with the order of events. I had to go back over everything; just as if I were rewriting *The*

187

Book of the River entire, from memory, having lost the manuscript. Which I had. Since it hadn't been written yet.

I was finding it increasingly hard to figure on Yaleen as a real person, or as the same person as myself. When she finally arrived, wouldn't she seem like some sort of living *fiction*? There she would be, saying her piece and doing her thing just as if she were the author of those words and deeds (which she was), yet with a few choice words of my own I could edit her life savagely and alter the whole story line!

If I did that, perhaps I would simply vanish out of her life, and her story. Then she would indeed be the free author of her destiny, and I would be . . . a blank. A page unwritten. Try as I might, I couldn't imagine what it would be like to vanish. But I surely wasn't going to take any chances on it!

About this time I realized that it wasn't sufficient for Yaleen just to turn up and get herself killed a bit later on. Before I could speak out, *The Book of the River* would have to be published, otherwise my words mightn't have the same impact. They wouldn't carry as much weight; so I told myself. (Weight to do what? Aha! If only I'd known the answer to that.)

Besides, what with Yaleen seeming so unreal, I felt that I needed the tangible reality of the book before I could become Yaleen again. It was as though her life was stored in there and could only become available to me when the book was issued. Ordinary memories grow fuzzy and mixed-up. Ordinary memories aren't the same as the experience of reliving a life in the *Ka*-space. Yaleen was a part of me which had fallen into the pool of time-past. She could only be hauled to the surface and regained, in the shape of her book.

Her reality had become the pages she would write. Meanwhile my own reality had shrunk to even less than book-size – down to matchbox-size. And all this while the whole cosmos was crashing silently and ever so slowly about me. Oh how the aeons flowed downstream, with me no more than a dayfly on a ripple.

Frankly, I'd say I deserve a bit of credit for not going crazy during this long waiting period. I merely seemed quite odd to my parents; rather out of step. (I'd started to take a few lurching steps.)

One day it rained. It poured, it bucketed. This was most unlike the usual Pecawar weather.

So I said, 'Wain.'

My parents were delighted. They were over the moon. (Ah, but we had no moon here, did we?)

So I obliged them with a few more ill-uttered words. But then I shut up again. I had to, hadn't I? Otherwise I might have spoiled everything. Still, Mum and Dad seemed satisfied with small mercies. For the time being they appeared relieved.

Whom did I pity more: them, or me? Them, I suppose. Myself, I was almost beyond self-pity. At times this whole charade even struck me as weirdly amusing. Yet how cruel of me – how cruel to Mum and Dad – to feel amused by it. What's more, if I let myself become too amused I might go mad, I feared.

So I soldiered on (as people would say, once the not-yet war was over). I spent my days wrapped in memories. I devoted less time to trying to chart unchartable options and alternatives, which in any case I didn't dare opt for.

'Wain.' Big deal.

Oh, but I'll make up for my silence by and by, Mum and Dad, I promise. Yet will that make you any happier?

Problem: I knew how Yaleen had reacted to Narya. I remembered, albeit fuzzily. But how had Narya reacted to Yaleen?

And what had happened in the house after Edrick

murdered Yaleen? I had no idea. If only I knew! If only Edrick had dropped some hint when we were in Eeden.

But no, no, no! Here yawned a trap into which I mustn't fall – and now I realized that I'd been sliding into this trap for months. The name of the trap was foreknowledge – the paralyser of initiative. It was *me* who was in peril of becoming a puppet, by following the story line exactly. Not Yaleen, but me! No wonder my parents often looked concerned, as though their Narya were missing some spark or other essential element of life: wilfulness, originality, whatever.

I made an effort to be more spontaneous and affectionate. I laughed and clowned a bit. Dad took me out for rides around town on his shoulders: I chirped appreciatively. I was sleeping in Capsi's old room by now. Dad added giant baby animals to Capsi's panorama of the west bank and coloured them in. I cooed and chortled.

Time sludged by.

We celebrated my second New Year's Eve with caraway cake and candles and gifts. Amongst other presents received by me – with wordless cries of delight – was a toy pussy-cat, which I could pull after me on a string. The cat wore a collar of tinkly silver bells.

Shortly after that party, Mum and Dad were discussing in hushed tones the amazing withdrawal upriver of the black current. Soon invasion was on their lips – and war . . .

Mum's other cousin Halba came to town on business at this time, when Pecawar was a-buzz with fearful rumours. She owned a spice farm up-country, and had never been especially close to Mum; though Halba did pay us a number of visits over the years, and when I was twelve years old Capsi and I spent several weeks' holiday with her – a vacation which I wasn't likely to forget in a hurry, since

190

Halba had fed us growing kids quite meanly and had made us toil for our keep.

Take the spice mace. Nutmeg balls, so sweetly smelling, come from little trees with yellowy blossoms. The blossoms are followed by a fruity 'droop' the length of your little finger – inside which is a stone, the kernel of which is nutmeg. But an outgrowth from the base covers the nut with a crimson network called the 'aril' – like a sort of thread fungus – which has to be picked off by hand, oh so carefully and painstakingly. And that's mace. Little fingers can get quite weary and knotted, unpicking the aril for a good few hours.

Take cloves. Cloves are simply the dried, unopened flower buds of a tree related to the nutmeg. Halba had a little plantation of these, and every bloody one of the blood-red buds had to be picked by hand, up ladders, double quick, before they could open.

Luckily, while Capsi and I were visiting, the vanilla orchids were still in bloom and hadn't yet set pods, or we might have been in for the treat of burying them in hot ashes and subsequently digging the shrivelled brown fingers up to rub them individually with olive oil. The corner of Halba's farm, where the vanilla orchids grew, did intrigue me, though. Hot water bubbled up from underground into rocky pools, so that the climate in that one particular spot was uniquely moist and steamy, unlike anywhere else for leagues and leagues. It was ideal for vanilla; Halba was the only local supplier of this spice.

Oh, and I'm forgetting the gentle art of peeling cinnamon, supposing that we had any spare time from unthreading aril and plucking clove buds. Capsi and I really needed those hot orchid-ringed pools to soak our feet in after a few happy hours spent rubbing the bark from the young cinnamon shoots with the soles of our feet, Halba's preferred method of unpeeling.

Halba was a stout, bustling woman who seemed jolly

and was actually downright mean; and on those occasions when she visited us she brought nothing by way of a visiting gift yet always heartily ate her fill and generally contrived to carry something off with her – an ornament, a bag of fruit, some dried fish, a book, anything which she fixed upon and decided was surplus to our requirements. The time when she bore Capsi and me off was, of course, designed to save wages at harvest time. And did she resent the waste of a day to bring us home again to Pecawar afterwards, with a bag of her best dried brittle quills of cinnamon which we had 'earned'! (We had, needless to say, eaten her out of house and home; as I recall my mother felt obliged to press some expensive candied blue-pears on Halba, which she accepted as her right.)

Anyway, Halba turned up in the midst of all the pother about the war – mainly to pump Dad about the likely long-term effect on prices and exports, a topic which he had no wish to discuss. (More about this anon.) After feeding herself generously at our house, and having commandeered a bed for the night, she then took herself off for the evening to visit 'her friends' (which presumably we weren't).

Mum immediately buttonholed Dad.

'How lucky that Halba's come!'

'Is it?'

'Yes, don't you see? You and me and Narya should be ready to quit Pecawar at a moment's notice – in case those savages invade here next. This new local militia of ours mightn't be able to cope. We could go and stay with Halba, where we'd be safe. *Nothing* must harm Narya! That would kill me.'

Dad sighed. I could see him weighing which argument was best, to pit against this folly. If he pointed out the truth about our 'friendship' with Halba – and how little she would want us roosting on her in the country – this might make my mother stubborn. It might stir her to prove that nobody could *not* want Narya and her. Likely she would accuse Dad of a failure of love; of not wanting to bother disrupting domestic routine even to save his family from peril.

Dad hummed and hawed for a while – till Mum grew quite peeved – before he found the right tack.

'Look, if there's an invasion, the riskiest thing would be to take to the roads. Supposing there's trouble – I don't say there will be, but supposing – if we stay indoors here at home, villains would have to make a deliberate decision to break in and harm us. But if they caught us out in the open, harming us would be the most casual thing. In fact, if you're an invader that sort of behaviour makes sense. It spreads fear and disorder. Don't you see? We'd be mad to flee up-country.'

'Maybe we should go right now, before those brutes have a chance to invade. Narya and I could leave with Halba tomorrow. You could sort out some leave and follow on.'

'I really don't advise isolating ourselves out there. Look at it statistically. In a place as big as Pecawar there's no reason why we especially should be harmed. But on a lonely farm, with fewer people thereabouts, it's more dangerous. Not less! Don't you see? If the enemy turns up there, you'll be in real peril . . .'

The argument rambled on for a while, without any direct references to Halba herself, and in the end Dad won. No request for sanctuary was put to the woman.

Yaleen was also mentioned that evening; speculatively, not too fretfully. Never once did I hear my parents refer to Capsi. Maybe they spoke of him in private.

No invasion came, of course. But came the day when Dad bore me out, shoulder-high, to see the rump of the junglejack army trudge into town.

Hitherto Mum had refused to let him take me to watch boats unload weapons or to view the advance guard of the army – the river-virgins, the first arrivals – performing their drill. She thought that the sight might scare me and upset my peace of mind. I, who was responsible for half of this! When it came to greeting the 'jacks who had tramped such a long way to our aid, Dad put his foot down. Both feet, in fact: one in front of the other, and me on his shoulders.

We took up station on Molakker Road – our southern approach – amidst quite a crowd, and Dad gave me a bright red kerchief to wave. Presently the troops tramped into view and did their best to put on a show for us. Oh, the glamorous, smelly, travel-stained warriors twirling their swords and axes, pikes and spears.

'Soldiers,' said Dad. 'Those are soldiers.'

'So-jers,' I repeated. I cried the word over and over as we watched the rather weary parade. How delighted he was with me.

Alas, there was an accident. As the rearguard made their way by, a 'jack with the build of a bull whose black hair was curled into horns by sweat tossed an axe right up in the air, to catch it by the handle. At that moment an older man in front, who must have been exhausted, stumbled. In an effort to recover step and poise, he pranced backwards. The two men collided. The toppling axe caught the older man on the side of the head. He screamed, fell, writhed in the dust clutching at his injury. Blood pumped from the ruin of his ear, bright as the kerchief I was waving.

Dad hastily reached up and clapped a hand over my face. With a groan, he whirled me away. When he set me down and let me see again, we were behind the high brick wall of a builder's yard hidden from the commotion in the road.

'See so-jers,' I said cheerfully, and flapped my red flag.

'Yes, soldiers. But we'll have to get on home now. Your mother will be wondering where we are. It was good seeing the soldiers, wasn't it?'

'Mmm. Mmm!'

There were other outings in addition, though never by way of the quayside itself. On this score Dad heeded Mum's wishes. Maybe he didn't want another daughter of his to be prematurely intoxicated by river life. Or maybe he was worried in case I might lisp some indiscretion when we got back home. Not that I had betrayed him regarding the soldier's mutilation; but he may have believed he had acted so promptly that slow, strange Narya noticed nothing horrid.

These were outings to Dad's place of work; and if I've never before mentioned the fact that Dad worked, or at what, there's a good reason – though I've only become aware of it now!

The truth is that during all the years while Capsi and I were growing up at home, we knew in the abstract that our Dad worked as a spice clerk, yet never once did we get close to his actual work; neither physically close nor mentally close.

Dad's job certainly left its aroma on his clothes and on his skin. However, this was no more and no less than the aroma of Pecawar town itself, fainter or stronger depending on wind direction, but always pervasive. Thus Dad seemed like a distillate of Pecawar, the centre of things, the origin. The spice warehouses, the drying and crushing and blending sheds and whatnot, were relegated to the edge of our mental horizon, as an effect rather than a cause.

Dad always held his work at arm's length, well away from our home life. Presumably he and Mum discussed work and money matters together; but we kids heard nothing of it. Nor did Dad hobnob in his spare time with any colleagues from work; we kids saw nothing of them or of their kids. We didn't mix. As a result there was simply no sense of connexion between our home and the place to which Dad went during the day. The work side of Dad's life was a blank. It was something carefully screened away.

Yet the screen hid no vital secret or romantic mystery. It just concealed something boring, something which didn't involve us.

Nor was the episode of our hardship holiday at Halba's farm an exception to this general rule. Dad neither escorted us to the farm nor brought us back. He worked in town, at the merchanting end of the spice business, and though he must have known all about arils and droops, when Capsi and I had recounted our harvesting experiences Dad had merely raised an eyebrow and soon changed the subject. I only remember him tousling our heads and saying, 'Well, you're home again; that's the main thing.'

Looking back, I believe this is one of the main reasons why I was so keen to sign on a river boat as soon as possible. And I guess this is what made Capsi scan the further shore in an effort to fill in its much more interesting blanks. Dad's workaday life didn't exist for us. By extension the workaday world of Pecawar wasn't for us either (a prejudice amply confirmed by our visit to Halba). It had no meaning.

Do you know, I'm not even sure whether Mum, in her youth, had brought Dad home from Sarjoy itself or from somewhere smaller on the way to Aladalia! No doubt we kids enquired, at the age when kids ask such things. No doubt Dad told us. Yet the notion of him being from somewhere else made very little impression. He went nowhere, to work. He must have come from nowhere too. Capsi and I had no desire to devalue those other magical exotic towns by overly identifying Dad with one of them.

As Capsi grew up, he of course came to understand that he could only ever visit foreign towns once in his lifetime – in the same manner that Dad had once voyaged to Pecawar as a young man to wed Mum. To do what thereafter? To tot up accounts or inventories or whatever. This realization turned Capsi against all of our shore, in favour of the other.

But then – so much for youthful rebellion! – what did Capsi do but run away to the Observers? To those who spent all their time totting up the account and compiling the inventory of the blank west bank, filling in the ledger of our ignorance. Capsi may have been rebellious, yet in a fateful way he was still the son of his father! Had it not been for me he might have spent the rest of his days up that Spire in Verrino, as a clerk of a different stripe.

I didn't consider that I was the daughter of either Mum or Dad in quite the same repetitive fashion. Except that by now I was their daughter *twice over*. Which was certainly a repetition!

In a surprise reversal of times past, Dad now took me several times to his place of employ. This, during a war! Yet here perhaps lay the key to this change of heart – rather than in any suspicion of his that he had lost his other children through a lack of workaday connexions. I'm sure Dad wanted to prove that he too was doing something significant, and that soldiers weren't the only ones who served. He wanted to show me this (as though I would understand, or even remember, at such a tender age!), and by so doing persuade himself that he was proud of what he did, and hadn't wasted his life.

Mum demurred at these trips to work, but Dad insisted. Now was a time when men were putting their feet down. Tramp, tramp. Quick march. About turn!

Since Dad was senior in his job these days, there was no bother about my turning up at work. He always chose routes to and fro which kept us away from the waterfront, but once at the counting house I had the run of the place and of the adjacent warehouses and processing sheds, some of which were seductively close to the river.

Generally the janitor, old one-eyed Ballow, kept his eye on me. Well, he wasn't really one-eyed; a milky cataract eclipsed his left pupil, and he wore a grey patch to cover it. Early on in our acquaintance he revealed his disfiguration, to warn me about the pair of ginger cats which slunk around the buildings (keeping these clear of shrew-bugs and of any intruding Golden Spritsail flutterbyes which would lay their eggs on spice sacks). Years ago Ballow found a hurt cat. Foolishly he picked it up, increasing its pain so that the animal struck out, puncturing his eyeball, letting in a disease. So he said.

'I often dream,' he told me confidentially, 'that I'm a cat – with the eyes of a cat. It's as though they owe me an eye, and repay me. When I'm awake, like now, I see everything flat. When I'm asleep, I see things deep as can be, the way they used to look. That's why I'm kind to the cats here, since it wasn't that sick one's fault. But don't you ever put your lovely little peepers anywhere near a pussy's claws, or your Dad would never forgive me.'

He pointed at one of our hunters, which had actually spotted a shrew-bug clinging on to a coriander sack – a fairly rare encounter. Ginger was arse-squirming towards its prey, taking his time, teasing the tip of his tail to twitches of delicious frustration. Eventually he launched, patted the shrew-bug to the floor, played with it till it was broken, then ate it.

'There's an old tale, you know,' observed Ballow, 'concerning three friends who only had one eye between them to see with. And one tooth between them to eat with. And one long fingernail to scratch with, and stir the porridge and pick your nose. When it came time to swap the eye and the tooth and the fingernail around, you might suppose as you couldn't trust the friend with the eye since he could see where the tooth and the nail were, so he might grab them and run off. But no. All three friends could see through that one eye at the same time, no matter whose head it was in, no matter if the three were leagues apart. Not that they ever were leagues apart, since without a tooth you can't eat, and without a nail you can't scratch; and they were always awful itchy, these friends, and they often had colds as blocked their noses up. But finally one day the friend who had the eye at the time – let's call him Inkum – he did seize the tooth and the nail by guile. He stuck the tooth in his gob, and the nail on his finger's end, and he took off at a run. His friends – whom we'll call Binkum and Bod – could see where he was running to, from his point of view, so they raced after him to keep up.'

Ballow sat himself down on the coriander sack. He slapped his hands on his knees and squinted at me. 'So what do you suppose happened next?' And he waited.

Now, I wasn't in the habit of answering anyone; and Ballow was really being quite a disgusting old buffer at the moment, though maybe he thought he was entertaining me or even educating me. But he just carried on sitting there on the sack, and every now and then he asked me again, 'So what happened?'

I could of course have walked away, and maybe I should have done, but I was thinking that Yaleen was my absent eye and I wouldn't be able to see or do anything effective till she turned up and surrendered her viewpoint to me.

I had an inspiration, and stuck my tongue out at Ballow.

He chortled and slapped his knees again.

'So you'd trade a tongue for an eye, would you, little girl? You'd trade a tongue for an eye! But it's you as needs a tongue, eh? Tell you what: if you'll give Ballow one of your eyes, Ballow'll give you his tongue to talk with. How's that?'

I revised my opinion sharply. Ballow wasn't daft or disgusting at all. What a perceptive old codger he was, to be sure. I wondered whether my Dad had put him up to this, having known Ballow for years; whether this was the real why and wherefore of my outing. But no, no, I doubted that. Dad, who had clapped a hand over precious Narya's eyes so that she wouldn't behold a wounded ear, would have clapped his hands over her ears if he had heard half of Ballow's banter.

I had to play this just right.

I flexed my fingers like claws. Said, 'Miaow!' – and hissed.

'Okay, okay', said Ballow. 'So you're hurting inside, like that pussy I mentioned. No need to scratch my other peeper out. What I see in you – with one peeper, which is better than most folks with two – I won't say to a soul. There, that's a bargain, eh? We're friends now.'

He stuck his hand out. It was big and tough as a cow's hoof and dirty. I wrinkled up my nose, but laid my little hand in his.

And we were friends from then on. Firm friends. One of us half-blind, the other one mostly dumb.

'I'll show you a game you can play with peppercorns,' he said. 'You have to build a pyramid . . .'

These excursions turned out to be the pleasantest hours of my phony infancy. What with the war and so many boats being used as a navy, the export trade was at a virtual standstill; though the clerks still had work enough on hand, analysing and accounting. Nevertheless, Dad always spared some time to walk me round the warehouses and processing sheds. I showed my appreciation by smiling and crowing, and touching and sniffing: the spices, and Dad. Connecting, connecting the two.

He too made a connexion one day – between time past and time present. I was in his little office, boxed off by a bamboo trellis from the rest of the spice-musty counting house. I was hanging on to the edge of his desk which was piled with open ledgers, crammed with figures in his neat hand, some fresh, some old and faded.

'Now supposing we'd fled to Halba's for refuge,' he remarked, more to his ledgers than to me, 'we'd have had to rely on her for charity, and repay her with labour, hoeing and pruning and hauling, wouldn't we? As our Yaleen had to, once, at harvest time. Instead of relying on ourselves alone. But maybe if you rely on yourself entirely,

200

that's what you become: alone. Then one day you break your leg, and who's there to help? Who's there?'

I drummed my fingertips on the desk top, as much as to say, 'I'm here.'

Dad laughed, and drummed his fingers too.

'Ah, what would we do without you, Narya? And what would we do without those brave 'jacks?'

Even after the war was won Dad continued, jauntily, with these treats. Yes, jauntily. For men of the east had marched far from their homes and gained a victory; and he was a man. So his heart quickened to the distant drumbeat. Thus maybe the Sons, in defeat, had gained one small, nasty victory; for what woman in her right mind would ever thrill to the clash of swords and the excitement of busting heads? To the looseness, violence and anarchy of it all? Oh yes, Dad had groaned when that 'jack lost his ear to the axe; but he groaned because his little girl might have noticed – and perhaps, perhaps, because that was the real outcome of wielding weapons, and he didn't wish to know.

Long ago, Yaleen had told that brother of Dario's that she sympathized with the frustrations of men. That was before she had been tortured in Cherub-land by frustrated Sons who bated women. True, those Sons were exceptions . . . mad dogs. Nor had the 'jacks who fought in our campaign exactly changed into crowing cockerels as a result. But there did seem to be an insidious equation between violence and the sporters of penises, when men were able to rule the roost. It had been so on the Moon, whatever Jean-Paul's secret intentions to preserve and protect his flock. (Though who had murdered umpteen Paxmen with a bomb? None other but the cherub Yaleen . . .)

And yet, and yet, men were diminished by our way of life. That was true, too.

Or had been true, till now. The war had loosened certain

inveterate restraints. Should those be bound up again tightly – or not? Maybe no debate was needed. The black current already stretched as far as Aladalia. Restless men could always walk to beyond Aladalia – where indeed they might be useful as soldiers, guardians of our freedom.

Meanwhile relations between man and woman were subject to a degree of flux, and Dad stepped out defiantly, perhaps unaware why there was a different spring in his step.

Then one day as he was bearing me along dusty crowded Zanzyba Road, just as we were drawing close to the Café of the Seasons, a voice cried, 'Dad!'

I saw Yaleen sitting there.

Dad broke into a gallop. I giggled with relief and nerves.

It was like a reverse of that time when I returned to war-wrecked Verrino and hastened up to the top of the Spire, only to find emptiness and nobody there (until Hasso turned up). Here was Yaleen at last, in exactly the right place. I felt hysterical. Hilarity welled up in me. The charade would soon be over. I could start being myself again, just as soon as there wasn't another self bumming around in competition. I could stop being Narya – and become . . . Naryaleen?

A tricky moment, this! Trickiest of all when I winked at Yaleen. She gave me such a peculiar look; but I couldn't resist the wink. Besides, I had already seen myself wink at me, a few years earlier at this very moment. I was grinning stupidly when I toddled over to the table, but I composed myself.

'Hallo, Narya,' said Yaleen. 'My name's Yaleen. I'm your sister.'

Supposing I said: 'Oh no you aren't'? Supposing I said: 'You and me are the same person'?

I didn't. I wasn't going to throw away two years' drudge on a wild whim. Would you?

Since I merely stood there mute, Dad and Yaleen got on discussing my supposed problems, over my head.

'Ah, she's my big darling, aren't you?' said Dad after a bit. He hoisted me aloft. 'Let's step on home, Yaleen.'

I steered Dad home by tufts of hair as though I were steering worlds. Or suns around the galaxy; keeping reality from colliding with itself by a hairsbreadth.

You already know the events of the next two weeks. During that time I was an arrow notched on a taut string, ready to fly to its target: namely that night when my parents would be away at Chataly's; and when I would lock Doctor Edrick and Yaleen in the bedroom together. But beyond that point I would be shooting blind.

Do you know, I'd been passive for so long that it even seemed possible to me during those last days that I might simply continue thereafter in the same vein? That this might be preferable?

I could start to talk more freely. I could grow up ordinarily. I could make believe that I was just like any other child. Ultimately I might even persuade myself that during my infancy I had been insane. Then, having duly grown up, I could steer well clear of Worms and rivers for the rest of my days, and nobody would be any the wiser . . .

During that same fortnight, Yaleen too had been going through similar mood shifts. She also had been thinking about opting out. She had nursed fantasies of marriage, or of becoming a hermit or a poet; now hadn't she?

Taut as I was – stretched like a banjo string – was I resonating in tune with Yaleen? Was I echoing her? Or had she perhaps been echoing *me* unawares? Had vibrations been passing up and down the same *Ka*-tree, on which we both were leaves, travelling through the ever-never?

It's odd: I only grasped this aspect of that last fortnight just now when I set it down on paper. Obviously there's some use in writing books; you discover things you didn't know before! Or do you perhaps invent them? Then convince yourself that they are and always were the truth, because they explain events more neatly than the confusion – the shooting in the dark – of the actual time?

To act or not to act? If I didn't act, I would forever just be the kid sister of Yaleen of Pecawar, author of *The Book of the River*. That wouldn't do at all, now would it?

So was my pride more of a spur to action than the threat posed by the Godmind and its burning lens? Perhaps! The Godmind and its concerns seemed far away from our little family home in Pecawar; from the smell of cinnamon coffee, from the gaudy barrel-gourds in the garden. My universe had diminished drastically, but at least I had my pride to see me through.

Chataly choked to death. Mum and Dad departed. Yaleen cooked a pudding, brewed cocoa, read to me and saw me off to bed with a kiss.

Before story-time I sneaked into the kitchen and unbolted the back door. Yaleen never did get round to wondering how Doctor Edrick had managed to enter the house without smashing and crashing. When he popped up, that was that. Busy! And after she was murdered, Yaleen had other things on her mind. Unbolting the door may seem a somewhat shitty thing for me to do. Hardly fair exchange for a pudding, a bedtime tale and a kiss? Well, if I can put it this way, it seemed a *likely* thing for me to do. When I locked the bedroom door upstairs I would close a trap; so presumably it was up to me to open the trap in the first place. It balanced out.

As soon as I estimated that Yaleen had settled down with the poems of Gimmo the Tramper, downstairs from my bed I crept. Yaleen would doze off before Edrick arrived, and I didn't know how long she would snooze. Hunkering down in the dark outside the door, I waited.

Not long, as I discovered.

Then everything happened very suddenly – just as it had happened once already. (Though this was the first, and only time.)

When Yaleen noticed me skulking there, I scrammed. I hid behind the urn in our entry hall. No sooner was I concealed than Yaleen came crashing through the door and scrambled upstairs pursued by Edrick. I counted slowly to ten and followed them. Opened the bedroom door, got the key, closed and locked it.

When I turned that key I locked another door as well: the door of foreknowledge. Suddenly the future was a blank, unwritten. Now the burden was gone; I was free. I felt as though I'd spent these last two years gaga in a trance . . .

Action, now! I hastened into my own room, to drag a chair against the open window. I climbed on to the sill. That was when I heard the bang of the pistol, muffled by Yaleen's mattress and a couple of intervening doors. (*Bye, Yaleen! Fly away!*) On the wall outside was a rickety trellis supporting a creeper which bore hosts of tiny flame-blooms every spring. The creeper pretty well hid the spars of the trellis, as well as holding them together. If the trellis had been easier to spot – and bear in mind – Dad would probably have torn it down to prevent precisely such an escapade as followed.

I edged out, latched on, and climbed slowly, feeling my way up to the flat of the roof. It was a good thing it was night. Apart from some escaping lamplight, the only light came from the stars. Just enough illumination, not too much. Any brighter, and I might have been *scared* – what with the cliff of wall above me and the gulf below and me only being little. One rotten spar snapped but I didn't lose my grip. The trellis sagged but didn't collapse. I soon humped myself over the guttering and lay a while, panting. Then I stood up on the roof and screamed my lungs out to the neighbourhood.

It's amazing how much noise a small child can make. And I made it all. I didn't bother with words, at first, just noise. Then I decided to switch to some words in case the neighbours thought I was merely a tom-cat with its dander up.

'Help! Murder! Enemy! Enemy! Help!' I shrieked.

By now Edrick had probably discovered that the door was locked, and kicked it loose. He'd be able to hear my shrieks, though since the noise was coming from overhead maybe this would confuse him. If he did dash into my bedroom and try to climb the trellis I was sure the structure would collapse; though come to think of it, Edrick only needed to stand on the windowsill to chin himself up to the roof. But why should he bother? Why should Yaleen's little sister matter to him now? He'd be best advised to cut and run.

Lanterns and lamps lit up in the nearby houses.

'Help! Help!' Raggedly; my throat was giving out.

People soon came pounding along the lane to our front door. I heard cries of 'Stop!' and half of the people rushed on by; so Edrick must have decamped. Pursuit receded into the distance. Very public-spirited, but hardly sensible! Why run after a killer?

Lantern light spilled into our garden from downstairs, supplementing the faint glow cast by Yaleen's reading lamp, so neighbours were inside the house by now; Edrick must have left the front door open in his haste.

In the distance I heard the crack of a shot.

I squatted on the edge of the roof to await rescue, while above me blinked the stars. My stars.

Death never makes things simpler. Oh what a fuss there was with Yaleen found dead! And Doctor Edrick also dead, as it transpired.

Needless to say, in the eyes of my saviours I was simply a shocked little child, so I had a bit of difficulty working

206

out exactly what had happened to Edrick. By and by I pieced it together. I gathered that his pursuers caught up with him in a blind alley, where Edrick fired his pistol, smashing someone's shoulder. Then the pistol must have jammed, or maybe it could only fire two shots before reloading; so our local heroes rushed him, and Doctor Edrick collected a knife in the guts.

No doubt this was a sign of the times in once peaceful Pecawar. Our local newssheet had published details of 'war atrocities' in Verrino. My parents had discussed these hushedly, other people not so hushedly, it seemed. Though the people of Pecawar hadn't themselves been injured by the war, this seemed to make them the more virtuously incensed on behalf of Verrino and its victims. It was noteworthy to me that the people of Verrino itself hadn't flooded out en masse to the prison-pens to try to massacre their former tormenters. They were numb with their sufferings. But Pecawar people had the energy to feel aggrieved. Thus a presumed absconding murderous Son armed with a gun and an offbeat accent deserved a quick reprisal, rather than citizen's arrest and investigation. (An investigation, just in case he was indeed a junglejack deserter, some poor wretch desperate to get home to Jangali.) When our citizens knifed Edrick, they didn't even know he had murdered anyone; not for sure. Such a thing wouldn't have happened before the war; but at least nobody openly boasted of planting the knife.

That was the least of the fuss; and I'm anticipating things, rather. That's because I want to tidy Edrick away quickly, since he has no further role to play in my story. So we'll put a speedy full stop to him right now, just as one of our good and kindly neighbours did that night with a blade. As the Godmind would say: 'Finish!'

Back to myself awaiting rescue. This was accomplished by one of the neighbours, Axal, husband of Merri. He fetched a ladder, brought me down to the ground and took me round to the kitchen, there to fix a hot spiced milk to distract my innocent mind; whilst upstairs the floor of my slaughtered sister's bedroom creaked underfoot. Merri also soon arrived, wrapped in a nightrobe.

Every now and then concerned faces appeared in the kitchen doorway, calling Merri or Axal (mainly Axal) into the living room to confer; there where Gimmo's *Songs of a Tramp* still lay on the floor. Bustle, bustle.

'Did you raise the alarm, Narya?' Axal knelt to enquire of me between whiles. I stared at him dumbly, clutching my cup for comfort.

Sadly Merri shook her head. 'It must have been Yaleen.'

'How did Narya get on the roof?' Axal asked his wife. This was a leading question.

'Yaleen,' I whimpered plaintively. 'Yaleen!'

'Hush, darling,' Merri soothed me. 'Your sister's gone away for a while.'

Oh yes indeed. Too true. Gone away for a while. (*Fly away, Yaleen!*)

'You can sleep at our house tonight, darling.'

I scrambled to clutch the edge of the sink. 'Home!' I insisted.

'No, no, it's a *good* idea to visit our house till your Mum and Dad get back.'

'Home!'

'The poor dear's had an awful shock.'

'Those sodding Sons,' Axal swore. 'Serves the swine right.'

'Shhh . . . ! Do you think there are any more about?'

'Militia'll be here soon. Carlo's gone to rouse the 'jack captain and the quaymistress.'

'At least,' whispered Merri, 'Narya's too young to understand. That's a blessing. But we must get her over to our place. And you're coming as well! I should think so, with runaway Sons around.'

'Of course, of course.' So what did Axal do but rush off

into the living room to talk to someone instead? Excitement, danger, action! It was quite some time before we left the house; and Merri had more trouble prising Axal away than me.

Mum and Dad arrived back late the following day. The neighbours knew where they'd gone to. (Just try to keep your business private in Pecawar! Well, Dad had always done his best, till recently . . .) The riverguild had sent a messenger. Chataly's funeral rites had to be somewhat rudely abridged; Mum and Dad returned hastily to tuck me back under their wings, and to grieve and bury anew.

To grieve; and not let me see how deeply they were grieving – blessing me the while with smiles and hugs and stray touches. But I saw. Oh all the grief!

I'd minimized this aspect of Yaleen's murder. I'd hardly given it a thought, in fact! Because Yaleen *had* to die; and I was her, anyway. But Mum and Dad didn't know.

I didn't – or rather, *couldn't* – console them. What a selfish shit I felt.

Not least when they took me into Yaleen's room a few hours before the funeral to say goodbye to her. The body was lying on bedding in an open box laid across trestles. A blanket was pulled up to Yaleen's chin. A crown of green leaves, pulled from the same creeper that grew on the wall outside my bedroom, was bound round her brow. I was supposed to cover her mouth for a few moments with my fingers. I was to hide her closed eyes with my hands. (The eyeballs had sunk in; the lids were flaps.)

Yaleen's bare arms were holding the blanket in place, her hands crossed above her breast. On her right hand, was my diamond ring. What a nerve! They were going to bury it with her.

After I'd covered her mouth and her eyes – rather perfunctorily – I seized her cold and waxen hand.

'I want this ring,' I said. 'It's mine. It belongs to me.' I started to haul the ring off; or to try to.

What a brat, what a brat.

Though goodness, I was *talking*! And in real sentences! Consequently the pain I caused by this misbehaviour was shot through with surprise and delight, judging by the glances Mum and Dad exchanged.

'No, Narya,' Mum said gently, 'you can't have it.'

'Oh but I must. Yaleen wanted me to have it. She was going to give it to me. She promised.'

Mum thought a moment. 'You wouldn't be telling us a little fib, would you?'

A *little* fib? Gosh no. I'd only been lying my arse off every day for the last two years; by omission if not by commission.

'Yaleen said so, when you went away. When you left us.' That should make them feel guilty. Insert one thorn of self-recrimination. How nice of me. But hell, I wanted that ring back. When all is explained, I told myself, all shall be forgiven.

'I don't *think* she'd make such a thing up,' murmured Dad.

'Darling,' said Mum, 'Yaleen probably meant it for you when you were grown up, and when she was an old woman.'

'A promise is an oath,' I said. (Dad raised an eyebrow.)

'A diamond ring isn't suitable for a young child,' Mum insisted.

'You can keep it safe for me,' I said. 'In trust.'

This time they really did exchange glances.

'Where did you hear that word?' asked Dad.

'Yaleen said it. She said "in twust".'

'It must be true.' Dad twisted the ring off Yaleen's finger. 'We'll keep this somewhere very safe till you're a little older, Narya. But it's yours, I promise.'

Mum began to snivel, then turned to hug me. 'Now

there's only you! But you're talking to us! It's like a little miracle. It's as if we've lost Yaleen but . . .' She choked.

Sure. But gained a real little girl; fitted with a voice and vocabulary.

'Perhaps,' said Dad, 'the shock has, well, made her bloom?'

'You *will* go on talking to us, won't you?' begged Mum.

What a question. I tried to look gaga and wide-eyed, and merely nodded.

'Say you will! Please!'

'My dear,' said Dad imploringly.

Maybe I ought to have let them bury the damn ring after all.

'She might be able to say what happened on that terrible night!'

Definitely it was high time for a bit of acting. 'Oh, night!' I cried. 'Bad man! Oh! Oh!'

Dad shook his head sternly at Mum. 'You shouldn't remind her of that. Let her think of the ring. The ring replaces Yaleen. Children are like that.' He held up my diamond. 'We'll put this somewhere safe, Narya. And soon we'll put your sister somewhere safe too, where she can sleep and dream of you.'

Sleep and dream, eh? Yaleen had told them a bit about the *Ka*-store of the Worm, but obviously it hadn't quite sunk in . . . as yet.

'Nice sister ring,' said I. 'Keep safe.'

So then it was time for the funeral; and quite a cortège hummed its way through the dusty streets. A lot of neighbours joined the procession. The local militia, led by their 'jack captain, paid their respects by carrying the death-box and by escorting it. The quaymistress – successor to the woman who had arranged my initiation – led a crew of riverwomen. Nice to know that I was missed!

Out to the graveyard we hummed our way wordlessly,

for death was a time when the talking stopped; when no more could be spoken. Of death itself, whatever personal fantasies or preferences one might have, nothing of value could be said in public. Or so these people all thought, for a wee while yet. Till *The Book of the River* came out; till they learned of the *Ka*-store of the Worm . . .

Meanwhile they hummed. They made a voiceless music to express love and sorrow; and by virtue of that hum, issuing from lungs which still breathed, the town breathed on, and everyone in it.

As ever, no one knew how the hum would develop; whether it would be soft, or loud; what sort of tune if any it would carry. No one in particular began it or led it. It arose. It gathered. It *was*. Grief and painful thoughts would die away in the living hum. Then after the death-box had been dumped in a shallow hole inside our sandy, walled cemetery, and after the 'Rods' had filled in the hole, the humming would die away. (Of course deaths are viewed a little differently nowadays; but you still have to dispose of the corpse!)

The death-hum at my funeral was a rich, loud plainsong. Presently it began to sound like the tune *Under the Bright Blue Sun*, no doubt thanks to the choir of riverwomen. I hummed along with glee till we arrived at our destination.

It was years since I'd visited the graveyard, but it hadn't changed. Worn stone windbreak walls wandered around the perimeter in a series of silted bays. Despite these walls the wind when it blew carved dunes and troughs. A fire-blackened fused patch at the far end marked where the Rods burnt whichever old death-boxes worked their way back to the surface, or were uncovered by the breezes . . .

For the benefit of readers leagues away from Pecawar, with somewhat different customs, I should explain that the Rods took their name from the way they probed the sand to find space for new death-boxes. Maybe a corpse would lie in the ground for a hundred years, or only a couple of years, but sooner or later it would surface in its box. The Rods would haul it away, and up it would go in smoke. That day, as ever in the cemetery, a few wooden edges and corners were poking up here and there like sunken vessels. This arrangement would hardly have worked in steamy, reeky Tambimatu! But it suited us in Pecawar. The dryness of the air and the sand soon turned bodies into leathery mummies. There was no smell.

So when Yaleen had been sunk in the sand and covered, the humming ceased. The militia marched off. Neighbours shuffled away homeward – increasing their pace as soon as they were out of sight, I don't doubt. The riverwomen departed, all except for the quaymistress. She lingered around the stone archway of the graveyard, and as we three family mourners emerged she approached my parents.

'Did Yaleen tell you that she left a memorial?'

'What do you mean?' asked Mum. 'A memorial? I don't follow you.'

'Yaleen wrote a book.'

'She never said!'

'It'll soon be published in Ajelobo.'

'How soon?' I butted in. 'My sister book, how soon?'

The quaymistress smiled down ruefully at me. 'Maybe twenty weeks.' She ruffled my hair. 'A long time for a little girl!'

Not really. I had an actual deadline now; a schedule for coming fully alive, as me.

'What sort of book is this?' asked Dad. 'What's in it?'

'Her life is in it. All of her life. I haven't read the manuscript myself, but that's the word on it.'

'And she never said!' exclaimed Mum. 'Never!' She glanced back towards the grave as though a hand might break surface, waving the book at us.

'Maybe when we read it,' said Dad, 'then we'll *really* know her.'

213

'Aye, when it's too late! First Capsi, now Yaleen. We're plagued.' Mum clutched me close.

'The Guild will see to it that you receive the very first copies.' The quaymistress went on more crisply, 'There'll likely be some income, too. Maybe a fair amount. Yaleen wrote the book for the Guild, but in the circumstances we'll remit you fifty per cent of any royalties accruing.'

This was really *crass*. And what a cheek: there would 'likely' be 'some' income!

'We don't need money,' Dad said coldly.

Oh, great!

'Take money, Dad,' I lisped. 'Fish are for catching.'

He stared at me oddly. 'We'll think about it,' he said with dignity.

'Do! Do! When you decide, just get in touch.' The quaymistress beamed. Mentally I consigned this particular specimen to a deep pool cram-packed with stingers. Then I hauled her out again, because in due course I would have to do business with her.

So we returned home. As soon as I reasonably could, and before Mum and Dad could nerve themselves to sort through Yaleen's few possessions, I slipped upstairs and into her room. I quickly found where I'd put my private afterword to *The Book of the River* and smuggled this into my own bedroom. Folding the papers up small, I stuffed them into a hole which I poked in the belly of my cat on wheels.

My afterword. Yes, mine. Now that Yaleen was safely sunk in sand, my two 'I's had flowed back together. The two streams of my life had rejoined.

Two years down, twenty weeks to go.

The weeks went. Not without strain, not without problems. Now that I'd begun to talk I couldn't very well stop as if struck dumb; but I had to watch every word I said.

What's more, Mum *treasured* me. Now more than ever. She acted as though I might suddenly succumb to ague, fever, paralysis, food-poisoning, night-chills, simultaneously or in any combination thereof. And whilst treasuring, she grieved, nobly and tight-lipped.

At last came the day when an advance copy of the book arrived by special messenger from the quaymistress's office. Mum didn't tell me what it was. She set it by in a safe place till Dad came home from work; she needed his company before she could tackle it. But I did catch a glimpse of the volume. It was bound in stiffened cloth, with a zigzag black and blue pattern suggesting waves, rivers, black currents. My name and the title were printed in silver lettering. The book looked handsome indeed. The Guild had taken pains.

That evening I was packed off early to bed so that Mum could settle to read the story aloud to Dad – all evening long and what seemed like half the night.

Upstairs, I stayed awake in the dark, latterly by pinching and slapping myself. Every so often I sneaked downstairs to check on progress. At long last I was in the belly of the Worm (in bookland). Mum's voice was sore and cracked. No doubt her eyes were giving out too. I settled silently on the stairs.

Finally Mum read out, *'That's what choices are for. To savour them while you can, and then to seize one. Or the other . . . That's it: the end,'* she said.

Before she could begin to weep, and soothe her eyes with tears, I ambled into the lamplit room.

'Pretty good, eh?' I said. 'Hullo, Mum, Dad. I wrote all that. I'm Yaleen. That's who I really am.'

What happened next wasn't quite what I'd expected.

Dad spanked me.

He delivered four thwacks across my backside – and though I can't pretend that this hurt me worse than being

215

tortured by Edrick and his boys, it had, um, impact. Whilst he was spanking me, Mum turned her head away, her hands still fondling *my* book.

Then Dad hauled me unceremoniously upstairs, stuck me back in bed and slammed the door.

Bloody hell.

At breakfast next morning I tried again. (Breakfast was spiced oats, nuts, bran and milk; the latest health fad for me.) Mum immediately looked fraught and remote.

Dad quickly interrupted.

'Narya! Last night you caused us a lot of sorrow, at a most precious moment. I realize you don't understand *why*, but I should have thought you learnt a lesson last night – much as I loathed having to teach you it. I'll do the same again if I have to.'

'Hang on, Dad! How do you explain I can suddenly talk like a grown-up?'

'I know you've become wonderfully precocious of late, Narya. And we're delighted. Truly! It's marvellous. You were such a slow starter. But I must draw the line at this . . . this unkind pretence.'

'There *is* no Narya, Dad! There never was. I've been Yaleen all along – I had to make believe till now.'

'Make believe,' he repeated tightly. 'Exactly! Just so. Children often make believe. But children don't think things through. You could hardly be Yaleen, when Yaleen was in the same house as you. So let's have no more of it, understand?'

Mum clasped Dad's hand. This at least stopped me from being thumped immediately. 'Might this be more serious?' she whispered. 'The shock of that night, do you think?'

'I was Yaleen all the time,' I insisted, 'because after I was shot by that sod Edrick – yes, that's who it was! – '

Dad shook his head at my foul language. Another symptom of my infantile brain-fever?

216

' – after that, the black current sent me down the psylink to Eeden, and I was reborn as a baby there. Later on I died in an explosion and started to come back here. But things went wrong and I twisted backwards through time . . .'

They listened. I think they were both trying to decide how ill I was.

'Enough, enough!' Dad broke in as soon as I began to fill in more details. 'Can it be that Yaleen's spirit has, well, taken possession?'

Mum shuddered. 'So where did our Narya go?'

'Nowhere,' I told her. 'You must realize: *she never was.* She was me, pretending. I'm sorry, but I had no choice. Why do you think I wanted my ring? Look, Mum, there's more to *The Book of the River*; more upstairs. I wrote an afterword to it. I hid it in that toy cat . . .'

Mention of something as comically banal and homely as the toy cat had a curious effect on Dad. He rose.

'I . . . I have to go to work. Or I'll be late.'

'That's true,' agreed Mum. Oh the comforts of the familiar, the balm of routine.

'You can't go to work today!' I protested. 'You have to take me to the quaymistress's office. Though I guess I could find my own way there. There has to be a conclave of the riverguild. And I need to contact the black current again. Because unless we can avoid it somehow, our world's going to come to an end!'

Dad stared at me bleakly. 'I think our world already came to an end.'

'No, no, don't you see? I'm back with you. This is a whole new start.'

'Of what? Of the end? What end? What are you talking about?'

'Oh, I'll have to write another whole book to explain! And I need to drink of the black current again. I'll have to . . . oh, there are oodles of things! But I must talk to the Guild in conclave first.'

'I suppose,' allowed Dad, 'I *could* stay off work today.'
He sat down again, wearily, confused.

Mum and Dad didn't suddenly accept me as Yaleen, in the
way I'd naïvely expected. There was no overwhelming
revelation, no abrupt and wild embrace. There was no
single moment of truth, joy and discovery. Instead: a
gradual shift, a slow slide in their attitude, away from me-
as-Narya, towards me-as-Yaleen. This went on for a
number of days, accompanied by occasional forgettings,
temporary lapses on their part. Perhaps this was a better
way to cope with the shock than the sort of dramatic climax
I'd pictured to myself.

Curiously, by the time that my parents *had* come to
accept me fully as Yaleen, the real and only, it was me who
felt most keenly the absent 'ghost' of Narya. It was me
who heard the footfalls of a shadow person next to me.
Narya had only ever been an invention – a character in a
fiction (of my own devising). Yet she had lived in this very
house alongside me, and I had fully believed in her, and in
her selfish little wiles. She had been real; now she wasn't.
She had never existed; yet indubitably she had. So therefore
somehow she still did exist – invisibly in some mirror world
of my mind, inhabiting some echo existence. She was a
different me, who might have been born if I hadn't been
born instead. Yet she genuinely had been born. And now
was unborn, once again. Thinking of her, I thought a lot
about the riddle of the raven and the writing desk . . .

Later that same morning – subsequent to my confession
over breakfast, and whilst our family relationship was still
in flux – Mum, Dad and I did set out together, nonetheless,
for the waterfront; there to beard that mercenary, calculat-
ing quaymistress in her den.

That particular woman's disbelief I finally dispelled by
revealing a certain kinky little initiation ritual of our guild
which I *had* kept quiet about when I wrote *The Book of the*

River, and which I intend to keep hush about here as well. (Always keep a card up your sleeve, eh?)

She believed. She set in motion the summoning of a conclave. Signals flashed up and down stream.

Four weeks later, in front of a conclave, I told all – just as it's set down here. I told of *Ka*-space and Eeden and Earth and the Moon; of Exotics and Flawed Ones and Alien stars; of the Godmind's scheme to build a lens of burning minds to pierce the dark mystery of existence. I told of seedships and rose shows. Of Venezia and California. 'Out of the mouth of a babe' – as precog myth put it!

And on board that schooner, *Oopsadaisy*, where the conclave was being held, I demanded and was given a slug of the black current to put me in tune with my old friend the Worm again.

I drank my slug on the third day of the conclave. That night, like the previous nights, I spent at home; and before falling asleep I fixed my mind on what I would like to dream. If you concentrate hard enough you can carry this trick off; though there'll always be changes which try to take you by surprise so that you're dumped into a different dream, not of your intention, where you'll forget yourself and just float along with the phantasmagorias.

I dreamed, as I'd intended, of a schooner sailing proudly on the river out near the black current. A conclave was taking place on board – since this was also uppermost in my mind – though alas, and unaccountably, this was happening in the open air on deck and consisted not of women but of beasts. Sows, bitches, ewes, turkey-hens and whatnot. Never mind! I paid no attention to the assorted bleating, yapping and oinking which might have tricked me into a farmyard fantasy; and presently from the water the Worm's head rose. The Worm had found me in my dream – to its considerable surprise!

Yaleen? It's you! But how? You aren't here. You can't be. She's –

The schooner's deck had emptied; all the animals had faded. The dream was of a different quality now: Worm and me, mind to mind.

Listen, Worm! Whatever you do, don't break the psylink with dead Yaleen! Don't lose your grip or you'll spoil everything! Got it?

Yes. But –

Just listen! I've carried out your little mission. I've been to Eeden and now I'm back again, but not in the way you expected . . .

I was getting rather tired of repeating all this! To Mum and Dad; to the Guild; now to the Worm. Obviously I would have to write a book. Then I could just hand out copies.

My account took a while, but a least I didn't have to worry about the dream fading out midway. By now the Worm was clinging on tight.

Worm, you still there?

Hmm? Oh yes.

Like the pillow talk of lovers, yet!

A fin for your thoughts?

Oh . . . You've flooded me, Yaleen . . . I'll have to think about all this. But well done, don't you know! Well, well done! Can you sail out to me so I can get all this directly from you in the Ka-store? I promise I'll return you safe and sound. You're so important to me!

Thanks. I'm flattered. Another swim in you: is that what you want?

It would be friendlier if you visited my head.

Off Aladalia? What, and wake up poor old Raf again?

I could come and collect you off Pecawar.

Withdraw yourself to Pecawar? That wouldn't make me very popular with people!

Do come to Aladalia! I'll reorganize my body. I'll provide excellent accommodation. You could stay a while.

I'd heard that kind of offer before. How about spending the rest of my life in a seedship pod?

We'll have to think about it, I said. *These one-night stands are sweet, but I wasn't exactly thinking of moving in with you.*

Oddly enough, to my amusement I found that in a weird sort of way I'd missed the Worm during my absence!

And maybe I'm a bit young for you yet? I said. *A bit tiny to go jumping into black currents, and down Worms' throats?*

If you came inside me, Yaleen, I could grow your body up – while your mind romped in the Ka-store.

How long would it take to grow me up?

I don't have vats and soft machines, I only have me. It would take as long as normal growth. Another twelve, thirteen years or so would see you all set up. You certainly wouldn't feel bored in the meantime.

Thirteen *years? That's hardly fair on my Mum and Dad, No, I couldn't possibly.*

Do try to take a swim in me at least.

Sure. Why not? Just so long as you'll promise to tell me what it's all about. What Ka-space is. How the psylink works. How we can stop the Godmind. And where you came from. And how time got twisted.

And why a raven is like a writing desk?

That too.

I may have enough clues. It could take a while to fit them all together.

So start trying, will you! There has to be a way to stop the Godmind from burning us all up.

Has there? What if there isn't?

Then I shall be quite annoyed with you, Worm.

Oh dear.

Mad, in fact.

Hmm, I think I'd best be going . . .

*In that case . . . goodnight, Worm. Be with me in my
dreams again.*

I will be. 'Night, Yaleen.

The next morning Mum walked me down to the waterfront
again to board the *Oopsadaisy* for the final session of
conclave.

There, in a cabin panelled in expensive ivorybone wood
and hung with a remarkable collection of fish-masks, I told
the assembled mistresses of my night-time chat with the
Worm, concluding thus: 'How about me having a swim? A
black sort of swim?'

Which is when, as ever, things started to go wrong.

I don't know whether I'd been putting these good ladies'
backs up during the past several days. Had I been acting
too pert by far? Truly I hadn't intended to. I thought I'd
become a whole lot more considerate, subtle and persuasive
recently. (Besides, in memory at least, my bum still ached
from Dad's smacks!) On the other hand, why had I dreamt
of these 'mistresses as a gang of honking geese and bleating
ewes?

'A swim? Not yet,' said one 'mistress.

'No, we can't have you running off and disappearing,'
agreed another.

The quaymistress of Pecawar, Chanoose by name, was
particularly adamant. (I'd already crossed swords with her
previously on the topic of my literary earnings.) 'When
all's said and done, you belong to the Guild, remember!'
She waved at the fish-masks on the wall to remind me.

Another 'mistress whom I knew from way back – two
lives earlier, at that other conclave held in Spanglestream –
was dusky old Marti of Guineamoy. She challenged me
with, 'How do we know you're telling the truth?'

'The Worm can back me up any time!'

'Oh, I'm not disputing that you're the same Yaleen as I
met before. Or that something truly remarkable happened

to you. You were murdered; then reborn. But when did you *really* come back to life? Can I credit that you waited whole years to reveal yourself? Maybe your spirit has possessed Narya, after all? And what actually did happen in between your death and resurrection? You may have dreamt all this business of your trip to Eeden in the *Ka*-store. Or even made it all up. Can you prove otherwise? *The Book of the River* is a somewhat inventive document in places, I suspect. I've read it, and I don't entirely believe in that giant croaker which tried to squash you in the jungle.'

'Oh don't you? Well it did!'

'Maybe you were hallucinating, from starvation and exhaustion. And maybe you weren't. But to my mind that part of your story *does* verge on romance, of the Ajelobo brand. Likewise I have my doubt about the dead man of Opal Island. Strange and marvellous things certainly happened, yet perhaps at times you also let your imagination run away with you? Which allows you to be as rude as you please, under the guise of honesty and frankness. I'm thinking now of your remarks *à propos* our other conclave at Spanglestream. 'Mistress Nelliam, with the face of a prune, indeed!'

'I didn't say anything rude about *you*, Marti.'

'No, but you blithely and impertinently made me an "ally" of Nelliam's. And whether or not I agree with your character assessments of Tamath and Sharla in *some* respects, you hardly do justice to the other fine qualities which deservedly made them Guildmistresses.'

'That's a matter of opinion.'

'True. And we're very tolerant of your opinions, are we not? But mightn't all your revelations about Earth and Eeden simply be . . . matters of opinion, too?'

'The Worm – '

'The black current believes what you told it. Or at least you tell us so. I suppose, since you rode the current all the

223

way from Tambimatu to Aladalia, we must allow a large degree of credence to this . . .'

What *was* Marti getting at? I felt perplexed. That other meeting of a conclave at Spanglestream had taken me on trust; they hadn't cast sly doubts. The present conclave seemed to be up to something. They were hunting around for justifications – but for what?

'Myself, I look around and I see our world; and the black current, yes indeed. We know what you say it is; and we accept this, basically. We know that originally we came from a distant star. But I don't see any concrete *evidence* of Eeden or Venezia or that huge moon.'

'What did you expect? That I'd bring back a rose, clutched in my soul's teeth?'

Marti pursed her lips. 'That might have helped. The problem for us is this: the happy balance of our world and the prestige of our guild have suffered upsets lately. I think we need a breathing space. Quite a long one, too. Approximately as long as it takes a little girl to grow up. Yet some things can't be gainsaid. Such as the *Ka*-store of souls. Such as the fact that a dead person can be reborn. Or the fact that the black current watches over us and knows us; as our Guild chapbook, handed down from forever, tells.'

'It's hardly handed down from *forever*. If you don't mind my saying so, 'Mistress Marti, you seemed a lot more analytical in Spanglestream.'

'Dear child, I *am* being very analytical – of the situation. Incidentally, your book is published now. Consignments arrived here yesterday in bulk.'

'Well, thanks for telling me!'

'You can collect your copies afterwards, from my office,' said Chanoose.

'It's already being read with the greatest excitement upriver,' Marti went on. 'You're becoming a heroine to people. Yes, a heroine, from the ranks of our Guild! We did worry whether people might assess your chaos-causing career uncharitably. Wonder of wonders, not so; from the reports we have already. A heroine,' she repeated softly, 'and a martyr too. What better way to speed a book to dizzy heights than the murder of its author? We're encouraging newssheets up and down stream to gossip.'

'Publicity pays,' said Chanoose. 'Expect to be famous in your home town presently.'

'A heroine,' Marti enthused, 'who has now been reborn out of the black current – as its, and as our, *infant priestess*. Reborn as she who proves that when we die into the bosom of the current, we live.'

'Oh no. Look: most people don't die into the Worm's bosom. Weren't you listening at all? Most people go to Eeden. To Godmind territory.'

'Against that, may the black current defend us . . . If your account should be real, and not fantastic! Yet doubtless with an intermediary of your calibre on tap, and given enough time, we may be able to offer the hope that everyone – woman and man alike – will benefit equally from the *Ka*-store – one day in the future. If everyone supports us.' Marti smiled. Wryly? No, slyly! 'The *Ka*-store sounds much more convenient than a trip to Eeden. So much closer to home. So much more convincing. Why, news of this may even convert those Sons across the river; it could make them see sense, and change sides.

'And *if* what you say about the Godmind is true, what better way to thwart it than to rob it of this world? How better can we save ourselves from this universal doom you speak of – should there be any such thing! – than by detaching ourselves from that Godmind? How better than by forging a compact with the black current on behalf of all our people? A compact to which our own guild holds the key – in the person of your own good self, Yaleen? Our own priestess.

'If you did indeed sabotage the colony programme on

that giant Moon and set it back – or rather, if you will do so in future – surely we have ample time. If doom there be a-waiting. And if doom there isn't, and it's all a fantasy of yours, no matter!'

'Oh,' said I. What Marti had just said made a crazy sort of sense. For this priestess scheme to work, it needn't even be based on truth.

I can't say I cared for it! What sort of life would an infant 'priestess' live? How could anybody who read *The Book of the River* be daft enough to imagine me as a priestess? And besides, outside of the pages of a few old fables hardly anybody knew what a priestess *was*.

Maybe that would make things easier. Maybe people would be daft enough. Suddenly the Worm's offer seemed almost attractive.

'Okay,' said I, 'I was lying all along. I admit it. I'm not Yaleen. I'm just Narya.'

Marti laughed. 'Too late for that! You've been far too persuasive. May you persuade many other people too!'

'This is the judgement of the riverguild sitting in solemn conclave aboard the *Oopsadaisy*,' said Chanoose formally. 'May the black current show us our true course. Through you, dear river-daughter, Yaleen of Pecawar.'

'You might at least make me a guildmistress,' I grumbled.

'What, a little girl a 'mistress?' asked Chanoose incredulously.

'Tush, this is much more important than being a 'mistress.' Marti favoured me with a dusky smile. End of conclave.

By the time Dad got home from work the evening after, a few townsfolk were hanging about outside our door, looking somewhat embarrassed and sheepish.

By the following evening, numbers had swelled. The hopeful spectators seemed more sure of themselves now, more ardent. They wanted to see us, touch us, hear us, just for a moment please. For this was the family home of Yaleen, heroine and martyr. On Dad's advice, which was sensible, we all stayed indoors. Some people kept up their vigil till quite late that night.

And on the evening after that, Dad fairly had to force his way home through a crowd packing out our lane. Mum and I were upstairs watching from behind a curtain. A lot of copies of my book were being brandished, clutched to bosoms, or still being feverishly read. A fair number of newssheets were flapping like flags. I recognized some neighbours in the crowd, amongst them Axal and Merri. Their faces looked different, changed.

'So this is what it's like being a successful author!' I quipped to Mum.

'Fame at last,' said Mum, trying to match my mood.

'How awful,' said I.

'How scary,' she agreed. 'Still, it's a great thing, isn't it?'

I only had myself to blame – plus the Guild, who had set up a fair old rumour factory, now working overtime. The day before yesterday, the newssheet had simply boosted my book. Yesterday, it went on about how I'd been murdered recently, and dropped hints of more amazing revelations to follow. Mum had folded those two newssheets away (after almost learning them by heart) as though they were printed on gold leaf. I don't know that she was looking forward quite so avidly to this evening's news.

But maybe she was.

Dad finally barged his way through and got safely indoors, shutting out folks with difficulty. He tossed the newssheet on the table and headed for the kitchen. I hung on to the table top on tiptoe while Mum spread the sheet out. I never knew that such large type existed as I saw bannered across the top. Maybe it had been specially made for the occasion. My resurrection was officially announced.

Dad returned with a bottle of ginger spirit and poured himself a stiff drink; which wasn't like him at all.

'Oh, I can't tell you what it was like at work after this came out! Didn't get a thing done for the last hour or so. I should have quit and come straight home.' He drank half the strong liquor in one gulp.

I shan't go into the *details* of the news story. Basically they were all perfectly true. Merely – how shall I put it? – angled somewhat.

Outside, we heard a rising murmur, which presently became a chant.

'*Ka . . . Ka . . . Ka*, Yaleen!' After a while this blurred into '*Ka*-leen!' as though my name had altered, from Yaleen to Kaleen. Maybe that would be my holy name; my priestess title.

Our front door began to rattle, and a few rude bold enthusiasts scaled our garden wall to perch there. We retreated upstairs. Even so, things were getting hectic when, at roughly the critical moment for us, and for the mob as well, through the curtains we spied the militia come marching along, forcing their way to our door. In their van was quaymistress Chanoose. Not the 'jack captain, no. The jungle guild weren't in on this power play.

The area before our house was cleared. Trespassers on our wall were hauled down and hustled back through the ranks.

We went downstairs again; Dad answered a rap on the knocker.

In strolled Chanoose. She bowed her head to me – I hoped *that* wasn't going to be catching. 'Good evening, river-daughter! You need protection from admirers. So here it is.' She glanced round. 'This house isn't suitable.'

'What's wrong with it?' growled Dad, invigorated by the ginger spirit.

'It's too small. Too modest. Too vulnerable. The Guild will build you a temple somewhere downtown.'

'A what?' I cried.

'A temple – dedicated to the black current. A *Ka*-temple. Your very own temple, Yaleen.'

'Oh I *see*: imitating the *Ka*-theodrals of the Sons? Except that we'll have the temples of the Daughter instead?'

'Something like that. We might as well call the place a temple. What would you rather we called it: a palace? I don't think our finances quite stretch to a palace. There's a war to pay for; and future defence.'

'Oh so the Guild is hard up for a few fish? How sad. How amazing. My heart bleeds. Better get the worshippers to bring offerings!'

'Obviously this is all rather unfamiliar,' Chanoose carried on, clearly enjoying herself. 'So we must extemporize. Your parents can live in the temple with you, if you like; and you'll have a permanent honour guard of attendants from our guild to look after the practical details, the daily routine. Right? You can also have some, um,' and here she had to jog her memory, 'yes, some acolytes – of your own choice. That should be nice and cosy. Maybe some of the friends you made on the river, as detailed in your book, hmm? Or even some of your enemies!'

'Will you take a drink, 'Mistress?' offered Dad.

'Why not indeed? How charmingly hospitable.'

Dad poured a glass for Chanoose, and a few more fingers for himself.

'Can I have a drink too?' I said. 'I've almost forgotten the taste, it's been so long.'

Chanoose's look reproved me. 'What, a little girl tippling strong liquor? I hardly think so! You'd make your stomach bleed. Or you'd faint.'

Dad didn't pour me any. Just as well, probably.

Chanoose raised her glass. 'To our reborn priestess! To Yaleen of Pecawar, intermediary of the black current, annunciator of the *Ka*, living proof of afterlives, star-traveller – '

'Oh stow it! I don't want a string of daft titles.'

'I'm just improvising, as I said. So: simply to you, Yaleen. May you show us the way.'

I pointed. 'The door's that way.'

'How witty. You know, Yaleen, you mustn't imagine that with all your funny little traits you're unsuitable to be a priestess. On the contrary! You're someone with whom ordinary folk can identify.'

'I want to write another book,' I said.

'Pen and paper will be provided. And even ink.'

'I want to bring my story up to date.'

'So write it! People will adore it. They'll believe everything in it that they wish to believe. But they won't stop believing in you. In fact, we want you to write another book. Say whatever you wish. Even about this part of it. Feel free to treat me as another Tamath – though frankly I flatter myself that I'm a bit more precise than her. Writing a holy book is just what you should be doing whilst you're a priestess. Everyone will be agog. Call it *The Book of the Stars*.'

'I certainly *shan't*.' Though the title did have a certain ring to it . . .

'That reminds me,' I said to Dad, 'I need my ring. I want to wear it.'

'Ah, so you still have your famous ring?' Chanoose crowed with delight. 'How excellent. Visitors to the temple could kiss it.'

'I'm not having people slobbering all over my hand!'

'Oh, I shouldn't think they would. Not slobber, surely? We're all civilized people. Ceremonials are always so nice, though, don't you think? I noticed you glancing at those fish-masks in the cabin. Bring back thrilling memories, eh? But let's not forget, Yaleen, that this isn't play-acting. If what you tell us about the Godmind is true, well, here's the way to defeat it. By mobilizing our world. By unifying.

230

By setting ourselves apart from Eeden forever. That's what you wished for, right?'

Alas, I had to agree.

'As priestess, you will commune with the black current – '

'And I'll try to persuade it to take everyone into its *Ka*-store – male and female alike – if we all drink slugs of it? Served up by me in a silver chalice?'

Chanoose frowned. Her look became distant. 'Everyone? We'll have to think about that.'

'Why? Oh, I see. That would muck your monopoly up! If men could drink of the current, they could sail forbidden waters whenever they wanted to.'

'We don't know that men can drink it – not yet. Anyway, we have to consider the Sons – '

'Not to mention their poor womenfolk!'

'Ah yes indeed. But the conversion of the Sons could take ages. It would be equivalent to a declaration of war. We can do without another war, don't you think?'

'You aren't by any chance thinking of doling out entry tickets to the *Ka*-store only to your *friends*? That wouldn't thwart the Godmind much! And once the shorelubbers over here who weren't your special favourites figured this out . . . well, there'd be riots. A bloody rebellion! Have you no imagination?'

'As I say, we'll have to think about this carefully. Softly softly, catchee fish. First of all we'll install you in your temple. We'll take things from there.'

And all of a sudden I put two and two together in my own head – and oh, but Chanoose did have imagination, all right!

When the Godmind created its lens, it wouldn't be setting fire to worlds themselves; merely to the minds of people on those worlds, all the people who were in psylink with it, all those whose *Ka*s flew home to Eeden.

No riverwoman's *Ka* ever flew to Eeden; nor any *Ka*

which the black current claimed. So therefore, when the Godmind finally made its move, everyone would be snuffed out with the exception of those protected by the Worm. All those pesky Sons and their ratbag population would be dead. Problem over; without us having to pick up a single sword.

Meanwhile at a stroke the followers of the black current would become the total human population of the galaxy.

Plainly Chanoose wasn't planning on riverwomen *alone* surviving (plus assorted men-friends and supporters). That would be both vicious and idiotic. If the Guild tried to play that game there would be a civil war. Besides, think of all that useful new land left lying fallow over in the west after the demise of the Sons and all their kin. No, we would need the whole mass of our own population alive and kicking.

But by playing a waiting game – by not opposing the Godmind outright, merely recruiting our own people to the black current cult – we of the east would inherit the whole world. That was why the Guild were going to think carefully; I knew it in my waters!

Yet that was all beside the point. The point, to me at least, was: what about the rest of the galaxy? What about all the other colonies with their millions on millions of people?

The trouble, here, was that nobody but me had bounced around the stars. Nobody but me had been to Earth or to any other planet. As far as the folks here at home were concerned, that world where the wench chewed snails or that colony where the crone crooned her eel-song might as well be fictions. If those worlds were all snuffed out, what did it matter? (But it mattered to me!)

The Book of the Stars, indeed! What a nerve Chanoose had to suggest such a title.

Now I was *determined* to call my next book just that. And I resolved that I would make the book as real as could be, so that readers would get the message that genuine people lived on lots of other planets.

But would the guild print the whole of it, once I'd written it in my temple in downtown Pecawar, surrounded by an honour guard? Whatever fair promises Chanoose made to softsoap me now, might they only print part? The part that suited them? There was only one way to find out.

'Right?' said Chanoose. She liked saying that word, since that's what she was in her own mind: right.

'Right,' said I. But what I meant, was: Write!

'It'll take us a few weeks to organize suitable premises. Might take longer, depending on the degree of grandeur. Till then, what with all this wild excitement I think the three of you would be better off on board a boat at anchor – '

'Hey, my Dad's a man!'

Chanoose peered at me. 'Fathers usually are.'

'So he can't board a boat. He already sailed once in his life.'

'Oh, I *see*. Couldn't you intercede with the current on his behalf? As a special exception? Then he could drink a slug and – '

'Chanoose! If you think I'm going to gamble with my own Dad's life and sanity, to test whether the current will allow men to – ! I swear I'll kill myself; then you won't have any priestess.'

'What a fuss you do make! In that case your father can bunk down in my office. You and your mother will come on board the *Oopsadaisy*. I'll post guards here tonight to keep the curious at bay. Tomorrow they'll escort you down to the quay in suitable style.' Chanoose turned to Dad. 'Don't worry about this house; we'll caretake it properly. And if you want to keep your job for a while, naturally we'll provide an escort to the spice houses.'

'Keep my job,' said Dad thickly. 'Not much point in

that, is there?' He looked shrunken and drained, as though instead of having swigged the liquor, it had swigged him.

But Mum looked excited. Proud.

That night in the midst of a dream of Port Firsthome the Worm surfaced. Like an ordinary soil-worm, but much huger, it burst up through the turf beside the Obelisk of the Ship. Its foundations disturbed, the Obelisk tottered and crashed down upon some picnickers: a capering old man, a kissing couple, two naked children, flattening them all.

Mud dripped from the Worm's dream-jaws. *Listen, Yaleen: you're going to blow up all the Paxmen on the Moon in another couple of years, approx? The prisoners of Hell will rebel and seize control?*

That's the general idea.

So then the Godmind won't be able to launch its last two seedships?

Not unless it can recapture the Moon. Against those laser-zappers.

But what if it over-budgeted the number of colonies it needs, just to be on the safe side? What if it already has enough people spread around? What if the lens mightn't be quite perfect – but nevertheless could be good enough? What if the Godmind doesn't need to recapture the Moon? What if it decides to go ahead with Project Lens right away? Directly, in a couple of years' time?

Gobbets of soil dribbled from its mouth.

One of the crushed, trapped children was still alive. A girl: she squealed piteously, like the voice of all the human worlds crying out for help.

A clammy feeling crept over me. *Are you implying . . . that I've buggered everything up again? Instead of slowing the Godmind's plan down, I've speeded it up?*

Could be.

There must still be a few ships en route.

Heading for stars close by. Maybe they're nearly there.

Shut up! I covered my ears. But the Worm's voice droned on inside my dreaming head:

There's another point I'd like to raise. What if you were right about the Godmind being able to zap me with its lens?

You mean, what I told it in the garden? Oh, that was all hogwash!

I know it was. But what if it's possible? What if you gave the Godmind a bright idea?

Oh.

What if you get it all fired up about that in a couple of years' time, and it sees how to do it?

If the Godmind could zap the black current, then obviously Chanoose's plan wouldn't work. Nor could any plan of mine. The *Ka*-store itself would be burnt out . . . Surely the Worm couldn't be serious! Surely I couldn't have planted the seeds of *that!*

You're joking, Worm.

Just think about it, eh? And down its mucky worm-hole in my dream my old friend withdrew.

Hey! I shouted after it. *If that's true, you've got one big vested interest in helping to save everyone!*

But the Worm had gone.

I thought. Hell, *how* I thought – even in my sleep. I seemed to be floating just below the surface of sleep for hours, my mind churning over and over while the rest of me got precious little repose.

I woke next morning with a thunderous headache, as though the Godmind had already tried to set fire to my brains and everyone else's.

After breakfast (for which I insisted on a greasy spicy omelette with a splash of ginger spirit on top) Mum and Dad packed a couple of bags.

Presently, came a polite rap on the door.

And before long we three set off on the first stage of

my latest journey, which wouldn't be nearly as long as any of my previous travels: this time merely to a schooner anchored offshore, and from there a few weeks hence to a temple. To become the lady high (infant) priestess of the Worm.

As we proceeded through town, flanked by our escort of militia, a clamouring procession just grew and grew in our wake till I felt I was wearing a tail of people as long as the black current itself.

The world's greatest science fiction authors
now available in Panther Books

Brian W Aldiss

To order direct from the publisher just tick the titles you want
and fill in the order form.   **SF781**

The world's greatest science fiction authors now available in Panther Books

Ray Bradbury

Fahrenheit 451	£1.95	☐
The Small Assassin	£1.50	☐
The October Country	£1.50	☐
The Illustrated Man	£1.95	☐
The Martian Chronicles	£1.95	☐
Dandelion Wine	£1.50	☐
The Golden Apples of the Sun	£1.95	☐
Something Wicked This Way Comes	£1.50	☐
The Machineries of Joy	£1.50	☐
Long After Midnight	£1.95	☐
The Stories of Ray Bradbury (Volume 1)	£2.95	☐
The Stories of Ray Bradbury (Volume 2)	£2.95	☐

Philip K Dick

Flow My Tears, The Policeman Said	£1.95	☐
Blade Runner (Do Androids Dream of Electric Sheep?)	£1.75	☐
Now Wait for Last Year	£1.95	☐
The Zap Gun	£1.95	☐
A Handful of Darkness	£1.50	☐
A Maze of Death	£1.50	☐
Ubik	£1.95	☐
Our Friends from Frolix 8	£1.95	☐
Clans of the Alphane Moon	£1.95	☐
The Transmigration of Timothy Archer	£1.95	☐
A Scanner Darkly	£1.95	☐
The Three Stigmata of Palmer Eldritch	£1.95	☐
The Penultimate Truth	£1.95	☐

To order direct from the publisher just tick the titles you want
and fill in the order form.   **SF981**

The world's greatest science fiction authors now available in Panther Books

Bob Shaw

The Ceres Solution	£1.50	☐
A Better Mantrap	£1.50	☐
Orbitsville	£1.95	☐
Orbitsville Departure	£1.95	☐

William Burroughs

Nova Express	£1.25	☐

Arthur C Clarke

2010: Odyssey Two	£1.95	☐

Harry Harrison

Rebel in Time	£1.95	☐

The To The Stars Trilogy

Homeworld	£1.95	☐
Wheelworld	£1.95	☐
Starworld	£1.95	☐

James Kahn

World Enough, and Time	£1.95	☐
Time's Dark Laughter	£1.95	☐

Christopher Stasheff

A Wizard in Bedlam	£1.25	☐
The Warlock in Spite of Himself	£1.25	☐
King Kobold	£1.50	☐
The Warlock Unlocked	£1.95	☐

Doris Lessing
'Canopus in Argos: Archives'

Shikasta	£2.50	☐
The Marriage Between Zones Three, Four, and Five	£1.95	☐
The Sirian Experiments	£1.95	☐
The Making of the Representative for Planet 8	£1.95	☐

David Mace

Demon 4	£1.50	☐
Nightrider	£1.95	☐

To order direct from the publisher just tick the titles you want and fill in the order form.   SF1282

All these books are available at your local bookshop or newsagent, or can be ordered direct from the publisher..

To order direct from the publisher just tick the titles you want and fill in the form below.

Name_____

Address _____

_____

Send to:
Panther Cash Sales
PO Box 11, Falmouth, Cornwall TR10 9EN.

Please enclose remittance to the value of the cover price plus:

UK 45p for the first book, 20p for the second book plus 14p per copy for each additional book ordered to a maximum charge of £1.63.

BFPO and Eire 45p for the first book, 20p for the second book plus 14p per copy for the next 7 books, thereafter 8p per book.

Overseas 75p for the first book and 21p for each additional book.

Panther Books reserve the right to show new retail prices on covers, which may differ from those previously advertised in the text or elsewhere.